the MUCKRAKER

MAGGIE SONNEK

MAGGIE SONNEK

THE MUCKRAKER

FOX POINTE PUBLISHING

Copyright © 2024 by Maggie Sonnek

All rights reserved. Published in the United States by Fox Pointe Publishing, LLP. No part of this book may be reproduced in any form or by any electronic or mechanical means, including information storage and retrieval systems, without permission in writing from the publisher.

This is a work of fiction. Names, places, characters, and incidents are either a product of the author's imagination or are used fictitiously. Any resemblance to actual events, places, organizations, or persons, whether living or dead, is entirely coincidental.

www.foxpointepublishing.com/author-maggie-sonnek

Library of Congress Cataloging-in-Publication Data

Sonnek, Maggie, author.
Olson, Sarah, editor.
Wagner, Kylie, designer.

The Muckraker / Maggie Sonnek. – First edition.

Summary: In this dual timeline novel, two journalists investigate the same prestigious family about one hundred years apart.

ISBN (hardcover) 978-1-955743-66-2 / (softcover) 978-1-955743-67-9

[1. Journalism – Fiction. 2. Historical Fiction – 20th Century – Fiction. 3. Multiple Timelines – Fiction. 4. Mystery & Detective – Fiction.]

Library of Congress Control Number: 2 0 2 3 9 5 1 6 0 7

Printed and bound in the United States of America

First printing March 2024

To James, Ada, Olive, and Eric.
Thank you for cheering me on during this process!

Chapter 1

SOPHIE

PRESENT DAY

MINNEAPOLIS, MINNESOTA

"Before we begin, let's set an intention for this class," my favorite yoga instructor, Jade, murmured in a soft voice. Tattoos covered her arms and her nose was pierced with a small gold hoop. The lights were set low. Lavender-scented candles flickered softly.

"Can my intention be to just lie here for the next hour with no one touching me?" Freya whispered. She was sprawled out on her lime-green mat wearing a faded, stretched-out t-shirt that read "Seniors 2007" across the front. I'm pretty sure I saw baby puke on it.

I rolled my head towards her. "You know what Jade says. You bring your own energy to your mat."

"But what if I have no energy?" she hissed back.

I stifled a laugh. "Some of us are trying to set our intentions?" I whispered with an eyebrow raised.

"Please," she shot back sarcastically.

"I am! I'm trying to calm my nerves," I said.

Jade instructed us into downward dog. I adjusted my high-rise Athleta leggings and tried to keep my heels on my mat.

"Girl! That's right. You start your new job tomorrow." Freya turned to look at me and lost her balance. She morphed into a cat-cow pose. "I'm so jealous. I'll be knee-deep in nursing a three-month-old while trying to keep a toddler alive. You have to text me every detail about your day." Freya hiked her maternity leggings over her postpartum belly.

"I'm seriously nervous," I whispered. My stomach—which was tight as I was holding a plank—flip-flopped. "I haven't done anything in front of the camera since...well, you know."

2 | THE MUCKRAKER

On cue, Jade murmured, "Let's rise to be the warriors I know you all are." I awkwardly stumbled my way to warrior pose while Freya resorted to lying on her back.

"I'm just going to hang out in Shavasana for a while," she mumbled, closing her eyes.

"Remind me why I'm leaving KOMO again?" I whispered to Freya.

"You're ready to tell stories...to do more than produce them. You got this."

I nodded and attempted a smile.

"Let's all fall back onto our mats and settle into Shavasana for a few minutes," Jade said. I closed my eyes, let out a deep breath, and tried to believe Freya was right.

When my alarm went off at six o'clock the next morning, I gasped and sat up. News Now Online. My first day. An hour later, as the C-line bus lurched to a stop at the Nicollet Mall Station, I was a ball of nerves. As executive producer at KOMO-TV, everything had been familiar and comfortable. Everyone knew me. I didn't have to prove my worth; my show ratings and Emmys did that for me. But now, in a new environment with new faces, everything was about to change. Swallowing my fear, I grabbed my green tote bag, hurried off the bus, and headed toward the Conley-Mass Building, home to dozens of businesses, including News Now Online.

"Hey!" A woman in her late twenties approached me. Her black hair was tied in a knot at the top of her head showing off her flawless, bronze skin. She wore an antique key strung on a long gold chain around her neck. "You must be Sophie. I'm Jen," she said, holding out a hand.

I smiled and returned the handshake.

"Here's your desk," Jen said, pointing to a laser-thin, white desktop balanced on what looked to be pieces of stacked wooden blocks. I ran my hand across the smooth surface. "Best part about this desk? It charges your phone and laptop. Just set your phone on top," Jen encouraged. I pulled it out of my green tote. Immediately, it lit up, charging.

"Wow," I murmured. At KOMO, our desks were from the 1960s. My drawers usually stuck together and I had to slam my hand down to loosen them.

"Alright guys, let's gather around!" I recognized Kase Reddy, the managing editor, from my interview. He came out of his office, one of the only workspaces that appeared to be glass-enclosed. The rest of the desks were lined up in an open-concept style, many of them against an exposed, red brick wall. I followed Jen to an orange mesh couch.

"Guys, this is Sophie McHale," Kase said, a pencil stuck behind his ear. He smiled at me. "She comes to us from KOMO-TV where she produced the ten p.m. show." A few people smiled and some nodded. "Jen will be showing her the ropes."

I offered a nod and a smile.

With that, Kase launched into the morning huddle. "Barry, will you follow up with Minnesota Cares about that health care policy? Our story last week about insurance premiums ruffled some feathers for sure. Let's keep that going."

Barry, a bearded, twenty-something, nodded.

Kase continued. "I'm loving the Insta-stories. Make sure you post at least one story a day." Insta-stories? I had to bite my lip. At KOMO, our news director was wary of using Twitter and Instagram for reporting. Freya was going to die from shock when I told her.

Kase continued assigning stories. Lastly, he turned to me.

"Sophie, this is a fun one. K!ng is in town for his sold-out show at the Downtown Center. Want to interview him?"

My mouth fell open. "Oh my gosh. K!ng? For real?" I sounded like a thirteen-year-old girl. "I mean, yes. Definitely."

Kase smiled. "Awesome. He only made time for a few interviews. You can get to the Downtown Center through the Skyway. Jen can give you directions." I nodded eagerly. An interview with K!ng. On my first day!

Jen and I walked back to my desk. "How awesome is this for your first day?" She jotted down a couple directions on a Post-it note. "The Downtown Center is just a few blocks from here. Take the Skyway from Conley-Mass to Fifth Street Towers," she said, pointing to her written directions. "That opens up to Downtown Center." She handed me the Post-it note. "Good luck! You'll do great."

I shuttled off a text to Freya: *First day and already have an interview with K!ng.*

Seconds later my phone pinged: *WTH?!?! SO jealous.*

When I joined KOMO-TV as an intern in my senior year of college, Freya was an associate producer for the morning show. After graduating, I joined her on the morning show team. The hours were brutal—midnight to nine in the morning—but the crew made up for it. A mix of quiet introverts and explosive personalities, they made sure the morning show was never dull. Eventually, Freya was called up to be the executive producer of the evening news. And she plucked me from the morning crew to be her assistant.

4 | THE MUCKRAKER

As I followed Jen's notes, I typed a message back to Freya: Can you believe it?!

Freya shot back: *I'm home watching Daniel Tiger reruns. Def not fair.*

When Freya left for maternity leave with Lucy, we all bet she'd be back in the booth within six weeks. Turns out, we were wrong. She never came back, shocking us all. That's when I took over as EP.

When I walked into the massive Downtown Center, a woman with the longest, slimmest legs I've ever seen teetering on three-inch heels walked over to me. Her blue eyes sparkled against her bronze skin.

"Name?" she asked.

"Sophie. From News Now Online," I replied.

She looked at her phone and nodded. "This way." I followed her, my heart beating faster with every step.

We approached a gray metal door. She knocked and then opened it. "Go on in," she said.

K!ng sat a few feet away, punching something on his phone.

"Hi, K!ng," I said, setting down my bag and grabbing my laptop. "I'm Sophie McHale. Welcome to Minneapolis."

He put his phone in his pocket and flashed me a smile. "How you doing, Sophie?"

I took in every detail of his dressing room so I could tell Freya. A plate of lemon wedges sat on the counter. Rose-scented candles flickered throughout the room. A frame holding a picture of K!ng and a young girl sat near his mirror.

I realized K!ng was waiting for me to start the interview. The only problem was, I hadn't prepared anything to ask. I was too focused on navigating the Skyway and texting Freya. I thought back to the headlines I'd seen while working at KOMO. Drunk driving.

"Can we talk about the recent allegation of reckless driving? I heard there were kids in the car with you and—"

"Nah, nah," K!ng said, shaking his head. "I don't wanna talk about that."

I cleared my throat. "Oh, okay. How about the vandalism charges that were filed against you?" My voice rose at the end of the sentence. "Um, at your daughter's preschool?"

K!ng let out a loud sigh and rolled his eyes. "No comment."

I nodded slowly. In the production booth, I'd be telling the reporter what to say, what to ask. But this time, I was the reporter. And there was no one telling me what to do next. Freya's words echoed in my mind: You're ready to tell stories…to do more than just produce a show. "Well…what about your thoughts on…climate change?" I inwardly cringed. Stupid question. I swallowed the lump in my throat and scrunched my toes inside my nude heels.

"Climate change? Girl, really? Do you know who I am?" K!ng stood up, his six-foot-something frame casting a shadow on me and my laptop.

Desperate to not lose this interview, I added quickly, "Well, what would you like to talk about, then?" A bead of sweat rolled down my back.

K!ng smiled widely. He sat back down in the leather lounge chair with his name embroidered across the back and crossed his arms behind his head. "There we go. That's K!ng's way." He flashed his custom-made, Pavé-diamond-set smile at me. "We're gonna talk about me. Did you hear I made the Forbes list? Again?" He jutted out his chin and smiled. "Yep. *Highest Paid Celebrities Under 30.* Six years in a row, baby. Only problem is, I turn thirty next year." He let out a chuckle. "Then what are they gonna give me?"

He waited for my response. "Um, oh wow. Turning thirty. Yeah, that's—that's a big deal." I cleared my throat. "So, how does it feel to be included on a list like that? Have you talked to the other celebrities who've also made the list?"

He shrugged. "Some of 'em. Most of 'em hate me," he raised his hands and shrugged. "I don't know why." Then, he stood up and slowly turned around. "What's there to hate?" He burst into fits of laughter.

"K!ng, it's time for your next interview," the woman in three-inch heels purred. "Then we have an eleven o'clock yoga class. That'll loosen you up for tonight's show."

K!ng nodded. "Sold out, baby!" He looked at me. "You hear my show is sold out?"

I looked down at the blank Word document on my laptop. My stomach dropped. I had nothing—not one word—to show from this interview... My first interview as a reporter.

"K!ng, wait," I squeaked. "Um," I racked my brain, desperately trying to think of something, anything to say that would give me a lead for this story.

"Sorry..." The gazelle-like assistant looked down at her phone. "... Sophie," she said, reading my name off an itinerary. "That's all the time K!ng has today." She held the door open for me.

I closed my laptop and stood to go. "Thanks for your time," I said quietly. "Good luck tonight."

K!ng didn't answer. He was too busy checking his reflection in his brightly lit, interactive smart mirror.

I left his dressing room and made my way to the Skyway, navigating back to News Now Online, the whole time cursing myself for letting him take control of the interview. The first rule of journalism is we ask the questions.

I pulled out my phone and punched Freya's contact.

"Hey girl!" she answered on the second ring. I heard Lucy shriek in the background. Then Freya said, "Luce, Mommy's right here!" To me, she responded, "Tell me everything."

Tears pricked my eyes. "Oh, Freya. I totally blew it. I have nothing—not one detail—to turn into a story." I walked by a Skyway restaurant that smelled of roasted chicken and garlic as chefs prepped for the lunch crowd. In a whisper, I muttered, "I would rip a reporter a new asshole if they came back with nothing."

Freya was silent.

"Freya, please say something."

"Soph, it's your first day," she murmured. "It's okay. Your editor will understand."

"Will he? I don't know," I said, hiking up the stairwell to News Now Online. "I guess I'll find out. I'll text you later."

"Soph, you are going to do great work. You got this," Freya said. I smiled, thanked her, and clicked off just before opening the sleek, frosted-glass door to News Now Online. Everyone was in the back of the office space, draped across exposed wood-framed couches and orange mesh chairs, all gathered around a long, retro-style Formica table.

"Sophie," Kase said. "Just in time for our noon huddle. How did your interview with K!ng go?"

"Um, it went okay," I lied as I sat in a white and orange chair and scooted up to the table.

"Great. Can't wait to see what you put together." He looked down at his notebook as my stomach churned.

"Um, I'd show you my outline, but I don't want to spoil the surprise," I squeaked out.

"I have to admit, I'm a huge K!ng fan. I love his new song, 'You Don't Care'," Kase said. Tonight's show sold out so fast, I couldn't get tickets."

Others around the table nodded and laughed. I squirmed in my seat. Kase waited for me to offer additional comments. When I didn't, he added, "Well, I know he only did a few interviews, so News Now Online will have exclusive content. Send it my way by the end of the day so we can get it posted before his show."

He then turned to Jen. "You up for another *Minne-story* live on Instagram today? Last week's live stream went great."

"You bet. The month of May celebrates both teachers and nurses. So I was thinking, let's feature a nurse and an educator in this stream. Check in on how they're doing. Like, collectively."

Kase nodded. "I like it. I mean, it could get ugly. Teachers and nurses have been through the ringer. Alright, guys," he said, clapping his hands and standing up. "Let's get to work."

I pushed my chair back and headed to the workspace kitchen.

"Coffee?" Jen asked, meeting me at the shared Keurig.

"Yes, please," I nodded, handing her a hazelnut-flavored coffee pod.

"I am so jealous you got to meet K!ng. I mean, we're all kind of jealous," she giggled, brewing coffee for me. "The newest girl on staff gets the biggest interview of the year?" She shook her head. "Not fair," she teased. "So, how was he? Was he cool? Was he nice?"

"Yeah," I laughed nervously. "He was pretty great. The only thing is," I stammered, "he didn't really answer my questions. Like, I tried to dig deep and ask him some tough questions but he just sort of deflected them."

Jen shrugged. "All the big stars do that. So, you just let 'em talk and capture the details you can. I mean, you shot some video, right?"

My stomach squeezed. "No. Was I supposed to?"

Jen looked at me quizzically. "Really? You didn't shoot any video? Huh," she said, removing my mug from the Keurig and handing it to me. "Well, just photos then? For News Now Online's Instagram feed?" She paused and looked up. "We should have done an Instagram takeover! K!ng takes over News Now Online's Instagram feed." She shrugged. "Next time."

My eyes widened. "I didn't," I muttered, panicking. "I didn't know I was supposed to get pictures."

"Sophie, really? News Now Online was one of the only news agencies to get an interview with K!ng," Jen said. Then, in a whisper she asked, "Well, what do you have?"

I shook my head. My eyes burned. I couldn't meet her gaze.

"Nothing?" Jen said, a bit too loudly. "Nothing?" she said again, this time in a harsh whisper.

A tear rolled down my cheek and I quickly wiped it away. "It wasn't my fault. I only got three minutes with him! He just took charge of the interview and kept talking about how he made the Forbes list and how great he is and…" My heart was pounding in my chest. My excuses sounded like a cop-out. "I think I blew it." I looked at Jen, hoping she'd comfort me.

Instead, she just stared at me, eyes wide. Then, she nodded. "Yeah. I mean, sorry, but yeah. It sounds like you totally blew it."

"Shit," I hissed.

Then, in a gentler tone, she said, "Maybe it's not the end of the world. See if you can get a story together. Try to remember any compelling details. I'll call in a favor from a friend whose boyfriend works security at all the big concerts. I'll see if he can sneak some photos."

A sigh of relief escaped me. "Thank you, Jen." I raced back to my desk, coffee sloshing, and racked my brain for details I could paste together. When Kase stopped by my desk around two o'clock to see how I was doing, I minimized K!ng's Wikipedia page and managed a chipper response to his questions. By four o'clock, I had something that might pass for a story. I included details about the previous six years K!ng had been on the Forbes list, how many times his tour had stopped in Minneapolis, and his flood of recent awards. Jen's friend miraculously came through and sent us a few pictures of K!ng in his dressing room and on his yoga mat…shirtless.

I sent the story and pictures to Kase and waited. By six o'clock, I still hadn't heard anything. I was getting nervous. I knew he wanted to post the story before K!ng's concert that night.

Then, I heard a gasp from one of the desks in the back. Jessie, an on-line producer, hollered out, "K!ng's three-year-old daughter has cancer?!" My head spun around. Jen and a handful of other reporters ran to Jessie's desk, surrounding him and looking at his computer screen. I joined them, hanging back.

"In our exclusive interview tonight, we'll take you deeper into the diagnosis that K!ng has kept hidden for months," a reporter's voice read over b-roll of K!ng. Then, the star popped up on the screen, crying. "I mean, I've tried to stay strong. I really have. Family first, right?" He stopped and rubbed his eyes. "But, God, when it's your kid, it's so hard. My little Yesika. She's my dream. She's my why." The petite, blond reporter came on screen. "See more of that emotional interview coming up at six."

My jaw dropped. Everyone turned and stared at me. "I…how…I mean, he didn't…" At that moment, Kase slammed his fist on the nearest table.

"Wow, they broke the story of the year." He made a beeline for his desk without looking at me. I walked back to my desk, aware that everyone was glaring at me—aware that I'd ruined my chance at proving I had what it took to be a top-notch reporter.

Chapter 2

BIZZIE

MAY 1920

HIBBING, MINNESOTA

"You don't want to go out there," the postman warned.

Bizzie protested. "One of my students lives there and he's been missing from school," she replied.

He shook his head, dismissing her. "The county poor farm ain't a place for a girl. Besides, bears and wolves prowl those woods."

Bizzie pursed her lips and balled her fists. "I grew up in these woods. I know how to protect myself."

"Grew up?" he scoffed. "You're still just a child."

Bizzie, just over five feet, straightened her back and squared her shoulders. "I'm eighteen," she responded indignantly. "And I already have my teaching license. I suppose I'll have to find directions from someone else." She turned to go.

"Wait," the postman said, shaking his head. He began scribbling directions on the margin of a newspaper.

Bizzie leaned over the counter. "Is that the *Tribune*? From Duluth?"

The postman nodded at her. She squinted to read the headlines. "I lived in Duluth while I was getting my teaching certificate and I read the papers every day."

"You're a strange girl, eh?" he said, the corner of his mouth rising. He slid the paper toward Bizzie. "Follow Main Street, past the old Kreye house…you know the one?" Bizzie nodded. "You'll see a gravel road a few steps after that. Follow that about a mile. Then you'll see a small path through the woods. That'll take you right to the farm." He shuddered. "Still don't think you want to go there."

Bizzie smiled and thanked him.

"Wait," he said, grabbing an iron lantern behind him. He struck a match, lit the candle inside, and handed the lantern to Bizzie. "Just in case."

When she got to the old Kreye house, a red, brick structure with a wraparound front porch, she searched for the gravel road. Behind some overgrown trees and a huge plot where a garden used to be, she saw it. By the time she reached the clearing in the woods—the county poor farm—it was dusk. Bizzie was grateful for the postman's lantern.

Rustic pine hand-hewn logs, notched at each end, formed the exterior. The roof was covered in wooden shingles. She smelled wood smoke and pine. Bizzie bit her lip, knocked twice, and held the Palmer Method Handwriting book close to her chest, remembering the postman's warnings. She knocked again, rocking back on her heels, hoping this treacherous trip through the woods wasn't pointless. Then, the door opened just a sliver. Bizzie could see a pale face in the crack of the door. A woman. Her hair hung around her face and down to her shoulders.

"Hello, I'm looking for Leon. My name is Bizzie Johansen. I'm his teacher," she said, hoping the woman—Leon's mother?—would open the door wider and let her in. But, instead, she stood as still as a statue and looked at Bizzie blankly. Bizzie pressed on. "Uh, he's been out sick for several days. I was starting to worry about him." She was speaking faster, wondering if it had been wise for her to come out here alone. Just when she started to back away from the door, she heard footsteps. Then a jumble of words in another language—Polish maybe?—that she couldn't understand. The door yanked open. There stood Leon in a ratty-looking shirt and wool pants that exposed his ankles and were patched three times over on his knees.

"Leon!" Bizzie blurted out, excited and relieved to see her student. Then, just as soon as her relief settled in, she was met with a stench so pungent that she instinctively covered her nose with her hand. It was as if an animal had died inside the house. She couldn't fathom how this family could be living amid a stench so powerful. She backed away a few steps and gulped in the fresh, spring night air.

"What are you doing here, Miss Bizzie?" Leon asked. He gestured for Bizzie to enter. Meanwhile, the woman skittered away, never meeting Bizzie's eyes. Bizzie took one more gulp of the evening air before entering the dimly lit house.

"I was getting worried about you, Leon," Bizzie said, folding her hands in front of her to keep from plugging her nose.

"Ah, it's no big deal. I had to help at the farm," Leon said. In his hands was a small paper crane. Bizzie smiled. At school, he was always tinkering and fiddling with paper. Making paper animals, paper cranes, little books. His gangly legs and arms never stopped moving. Here, just like in school, he was fiddling with something.

"Don't they know you have school to attend?" Bizzie asked.

Leon shrugged. "Mr. Selco says it's better I help here. He says I'll learn all I need to know working in the fields."

Bizzie furrowed her brow. "Mr. Selco? He's the owner of the farm?" Leon looked at his feet and nodded. "But surely, he cares about your future. What if you want to do more than work in the fields when you grow up?"

Bizzie heard heavy footsteps. Leon's wiggling stopped and he stood still.

"Leon, what are you doing talking to some strange lady?" a booming voice hollered. Then, a big-bellied man with a bushy beard appeared.

"Hello, sir. I don't mean to cause any trouble," Bizzie stammered. "I'm Leon's teacher, Miss Bizzie. I came to check on him and deliver—"

"He don't need no teacher snoopin' on him. He's fine. He's helpin' me on the farm," the man spat. "Spring is our busiest time of year. Plantin' after the winter."

"I understand. With all due respect, he's only nine years old. Don't you think he should be in school? Learning with his friends?"

"Bah!" the man hollered.

Bizzie teetered back on her heels while her stomach fell to her toes.

"I'm the supervisor of this here farm. You know how that came to be? Hard work. Real work. Not book learning." He turned and grasped Leon by the shoulder, pulling him under his sausage-like arm. "From now on, Leon won't be returning to school. He'll be here. With me."

"But, sir, I really think—"

"Enough. That's it!" The man shoved Bizzie out the door and slammed it in her face. Bizzie felt her eyes stinging. Tears streamed down her face. She stood there for a minute before turning to go.

"Miss Bizzie!" Leon's voice caused her to turn.

"Oh, Leon!" Bizzie said, grabbing the boy in a hug. Her tears plopped onto his stringy, dirty hair.

"Don't worry about me," Leon said, smiling. "I'll be fine. Besides, the school year is almost over. And Mr. Selco isn't so bad. Plus," he gestured at the log house, "it's a roof over our heads. That's better than what we've had before."

Bizzie smiled, tousling his hair. "Well, here. Take this." She shoved the handwriting book into his muddied, stained hands. She sniffed and opened up the book. "I think this is where we left off in school." Leon took the book and nodded.

"I made this for you," Leon said, shoving a small paper crane into her hands. Then, he stretched his gangly arms around Bizzie's small waist.

"Leon!" Mr. Selco hollered from the log house and Leon backed away.

"Thanks, Miss Bizzie," Leon whispered and ran back inside.

Bizzie let the tears stream down her cheeks. Leon! Stuck in a place so horrible. She trudged back through the woods, somehow remembering the path to take her back to town. As the wind blew through the trees, she couldn't help but think it was calling her, guiding her to be something more.

Chapter 3

SOPHIE

JEN CAME OVER TO MY DESK and touched my elbow. "Well, this sucks," she said.

I closed my eyes and nodded, not trusting my voice.

"And K!ng didn't mention anything about his daughter during your interview with him this morning?"

I shook my head and whispered, "No. Nothing." The picture frame of the young girl flashed through my mind. His daughter. I should have just asked about that picture.

Then, from the corner of the room, I heard Kase. "Sophie, let's talk." He jerked his head toward the direction of the conference room. I took a deep breath, balled my fists, and followed him into the room, watching him close the door and sit down. He pursed his lips.

"I'm going to cut to the chase. They beat us today," he said, pointing towards Jessie's computer. "At News Now Online, we take the time to research, to find outside sources, to take a goddamn picture!" He smacked his hand down on the table. I jumped. "But what you sent me? That was crap. Absolute crap!"

I bit my lower lip and felt the familiar bump of an old scar I got as a kid.

He shook his head. "Any journalist in this office would have loved to interview K!ng today." He drew out the word "loved." "But I thought, no, I'll give it to my newest reporter. Let's throw her a bone. Let's see what she can do." He crossed his arms and looked at the floor. "The worst part? Mainstream media beat us. We're supposed to outsmart them." At the mention of mainstream media, my face fell.

That's where I came from. Was he saying I wasn't cut out for this? "I mean, what…what were you thinking?"

My voice caught in my throat. I thought I was ready for a new challenge. I thought I was ready to become a reporter. Maybe I was wrong. I let out a stream of air and shook my head. "I don't know. I'm sorry." I stared at my hands. "I think I froze up."

Kase nodded and scratched his chin. I waited for him to tell me to get my belongings and leave. Instead, in a gentler tone, he said, "I get it. I've been there." He folded his hands in front of his face. His empathy surprised me. "Try again tomorrow?"

I looked at him with wide eyes. "Really?"

Kase smiled. "Yes, but know this: Working at News Now Online is a privilege. We have a duty to report the truth to our readers and followers. They are counting on us to ask the hard questions. To push a little further. To report news differently than how it's previously been delivered."

I nodded. "I understand."

Kase stood and held the conference room door open for me. Everyone was still gathered around Jessie's desk, eyes glued to his computer screen, as the reporter wrapped up the story about K!ng. I hung back quietly and watched. "We've heard fans have already started a GoFundMe campaign, while Twitter is blowing up with the hashtag #CureforYesika. As for what K!ng thinks? We just got a text from him," the reporter said. She held an iPad and stood in front of a large screen, showing a picture of K!ng and Yesika. She read, "To all the reporters at CBS 10: Thank you for sharing this story about my pride and joy, my life. I am forever grateful to you." The reporter flashed a big grin at the camera. "We're here for you, K!ng and Yesika, as you navigate this path to healing. Live in Minneapolis, I'm Kelly Katchaway."

Before any of my coworkers noticed I was still in the room, I hurried over to my desk, grabbed my things, and rushed out to the bus stop. Gathered with the other commuters, I texted Freya.

Wow. What a first day. Totally f'ed up.

A few seconds later, Freya responded: *It's a first day. First days always suck.*

I smiled, then punched back: *Get this. My desk charges my phone and laptop. And it's stacked on wooden blocks that look like Jenga blocks.*

Freya: *Seriously? At KOMO we were lucky to have a desk with drawers.*

It took a couple of days, but the K!ng story eventually blew over. My coworkers were even starting to look at me again.

"Laura, let's have you cover the Uptown shooting," Kase said at the morning huddle without looking up. Laura's lip and nose were pierced. Her hair was parted down the middle. One half was shaved close to her head. The other half, dyed a bright blue, was bluntly cut and rested near her chin. She wore hot pink pants with gaping holes in the knees and black combat boots. Kase added, "If protestors are still out, make sure you include them in your Instagram feed. And I think local artists are starting to work on a mural on 35th and 10th. Might be a good visual."

"Barry, you keep working on that health insurance story. Call our source at Care Coverage and talk about the customer's journey—how easy the new enrollment site is to navigate, that kind of thing. Maybe a live Q&A on Instagram? Customers can ask their questions in real time." Kase jotted down more notes in his notebook and Barry nodded.

"Chandra, what do you think about doing something on summer safety? I'm thinking a reminder about swimming, boating, all that stuff." Kase looked up. "We could do a cool, shareable graphic."

"Yeah, that works." Chandra's brown skin was bronzed and golden. Her hair was the color of dark chocolate and was cut short to her head. Gold bangles hung in her ears. She looked mildly interested in the story.

Kase scratched out more notes. "Jen, you're on features today. What do you think?"

"I just got a huge tip from the Mall of America. They just dropped their 'Best Toys of the Year' list. What if I do a teaser for that? I'm thinking we could get lots of hits."

Kase nodded. "Sounds great. If you head over there, grab some video. Maybe a few interviews with shoppers. Oh, I wonder if we can partner with the shops to do a giveaway too?" he offered.

Jen nodded and gave a thumbs up.

"And Sophie," he tapped his notebook with the eraser side of his pencil. I felt all eyes on me. "Morris Hartman is announcing his candidacy for governor next week. What if you reach out and do a sit-down with him?"

I froze. Another one-on-one?

Kase must have sensed this because he said, "Relax. Nothing crazy here. Just a few soundbites and some photos."

I let out a breath and nodded. After the huddle, reporters dispersed and got to work. Jen caught me before I headed to my desk.

"Coffee?" she asked, pointing to the kitchen. I followed her there and popped a coffee pod into the Keurig.

"I've worked with Hartman for the last couple years as he's geared up for this," Jen said, stirring a packet of sugar into her coffee. "He's a really good guy. I think you'll like working with him. He could be an asset down the road. Plus, his family's like royalty in Minnesota."

"What do you mean?" I asked.

"Well, you know his grandfather was Dr. Hartman, right? Of Hartman Clinics?" Jen said. "He's the one who opened that huge medical center west of here."

"Ahh, yes. Of course. Morris Hartman, Dr. Hartman's grandson."

Jen nodded.

"Okay, got it. Well, as long as I don't blow this like the K!ng story, I'll be happy," I said. She squeezed my elbow and headed back to her desk.

"Hey Sophie, have a minute?" Kase asked, catching me as I poured cream into my mug of coffee. His teeth were slightly crooked, but sparkly white. I could smell his minty breath.

"Sure," I answered, taking a sip.

"Lots of reporters around town are covering Hartman's announcement this week. Let's try to get a different angle. Like more of an investigative approach. Do you have any ideas?"

I hadn't had time to give my story much thought. I'd barely had time to get coffee. But I wanted to prove that I *could* think like a reporter. The memory of my failed live reporting attempt from five years ago—and my failed K!ng interview—sprang to mind. My hands clammed up and I felt my heart skip a beat. "I know we're already covering health care," I stammered, remembering Barry's story. "But what if we take a look at how, or if, businesses like his are providing their employees with family medical leave." It was weak, but at least it was something.

Kase ran a hand through his red hair and then snapped his fingers. "That gives me an idea. Come over to my desk for a second." I followed him to his office. His desk, also a charging station, was immaculate. A simple wooden frame with a picture of a golden retriever sat on the desk's corner. He opened his laptop and started punching the keys.

"I like that you're thinking big picture," he said.

My shoulders relaxed a bit.

He gestured to his screen. "But instead of health care, let's look at education." He pointed to an article from News Now Online's archives. "We have Hartman on record for saying he believes Minneapolis Public Schools are headed in the right direction. He said he has full confidence in the system, or something to that effect. But look here." He pulled up the roster of a high school hockey team from an expensive and exclusive private high school in the western 'burbs. The goalie was Kincaid Hartman. "He sends his kids to the most expensive private school in the state." He looked up at me.

"So, even though he lives in Minneapolis and says he believes in the system, it's obviously not good enough for his own kids," I said.

"Bingo. That's our angle. Or at least a good start. What do you think?" Kase asked. "Do you think you're up for it?"

I tried to shake off memories of my failed interview with K!ng and managed a cool, "Yeah. I can do it."

I returned to my desk and did a quick Google search, typing in "Dr. Hartman Minnesota." Jen was right; there was a Hartman Clinic in nearly every small town across Minnesota and in every suburb of the Twin Cities. I was a little embarrassed to admit I didn't know much about the Hartman family. In less than a second, more than two million results popped up. I zipped through the queue. A Wikipedia page, the Dr. Hartman Foundation website, and a site dedicated to his legacy were at the top of the list. I scrolled through his Wikipedia page:

> *In the 1920s, when rural towns throughout Minnesota were hit especially hard by influenza, Dr. Hartman pushed for proper care and medication, especially in Crab Orchard, where he set up his first clinic. He continued visiting patients at their homes throughout the outbreak, even once during a tornado. In 1955, Dr. Hartman received the Nobel Peace Prize in Medicine.*

Wow, I thought. I knew Dr. Hartman was a big deal, but I didn't realize he'd won the Nobel Peace Prize. I typed "Morris Hartman" into a new tab. A headshot popped up. He had dark, sweeping hair and was wearing a navy suit. Turns out he owned three businesses: Hartman Metalworks, Midwest Steel Group, and Midwest Forging. He also served on a few boards of directors for some nonprofits and sat on the board for the Mining Corporation of Minnesota.

I pulled up the News Now Online shared drive that Jen had shown

18 | THE MUCKRAKER

me and clicked on the Contacts folder. There was the email address and phone number for Hartman's campaign manager, Hines Oberg. I dialed the number listed and waited. On the third ring, an answer came.

"This is Hines," said a nasally voice.

"Hi, Mr. Oberg," I said. "My name is Sophie McHale. I'm a political correspondent for News Now Online." I took a breath and charged ahead, "I'd love to schedule a sit-down with Mr. Hartman. We understand he's announcing his candidacy for governor next week."

"What's your name again? I don't think we've spoken before."

"Sophie McHale," I said, my voice betraying me and rising as I said my last name. I cleared my throat. "I'm new to News Now Online."

After a minute, he replied, "We're setting up interviews for Thursday and Friday." He paused. "Looks like he could meet with you at ten o'clock Friday morning."

"Perfect," I said, scribbling that in my spiral-bound planner.

"OK. I've got you down. I like to send over a list of issues important to Mr. Hartman prior to any interview. What's your email address?" I gave it to him and we hung up. I waved Kase down.

"All scheduled for Friday morning," I said.

"Great. Do a little more research about the education thing. Dig a bit deeper. See if you can find out why he sends his kids to private school, just so you're prepared for the conversation," Kase said.

I nodded.

"And why don't you scroll through the wire and see if there's any national news you can cover in the meantime," he said and started to walk away. "And Sophie? Great job."

My heart soared.

Chapter 4

BIZZIE

THE NEXT MORNING, Bizzie crunched along the gravel road that connected her family's cabin to the main road into Hibbing and the schoolhouse there. She was lost in thought over Leon and the poor farm he called home when she heard someone calling her name. She turned around to see Sloane, a bubbly seven-year-old in pigtails, running toward her.

"Oh, Sloane," she said, breathing a sigh of relief to see her favorite student. "It's you." Instinctively, she searched for Sloane's brother, Collin. The little girl must have noticed.

"He's comin'," she said with a smile. Sure enough, his tall frame appeared a minute later.

"Morning, Miss Bizzie," he hollered, his deep voice filling the empty and isolated gravel road.

"Good morning to you, too!" Bizzie said, a little too eagerly. To Sloane, she said, "We'll catch up to you." The little girl ran ahead toward town, turning back once to peek at her brother and her teacher. Bizzie turned to Collin. His familiar scent—fresh meadow, sweat, and mud—comforted her. She loved having him near. His broad shoulders, his square jaw, his dark hair that fell over his eyes. But, when she caught a glimpse of his eyes that morning, they looked dark and sleepy. "You didn't sleep well?" she asked.

"No. But that doesn't matter now." He pulled her in for a hug. "Maybe we could sneak away for a little nap? What do you say?"

Bizzie felt a shiver run up and down her spine. But she swatted him away. "You know school starts in a few minutes." They started walking

20 | THE MUCKRAKER

in step toward the schoolhouse.

"You okay?" Bizzie said, taking Collin's hand. Friends since they were ten years old, it had been just six months since Collin had first taken Bizzie's hand and kissed her on the cheek. Since then, he'd walked—or snowshoed—with his little sister and Bizzie to school every day.

He shrugged. "We lost one of our best milking cows last night." He rubbed his eyes and shook his head. "Pa thinks she got into a patch of goldenseal." He looked up at her. "Now he's real worried about making our supply."

"Goldenseal?" Bizzie asked.

"It's a plant that sprouted in a patch of the field. Way out. Most of the cows don't ever go that far," he shook his head again. "Don't know what happened or how she even found it."

"I've never heard of goldenseal. It's poisonous?" Bizzie asked.

"Can be in large amounts when it's not diluted," he said. He laughed at Bizzie's horrified expression. "It's not all bad. Here, I probably still have the scent on my hands. Smell it." He jabbed a hand in Bizzie's face. She immediately stepped backwards. Collin laughed. "It's not poisonous in small amounts. In fact, Ma will add it to our tea when we have a fever or a cold. Clears it up right away." He gently placed a hand behind Bizzie's lower back and again pulled her in toward him. Then, he placed his other hand on her cheek. "See? Smells good, doesn't it?"

Bizzie could hardly breathe. Her heart pounded. She looked into Collin's eyes and breathed in the goldenseal. He was right. It did smell good. It smelled like clover. Like a meadow. Like his farm.

"The shape of the leaves is like this." He kissed Bizzie's hand and traced his finger in the shape of a star. "Like little green stars with a white blossom on top. That blossom turns into a berry." Bizzie's hand tingled as he continued tracing his finger. She heard Sloane ring the school bell and jumped back.

"I guess it's—it's time for me to go in," she stammered.

Collin smirked and shrugged at the same time. "Oh, I almost forgot," he said, handing her a copy of a folded-up newspaper—*The Minneapolis Journal*. Bizzie squealed. She would devour the *Journal*, reading every page twice, imagining what it would feel like to have her name printed under an emboldened headline.

"Your uncle got this?" Bizzie asked, running her fingers over the smooth, black print.

"Yep," Collin replied. Collin's uncle worked on the Northern Pacific Railway and would pick up the latest edition of the *Journal* while shuttling through Minneapolis. It was on their walks to school that she'd begun to tell him—just a little at first—about her dream of becoming a writer. A journalist for a real newspaper. While she was living in Duluth studying to become a teacher, she got to know a reporter: Ms. Sally Salter. Sally lived near the teacher's college, and Bizzie would often walk with her and her dog, Daisy. Sally was known throughout the Iron Range for her smart writing.

"Well, you should become a writer," Ms. Sally told her matter-of-factly after Bizzie had confided in her, expressing her love for writing. "If I can do it, anyone can."

Bizzie just laughed and shook her head. "I need to support my family. Becoming a teacher is the best way to do that."

Ms. Sally nodded. "That may be true, but never forget what gives you life."

"You comin', Miss Bizzie?" Sloane stood near the schoolhouse door, waiting. She waved to Collin and hopped up the steps.

At lunch, while the students ate their sandwiches outside on the grass, Bizzie stole a few moments of silence at her desk. Eagerly, she flipped through the pages of the newspaper. A story on the third page caught her attention. It was about Hibbing—her beloved hometown. Her eyes were glued to the black ink as she read:

> *Hibbing in the winter is like a second Siberia. It's unfit for human habitation. The unbearable frozen land marked by the gray unrelenting sky is as unfriendly as a wicked headmistress.*

Appalled, she read on, learning that the reporter had passed through Hibbing on his way to Thunder Bay to visit a fur trading camp. He vowed to never return to northern Minnesota.

"Another Siberia?" she muttered to herself.

Shocked and indignant, Bizzie whipped out a piece of crisp printing paper and a pencil from her desk and angrily began to write.

> *Dear editor of The Minneapolis Journal,*
>
> *I read your reporter's most unflattering remarks about my beloved hometown of Hibbing. I nearly think he should be fired on the spot for slander. Each November, when the frost kisses the*

windowpanes of our log cabin, the Winter Carnival sprawls open. Sculptors carve intricate animals and beasts out of blocks of ice. I snowshoe the half-mile to and from work, meeting the peacefulness and stillness in the woods. And on crisp, December nights, there is nothing gentler than snowflakes falling silently to the ground.

When she was finished, Bizzie smiled at the completed letter. Practicing her signature on the blackboard behind her, she wrote "Bizzie Johansen."

"Sounds like a child's name," she muttered to herself. She erased that and tried again, thinking of Sally Salter. This time she wrote: Elizabeth Johansen. She frowned. She wanted to be taken seriously, to sound authoritative. She grabbed *The Journal* from her desk and flipped through it. Full of male reporters. She tried a third time: E. Johansen. She smiled. That would work.

Before the students returned for afternoon lessons, she signed the letter and tucked it into her bag just as the children filed in from lunch.

After a tedious math lesson, twenty minutes of reading, and a spelling quiz, Bizzie opened the wooden door, letting sunshine and fresh air stream in, a sign of the end of the school day. Her students jumped to their feet, grabbed their books, and bolted out the door. All except for Sloane. She helped Bizzie erase the math lesson on the blackboard. A deep voice made them both turn.

"Hi, Collin," Sloane greeted her older brother.

He smiled at them both. "Sloane, want to pick some dandelions for Miss Bizzie?"

The girl smiled and flew out the door into the meadow. While Bizzie continued cleaning up the schoolhouse, Collin sat down at her desk and crossed his feet on it. Mud from the farm splattered across her papers.

"Collin!" she said, swatting him with *The Minneapolis Journal*.

"Did you already read through that?" he asked her.

"Of course," she smiled. "And I loved it. Except, one of the reporters wrote a terribly unflattering article about Hibbing during the winter." She folded her arms. "I wrote to the editor, telling him the good things about our little town."

Collin smiled, clearly amused. "Good things during the winter? Like what?"

"Well, for one, the Winter Carnival. I told him about snowshoeing to school and the gentleness of snowflakes falling to the ground."

"So, you wrote a letter to the editor." He was up now, pacing across the scrubbed, pine floors. In a high-pitched voice, Collin said, "'Dear editor, I live in the best town because a handsome man walks me home every night. His name is Collin Lancaster.'"

"Oh, is that what makes Hibbing so great?" Bizzie giggled.

Sloane burst in with a bouquet of dandelions and set them gently on Bizzie's desk. Then, turning to Collin, she said, "Are you ready? I want to see how my baby kittens are doing back at the farm."

Collin nodded and stuck out both of his elbows. To Bizzie, he said in a deep voice, "Miss, Bizzie, may we accompany you home?"

She and Sloane rolled their eyes and laughed. Each of them took one of his arms and off they went.

Bizzie walked into her family's log cabin and found her mother, Alice, standing over the stove. She turned and looked Bizzie up and down, then turned back to her cooking with a frown. Bizzie could count on one hand the number of times she'd seen her mother smile. And after the mining accident the previous year, things had only grown worse. Bizzie knew her mother longed for a life of nice things. Instead, she'd married Bizzie's father, the son of a miner. Despite his wife's pleading for a comfortable existence in St. Paul, he longed for the mines. He'd promised Bizzie's mother they'd only stay on the Iron Range for a couple of years. But a couple of years turned into five, ten, now twenty, and Bizzie could chart the way her mother's bitterness steeped into a roiling undercurrent of fowl moods and dissatisfaction.

"Hello, Papa." She went over to her father who was nestled in his favorite chair. A family of birds had built their nest on the tree right outside. Bizzie's father delighted in listening to them chirp and sing. Even though the mine accident had taken his sight, he always knew when they flew south for the winter. The nest would turn silent, a sign of the colder weather to come. Bizzie set down her bag, knelt down next to him, and grabbed his hand. He lifted her small, smooth hand and rubbed it against his scratchy beard.

"My Bizzie is home, my Bizzie is home," he sang in his rich, deep voice, something he did every afternoon when Bizzie returned home from teaching. "And how are the young scholars today?"

24 | THE MUCKRAKER

Bizzie sighed. "Henry O'Teale is causing trouble again. He brought a frog to school and set it on my desk." Bizzie's father burst out laughing, a welcome sound in the dreary, dark cabin.

"Oh, Henry, my lad, you'll get what's coming to you," he smiled. Then gestured for Bizzie to come closer and whispered, "Did you steal away some time to write today?"

Bizzie smiled. Then, glancing toward her mother, she reached into her bag and took out her brown leather journal. The letter was tucked neatly inside. Bizzie explained that she'd written a letter to the editor of the *Journal*, expressing the beautiful yet brutal parts of a northern Minnesota winter.

"Will you read me the letter you wrote?" Bizzie's father asked. He settled back in his chair, closed his eyes, and rested his hands upon his stomach, as if he was preparing to listen to a beautiful symphony.

When Bizzie finished reading it, she looked up to see tears sparkling in Papa's eyes. "I'm glad you can see the beauty I do," he patted his heart. "I can still see it in here."

"Elizabeth, it's time you helped me get dinner on the table," Alice snapped. She was wearing a white apron, and her hair was pinned in a tight bun. After Papa's accident, Alice had to find work. She knew the owner of the Chatsworth Hotel, Hibbing's only inn. He offered her a job as a housekeeper. That, paired with Bizzie's teaching salary, fed and clothed the three of them. Bizzie squeezed Papa's hand, tucked the letter inside her journal, and hurried over to help her mother. Until she found a way to make as much money from her writing as she did from teaching, she was just as stuck at her job as her mother was at hers.

Chapter 5

SOPHIE

I SURVIVED THE NEXT FEW DAYS with lots of coffee in the morning and wine at night. At work, I spent my time rewriting a few stories that came through on the Associated Press wires; I could soon spout off more details about healthcare reform and budget proposals for a nationwide infrastructure bill than most would care to know. I learned how to write in News Now Online's tone. The brand standards document was like a dictionary. At KOMO, the brand standard was this: Use the new logo and always say "alleged" until the suspect has been formally charged. At News Now Online, an entire page was dedicated to words to use instead of "was."

At home, on my Pottery Barn sectional I bought when our team won our first Emmy at KOMO, I lounged in my decade-old, college sweatpants and flipped on *Outlander*. Then, I snatched up any dirt I could on Morris Hartman…which wasn't much. For a white Republican businessman from the suburbs with a pretty wife and three kids, it was no surprise his record was spotless. I jotted down a few notes while sipping moscato and admiring Jamie Fraser's kilted legs on my screen.

On Friday morning, I headed straight for Hartman's campaign office for the hour-long chat. Kase told me to call or text if anything came up. Flashbacks of my failed interview with K!ng danced through my head. I brushed those off, pulled on my favorite zebra-print blazer, and swiped on some nude lipstick. I tied my hair in a neat bun on top of my head and slid in some red, leather teardrop earrings. Because his office was in the suburbs, I ditched the bus and hopped in my red

Kia Optima that was parked in the dimly lit apartment garage.

The campaign office was sandwiched between an autism therapy center and a donut shop. I was tempted to swing in and grab a treat, but instead I took a sip of my lukewarm coffee and pulled open the door to Hartman's headquarters. Gray carpet covered the floor. Posters with Hartman's logo, the letter "M" inside the state of Minnesota, were pinned on the beige, cubicle walls. A short, pink-faced man talking on the phone wearing a "Morris for Governor" t-shirt waved me in. I sat in one of the plastic chairs against the window and pulled out my notes and laptop. A minute later, the man came over.

"Sorry about that." He held out a hand. "Hines Oberg." I stood and shook his hand. At my height of almost six feet, I towered over him. He looked to be in his early forties and squinted when he talked. It appeared he was trying to grow a mustache above his lip, but the attempt reminded me of a middle school boy.

"I'm Mr. Hartman's campaign manager. He'll be out in just a minute." Mr. Oberg told me he'd be at his desk if I needed anything, and I returned to my notes. I could hear him make another call.

"I don't care if that doesn't work," he shrieked. "Make it work!"

A minute later, Morris Hartman walked to the entryway where I sat. He was taller than I anticipated. And better looking. His brown hair was peppered with a few grays and fell just above his blue eyes. Wearing a navy suit, he looked almost presidential. When he came over to me, I smelled his aftershave—a mix of cedar and lime.

"Sophie?" he asked, smiling. He stuck out his hand. I stood and we exchanged greetings.

"I'm so sorry I'm late. Let's go back to my office," he said and led me through the space. He stepped around an opened, cardboard box filled with "Morris for Governor" t-shirts—the same one Hines was wearing. Inside his office, an L-shaped desk made of distressed wood and dark iron legs sat in the corner. Instinctively, I reached my hand out and slid it across the smooth surface. *Nice, but does it charge your cell phone?*

"Nice, right?" Morris said, motioning for me to sit.

"It is," I said, impressed.

"Thanks. I made it with my son, Kincaid," he said. "It was our summer project." He shrugged, as if it was no big deal.

"Really?" I smiled. "That's amazing!" A flashback of my interview with K!ng popped into my mind, and I tried to return to my ball-buster reporter facade while Hartman kept on about the desk.

"My grandfather, Dr. Hartman, had a farm west of here. We had to tear it down but were able to save some of the wood." I perked up at the mention of Dr. Hartman. *Should I lead with questions about the medical clinics?* I wondered. *No*, I brushed the thought away, going back to my prepared notes.

"So, let's talk," he smiled, then folded his hands and set them on his desk.

"Well, I want to ask you a few questions about your, er, Support the Schools plan." I glanced down at my notebook. "You say within the first sixty days of your administration, you want to introduce this program to all the schools in Minneapolis. You say it'll bolster technology funds and aim to give all tenured teachers salary increases. We have you on record saying that you have complete faith in the school system, and that it's headed in the right direction." I paused and glanced up. Morris nodded. "But you send your kids to a private school—Northwest Academy—in one of the wealthiest suburbs in the state."

"You know what, Sophie, I'm glad you brought this up. I've been wanting to address this for a while." He sat back in his chair and crossed his legs. "I actually feel like a hypocrite. I mean, I'm all about empowering the public school sector in Minneapolis, but I'm not sending my own kids there."

I didn't respond. This wasn't the response I was expecting—nor was it the one I was hoping for. I was hoping to catch him off guard, not get some politician-slick answer.

"My wife and I are actually in the midst of a conversation about our kids' future. We want them to be agents of change and be part of this movement for bettering our schools and our communities." He paused. "Let me just say this. And it doesn't sound very polished. I'm sure Hines would kill me for saying this to a reporter." He laughed and rolled his eyes. "But I trust you. Look, I know that I look like a hypocrite." He held up his hands like he had nothing to hide. "I'll fully admit to that. And—on the record—my family and I are working to create a more streamlined plan that works for us and, at the same time, supports my education plan."

I nodded.

"So," I bit my lip. "It works for you. Your family. But what about them? Every kid in the public school system?" I held my breath, terrified that he might take offense to the question, but also desperately wanting him to reveal something deeper that I could bring back to Kase.

Morris nodded and sat up straighter in his chair. "That's an excellent point. Yes, we—my family—want to find a path forward that works for all of us—those who live under one roof. But we—my family—also need to remember that we are representing every one of them—the students in the public school system. And that's what really matters."

"So, you're saying your own kids care about the well-being of other kids they don't even know?" My heart was pounding.

Morris chuckled. "I know, I know. Get teens to look up from their screens and it's a miracle, right? But, honestly, yes. Kincaid and Euphegenia really do care. Kick coaches lacrosse to underprivileged athletes in the city, and Effie teaches violin lessons to kids who want to learn but can't afford the instrument. She's set up this whole renting system and everything. In fact, last year," he pulled out his phone and began scrolling, "they were both invited to speak at Minneapolis' Youth Volunteer Summit." He showed me a picture of two beaming, seemingly perfect teenagers.

I forced a smile and mumbled, "Could you send me that? We'd love to use it with our story." I typed some worthless notes into my blank Word document, cursing myself for yet another failed interview. This time I came prepared and still only ended up with fluff.

For the next half hour, Morris rattled off everything that was in the media kit Hines sent over earlier in the week. My palms were sweaty as I wondered what I would say to Kase. This was my chance to make a good impression and prove that I really could ask the tough questions. Before our conversation came to an end, I did ask Morris if I could snap a few photos for our Instagram feed. He smiled and posed, looking natural and comfortable behind his desk. When Morris walked me out, I noticed Hines was on his phone again. He nodded a good-bye in my direction. Morris shook my hand and told me to call anytime.

I didn't bother texting Kase. I figured I could break the news to him—that I wasn't breaking any news—when I returned to the office.

For the second time that morning, I skipped the donuts. I climbed back into the Kia, punched in Freya's number, and the phone rang through my car's Bluetooth.

"Hello?" Freya answered breathlessly.

"Bad time?" I asked.

"No…just trying to change a toddler's diaper and nurse an infant at the same time. How's your day going?"

I laughed. "Yours sounds harder. I just had an interview with Morris Hartman. He's announcing he's running for governor next week. But I think I bombed this one too," I moaned as I merged onto Highway 394.

In a calm voice, Freya said, "Tell me what happened."

I explained how Morris was uber-prepared to answer all of my questions. "Everyone at News Now Online is revolting against the status quo. And I'm like, 'Hi! I'm new here. I don't know how to be a reporter.'"

Freya laughed. "Stop that right now," she murmured to one of the kids. "Sophie, when I brought Lucy home from the hospital, she wouldn't sleep. Like, THE CHILD DID NOT SLEEP. After three sleepless nights, I called my mom, bawling. I was legit going insane. You know what she told me?"

I smiled. "Something wise, I'm sure."

"No! She said, 'Freya, get your shit together.'"

"Wow. That's not what I was expecting."

"Well, that's my mom for you. Sophie, get your shit together. You're an Emmy-award winning producer. You know how to ask a few hard questions. Quit doubting yourself." I heard a wail in the background. "I gotta go. Baby needs me."

I laughed and hung up just as I pulled into the Conley-Mass parking lot. When I walked into News Now Online with a burst of confidence thanks to Freya, the place was bustling with an energy I hadn't seen all week. Kase saw me come in and waved me down.

"Sophie!" He came over to me, his phone in his hand. "Did you hear? DFL candidate Jim Jansrud has been accused of sexual misconduct via Twitter."

Shit. "No, I hadn't heard. I had my sit-down with Morris Hartman this morning."

He looked up from his phone. "Oh, that's right. How'd it go?"

"Um, it went well," I squeaked, the newsroom's energy of *real* reporters working and Kase's voice shredding my confidence. I couldn't help but feel like an imposter. I stammered, "I think it'll come together into a good story."

"Sounds great," Kase responded, looking back at his phone. He was clearly preoccupied with this Jansrud news, which worked in my favor. "Right now, our entire team has scratched their assignments and is working on the Jansrud story. The alleged victim's Twitter handle is JanAnon. Like Jansrud Anonymous. We're trying to figure out who might be behind the account." Jen walked by and handed him a stack of papers. She smiled at me. Kase said to both of us, "Gotta run to a meeting. I'll catch up with you both this afternoon."

When Kase walked away, I let out a sigh of relief.

"You met with Morris this morning, right?" Jen said, walking with me to my desk.

"I did," I nodded. "It was great. He was super nice. I just don't know if it makes for a compelling story."

Jen shrugged. "Sometimes we just share the facts, and that's okay."

I tucked this nugget away. Although it seemed against News Now Online's brand and ethos to "just share the facts," it did make me feel better. I sat down and pulled out my laptop, reading through my fruitless notes from the morning. As I ran my hand along the white laminate workspace that was charging my phone, I thought of Hartman's reclaimed wooden desk. Curious to learn a bit more about Dr. Hartman while the rest of my team dug into JanAnon, I did another Google search.

This time, I punched in "Dr. Joseph Hartman, Crab Orchard, farm." I scanned the results and clicked on a hit from the *Crab Orchard Tribune*—something about celebrating his legacy.

> *Dr. Joseph Hartman moved to Minnesota in 1920 after graduating from medical school in New York City. He began a small country clinic in Crab Orchard. Soon, he became known as 'Good Doctor Hartman,' because he would make house calls whenever necessary. But a year later, disaster struck. A tornado demolished Crab Orchard, including Dr. Hartman's clinic. With the help of the community and a few wealthy investors, Dr. Hartman rebuilt his practice. He was able to buy land and hire renowned architects who created custom buildings and furnishings. Ten years later, the Crab Orchard Health Center, Spa, and Sanitarium became known as the Oasis of the Midwest, offering cutting-edge cures, medications, and research.*

I noticed a link to another article, also featured in the *Tribune*. "The Oasis, Founded by Dr. Joe Hartman, to be Demolished." I clicked on it. According to the paper, the Health Center—known to Crab Orchard residents as the "Castle on the Hill"—had been vacant for the last twenty years. Because none of the redevelopment proposals had been successful, the article—dated a month earlier—said the city council was considering demolition. Doubtful that any substantial story could come from this but desperate to avoid another K!ng debacle, I dialed Hines' number.

A stilted voice answered.

"Hi, Hines. Sophie McHale here. You know, I forgot to ask Mr. Hartman one question. I'm wondering if I could chat with him. It'll only take a minute."

A pause on the other end. Then, "Let me see if he's still here." Silence. A minute later, a friendly voice said, "This is Morris."

"Hi, Mr. Hartman. This is Sophie McHale. I'm sorry to bother you." Nervously, I doodled designs on my notebook. "I was thinking about Dr. Hartman, your grandfather. You mentioned him today when you talked about your desk. You said he lived on a farm, where he developed a country clinic into the Oasis?"

"That's right," Hartman said.

"I read that it's slated for demolition. Just wondering if you care to comment about that. I'm sure it's all a bit sentimental," I said.

Silence on the other end. "I'm sorry, Sophie, but I have another call coming in. Let's talk about this next time we see each other, okay?"

With that, he hung up.

"That's strange," I muttered to myself.

I reviewed the demolition article again. Community preservationists were trying to save the Oasis. Calling themselves "Friends of the Oasis," the article named Greg and Ida Kirkbridge as the leaders. I found their phone number at the end of the article and gave them a call. Within a few minutes, I had set up a tour with Ida. I snuck out the door while Kase and my other coworkers were getting nowhere investigating a Twitter account.

Chapter 6

BIZZIE

BIZZIE ARRIVED AT SCHOOL EARLY so she could prepare the day's math lesson. It was no easy task. With students from young Henry—an adorable, blue-eyed, five-year-old who didn't yet know his ABCs—to sixteen-year-old Clara, who was a bit too smart for her own good, Bizzie struggled to teach so all the children would understand the lesson and be challenged by it.

When the school door banged open, Bizzie nearly fell off her chair. She looked up to see Collin and Sloane, both breathless, holding a newspaper.

"Collin, what is it?" she said, standing up and meeting them in the middle of the small schoolhouse.

"Bizzie! You're not going to believe it," he said, his eyes twinkling. Sloane stood by his side, grinning ear-to-ear.

He flipped open the paper—*The Minneapolis Journal*—and set it down on one of the wooden desks.

"Look at this!" He pressed a stained and calloused finger in the middle of the paper. Bizzie peered over his shoulder, smelling sweat and dust.

> *Notice: Will the gentleman who wrote a letter to the Journal, criticizing our editorial of "Hibbing During the Winter" please send his name to the editor? Mr. Kavanaugh, editor, wishes to discuss with the contributor the possibility of him writing a feature article on the benefits of living in the northern part of the state, even during the winter.*

Bizzie shrieked, then jumped up and down. She hadn't expected the editor himself to respond to her letter. She hadn't expected a response at all.

"You have to respond right away!" Collin said, guiding her back to her desk and settling her in her chair. He shuffled papers around her desk, trying to find one that didn't already have writing on it. Bizzie laughed and shook her head.

"Let me," she said, grabbing a piece of blank paper from her desk drawer. She tapped her pencil against her chin. She wrote:

Mr. Robert J. Kavanaugh, Editor of The Minneapolis Journal

Dear Sir,

In answer to your printed request for the name of the person who answered your "Hibbing During the Winter" editorial, I am that person. I am most interested in writing articles for your paper. I realize you are not expecting to hear from a woman, but it truly makes no difference whether I am a man or a woman. I beg of you to give me an interview

Bizzie shook her head and stopped mid-sentence. "This is hopeless," she muttered, then crumpled the paper and threw it on the floor. "He'll never interview me—a woman. Not even a woman. A girl."

"Well, he read your article, didn't he, E. Johansen?" Collin raised his eyebrows at her. "He can't refuse an interview to *that* person."

"But—but, he'll think I'm a man," Bizzie sputtered.

"Let him think that. Show up for the interview and *make* him give you the job." Collin grabbed her small, smooth hands. "Bizzie, this is what you've always wanted. This is what you've dreamed about." He paused. "This could be your ticket out of here." He chewed those last words and spit them out; she knew just uttering them pained him.

Bizzie thought for a moment. "He will at least have to give me one moment of his time."

She grabbed a new piece of paper and determinedly began to write.

Dear Mr. Robert J. Kavanaugh,

In reply to your request, I am the person who wrote to you about "Hibbing During the Winter." May I suggest next Friday afternoon at three o'clock for our appointment? I will be at your office promptly at that time.

Sincerely, E. Johansen

She nodded, pleased with the note.

"By next Friday, school will be out for planting season and I'll have the time to go away to the city for a few days," she said.

Collin nodded. "Quick, address it and I'll run it to the post office. Mail goes out this morning," he said.

Bizzie smiled and wrote down Mr. Kavanaugh's address. She grasped the note to her chest for a moment before handing it to Collin. "Sloane, do you mind laying out new pieces of chalk for the day?" Bizzie asked.

The girl nodded, her pigtails bobbing. Bizzie grabbed Collin's hand and walked him towards the schoolhouse door.

"Thank you," she said. "You've always believed in me."

Collin grinned. "Since fifth grade. Remember? You helped me finish that darned math problem. Everyone else just laughed at me. But you never gave up on me either."

Bizzie smiled, then opened the door for Collin. "Mind ringing the school bell on your way to the post office?"

He nodded and tipped his hat to her. "Not at all, ma'am. Or should I say, E. Johansen?" With that, he was off, her future in his hands.

On Friday morning, Bizzie kissed her Papa goodbye while he sat in his armchair.

"I'm off to Minneapolis for a conference," she lied. For once, Bizzie was grateful Papa couldn't see her. Tears streamed down her face, and she silently wiped them away with the back of her hand. Doubt crept into her mind. *Should she really leave behind this life? She was, after all, comfortable. Her basic needs were met.* She looked up just in time to see her mother peeling potatoes. Her frown was, as usual, plastered on her face. There was a look in her eyes that gripped Bizzie's core. A look of misery. Desperation. Nothingness. An unfulfilled life. Bizzie swallowed and gritted her teeth. If she wanted a life different from this—from that of her mother's—this, right now, was her chance. She squeezed Papa's hand and grabbed her small satchel. She carefully filled it with her two best dresses, two picture frames, her journal, and a blanket. On the table was a brown leather journal tied with a piece of twine. She looked back at her father, lovingly. How did he know she'd need a journal? She held the journal to her chest and took one last deep breath.

She paused near the kitchen stove. "Well, I'll be off, then," she said quietly.

Her mother turned around, raised her eyebrows, and shrugged. "Look after yourself," she said. She turned back to the potatoes without another word.

Collin met her outside the cabin, ready to walk her to the Hibbing Train Station. The train was slated to make one stop in Duluth, then it would head non-stop for Minneapolis. Bizzie's heart fluttered with nerves and excitement. Collin must have noticed. He grabbed her hand and they walked in step.

"You are fearless, you know," he told her after a few minutes, still holding her hand.

Bizzie scoffed. "Not me. I'm terrified right now."

"You might be scared, but you're still fearless. I don't know many other young women boarding a train bound for Minneapolis, ready to meet with an editor and ask for a job."

Bizzie laughed. "I don't think you mean fearless. I think you mean thoughtless and silly."

Collin gestured at the train platform. "Look," he waved his hand. "Almost all men. Or families."

Bizzie looked around. He was right. She was the only young woman riding alone. The train let out a high whistle, and Bizzie took a deep breath and nodded.

"Good luck, E. Johansen," he whispered into her ear before backing away. Bizzie grabbed her satchel and boarded the train bound for the city. Her life was about to change.

Minneapolis was a shocking clash of noise, movement, crowds, and languages. The streets were filled with huge wooden carts pulled by stomping horses, dainty carriages, pushcarts, streetcars, and automobiles all tromping noisily over the uneven cobblestones, raising clouds of dust. Hawkers cried out, selling their wares. Women stood behind booths of flowers and scrubbed potatoes. Peddlers selling buttons and handkerchiefs and bars of soap paraded through the streets. Men pushed bricks of ice in wheelbarrows, chipping off bits for paying customers. People flowed in every direction, jostling each other and carrying bags and packages tucked under their arms. The city was both stimulating and thrilling, terrifying and overwhelming. Bizzie had dreamed of coming to this place and working as a writer for so long, she nearly had to pinch herself to believe it was actually, finally, coming true.

When she strolled past Dayton's, Bizzie paused and cupped her hands to peek inside the windows. She'd heard her mother often mutter, "A woman could get used to shopping at Dayton's." Then, she'd look at Papa and say, "But not me. I have to make all my own clothes." At that, Papa would sigh and pat her hand.

Inside, Bizzie saw a woman holding a sweater. Another held up a coffee-colored, silk dress. She longed to step inside, just to take part in the magic of it all.

Newsboys startled her, hollering from the corner of Fourth and Hennepin, their voices loud and grating. From where she stood, she could clearly see The Minneapolis Journal building. She felt a zing of excitement run through her body—almost a shock—as she looked on at the competing papers and print shops lining Fourth Street: The Penny Press, The Minneapolis Tribune, Leighton Bros. Printing, The Times. She'd read stories about Newspaper Row, but to see it in person was almost magical. Ten minutes before three, she walked through the doors of The Minneapolis Journal building.

She pulled open the heavy, wooden door and was smacked in the face with the smell of tobacco and ink. The receptionist, short with a thin mustache, greeted her behind a counter.

"Afternoon, ma'am. How can I help you?" he asked.

"I have a meeting with Mr. Kavanaugh," Bizzie murmured. "My name is E. Johansen," she added. The receptionist looked her up and down and said nothing. Bizzie's heart pounded. Just as she was about to stammer an excuse and run back out through the door, he nodded.

"I'll send for his assistant, Charles."

Minutes later, Charles, a tall and lanky man in his early twenties, appeared. He wound her past ink-stained desks to an office in the back corner with a nameplate that read 'H. Kavanaugh.' Bizzie could hear the steady clack-clack of the presses beneath her feet.

Charles knocked on the editor's door. It swung open to reveal a balding man with spectacles hanging from his neck. Charles shrugged and pointed to Bizzie.

Finally, the balding man sputtered, "Can I help you?"

Bizzie cleared her throat. "I believe I have an appointment with you, Mr. Kavanaugh." Bizzie pointed to the nameplate on the door.

"You're E. Johansen?" Mr. Kavanaugh asked.

Bizzie nodded.

No one said a word for a good five seconds.

Finally, Mr. Kavanaugh ushered Bizzie into his office. "Uh, please sit down," he said, clearing the newspapers off the shabby couch and thrusting them at Charles' chest.

"Charles, get this young lady a glass of water," he demanded, not taking his eyes off Bizzie who was now perched on the edge of the couch. The men in the office had caught wind of her presence and huddled together, peering through the door that was left ajar. "And close the door!"

Charles shook his head and slammed the door a little too hard, causing Bizzie to jump.

"What is your name, young lady?"

"Bizz—" she started, then cleared her throat and with her fingertips, smoothed the invisible wrinkles on her skirt. "Elizabeth. Elizabeth Johansen."

"Miss Johansen," Mr. Kavanaugh said, sitting back in his chair and putting two fingers to his graying temple. "How old are you?"

Bizzie responded a bit too quickly, her words coming out jumbled. "I know I look young, but I'm a good writer. It's the only thing I want to do." She sniffed once and then sat forward on the edge of her seat to continue. "I teach school to the north of here and have learned writing skills that could help me. I know I'd make a good reporter."

"Reporter?" Mr. Kavanaugh laughed.

"Mr. Kavanaugh," Bizzie said, her voice a little stronger and a little brighter. "I have ideas. More than just how to handle the brutal winters up north. My father was in a mining accident last year. The conditions inside the mine are deplorable. But no one knows that because those stories aren't told."

She paused as Charles stepped in with her water. He glanced sideways at Mr. Kavanaugh who waved him away.

"Newspapers are supposed to report about big people," Mr. Kavanaugh said. "People buy *The Journal* to read about rich people.

Influential people."

"But Mr. Kavanaugh," she said, "my father is influential in *our* town. And I think his experience could help other miners. And factory workers. And suppressed laborers. Don't you see? Writing about real people—real stories—could bring life to your newspaper."

Bizzie noticed Mr. Kavanaugh flinch at her last line.

She dared to proceed. "With half a dozen papers on Newspaper Row, aren't you looking for a way to make sure folks notice *The Journal?*"

A brief pause, then she plunged ahead. "Some of your readers are wealthy, yes, but lots are working class," she said, thinking about Collin's uncle, hopping off the train to fetch a copy of the latest news. "They want to read about real lives, real people just like them! What about the county poor farms here in Minnesota?" Bizzie asked with intensity. She thought of Leon, the sweet boy sentenced to a life of despair, living in such awful circumstances. "I've been to the Hibbing County poor farm and let me tell you, sir, that's something one never forgets. Eight people crowded in one tiny room, huddled around a measly fire. Children's feet wrapped in dirty cloth." Bizzie shuddered. "They deserve to be heard, Mr. Kavanaugh."

Just then, Bizzie was struck with another idea. Her eyes wide, her hands gesturing wildly, she got up and paced back and forth in his office, seeming to almost forget he was there. Bizzie felt Mr. Kavanaugh watching her.

"What about illiteracy in America? Try teaching young children to read when their own parents can't even help them at home or read them a bedtime story," Bizzie said tenderly. "These are issues that real people are dealing with, Mr. Kavanaugh. And they must be told. So those big men with influence and power can be inspired to do something about it. At least we can give them that." With that, her speech was over, and she sat. Her hands folded in her lap, she appeared to transform back into a timid, young girl.

"Well, Miss Johansen…" Mr. Kavanaugh shook his head and furrowed his brow.

Bizzie braced herself for the worst. Then, she noticed him glance at a photograph on his desk. It was a picture of a girl.

Bizzie nodded toward the photograph. "Your daughter?"

Mr. Kavanaugh didn't say anything. Instead, he sat down and scratched his chin. A moment later, he responded, "That is my daughter. She's, well, she's a lot like you, to be honest." A slight smile came over his face. "We can start with just one story. You prove you're up for the challenge, we'll talk about another."

Bizzie's eyes grew wide. She stood, enveloping Mr. Kavanaugh's right hand with both of hers. "I won't disappoint you, sir. I will make you proud."

"Now, which issue shall we tackle first?" Mr. Kavanaugh said out loud, though not quite in question form. He sat down at his desk and tapped his chin. "There's a county poor farm east of St. Paul. It won't be as impressive as the one you speak of in Hibbing," he said. "But it could work. I'll assign a photographer to accompany you. Meet here tomorrow. Eight o'clock sharp is our morning corral."

"I'll be ready," Bizzie said, beaming. "Oh, what about pay, Mr. Kavanaugh?"

The question seemed to catch him by surprise. "Well, uh, two cents a word."

"Ten," Bizzie countered.

Mr. Kavanaugh let out a blast of laughter. "Not even our famous Teddy Solberg gets ten cents a word!"

"Well, how about five cents then?" Bizzie crossed her arms, willing herself to remain unwavering.

After a moment, Mr. Kavanaugh nodded. "Five cents a word."

He opened the door of his office and Bizzie tiptoed out. She noticed all the male reporters sitting around, chewing tobacco then carelessly spitting into their cuspidors, tobacco juices spewing from their mouths. One of the men sneered at Bizzie. Another winked. Mr. Kavanaugh guided her out of the office. He scraped a hand through his thinning, gray hair and turned to face the reporters.

"You there!" he called to one of the men. "Where's that article about that Catholic high school? What's it called?"

The reporter sputtered and coughed, rummaging through the mound of papers on his desk. Bizzie watched in awe as he handed a crumpled piece of paper to Mr. Kavanaugh. "Here it is…DeLaSalle Institute, sir."

Mr. Kavanaugh snatched it out of his hand and scanned the copy. He turned and began pacing back through the men, tapping his finger on his chin. Bizzie noticed the reporters exchanging confused glances.

Mr. Kavanaugh stopped abruptly and stuck his bluish, ink-stained index finger to the second paragraph, nearly punching a hole in the paper. "Here you write, 'The Institute will be home to fifty young boys from mostly immigrant families.' Let's get to know these young men! Let's get to know their families!"

Mr. Kavanaugh was nearly running across the room now. "Yes! Yes! You see it, don't you? A full-feature piece on one of the families who will be sending their son to DeLaSalle Institute. They moved to Minneapolis from Ireland, seeking a better life. Why are they seeking out a Catholic school?" Then, almost to himself, he muttered, "You won't see The Penny Press running a feature story like that."

Bizzie saw Mr. Kavanaugh turn to face the men with blank stares on their faces.

"Damnit! What is wrong with you? I thought I hired reporters—real journalists." He crumpled the paper and threw it on the ground in front of him. "Search for the details that make news compelling. Search for the stories that sell newspapers. Search for the stories that will set us above the rest."

When no one responded, he threw his hands up, stomped back to his office, and slammed his door, forcing Bizzie to see herself out alone.

Chapter 7

SOPHIE

I LEFT THE CONLEY-MASS PARKING LOT and headed west to Crab Orchard. *Should I stay and sift through potential Twitter leads?* I wondered. I desperately wanted to prove to Kase and the other reporters that I could dig up dirt. That I could ask the hard questions. That I belonged at News Now. I took a deep breath and sped onto the highway. Besides, Ida Kirkbridge would be waiting for me.

Turns out, Crab Orchard was further from Minneapolis than I had thought. When I got to the Highway 6 exit, I had been driving for almost an hour. A gentle rain started to fall, and I flicked on my wipers and headlights. I understood why residents in town called the Oasis the "Castle on the Hill." It was the first thing I noticed. I passed a McDonald's and Subway before driving through Crab Orchard's quaint downtown. I spotted a diner, an art gallery, a community center, and a coffee shop called The Coffee Fox. I stopped at a four-way intersection where an older couple slowly crossed the road, arm-in-arm. Absent-mindedly, I drummed my fingers on the steering wheel.

"Hurry up," I muttered. I sped through a string of big, old, Victorian houses, keeping the Oasis in my line of sight. The road stretched out for a bit. Then, a driveway appeared, leading up a hill. Someone had already unlocked and unhooked a rusty chain that lay scattered on the ground. I turned up the steep and winding path. I could see at least six buildings, with the largest being a tall, austere-looking structure. According to an article I read online, that was the Grand Hall. Two long, straight wings radiated from it, forming a U-shape. Three ornate, brick towers stood in the center. What was once, I assumed, a grand and comforting retreat

42 | THE MUCKRAKER

was now foreboding and sad. The Grand Hall, a colossal five-story structure, looked like its very heart had stopped beating. Most rooms didn't have any windows left intact and the ones that did were cracked or shattered. Years of water damage had bleached the brick's exterior.

Two cars sat in the gravel parking lot. I pulled up and parked next to a green Toyota. Crunching on the wet gravel, I couldn't help but gape at the vast architecture and grounds. I had forgotten an umbrella, so I awkwardly held my green tote bag over my head to avoid the raindrops.

Pulling open the heavy, wooden front door, I was hit with a musty, sour smell so strong that I instinctively covered my nose. A stout woman with short brown hair and stringy bangs stood in the immense entryway. She smiled when she saw me. Despite the crumbling building around her, she seemed content to be in this creepy, haunting space. That fact alone made me a little unnerved.

"Sophie?" she said, holding out a hand. "I'm Ida Kirkbridge." We shook hands and I let my eyes adjust to the space. Two decaying Romanesque-style pillars, which I'm sure were once beautiful but now were covered in spray-painted graffiti, welcomed me. Straight ahead, I saw a pile of crumbling bricks. To my left, a patch of loose plywood boards. To my right, a rickety staircase. Ida must have seen my face.

"I know," she said. "The condition…the deterioration…it's a bit of a shock."

"Yeah…" I managed. "I'm not sure what I was expecting. Wow." I wanted to turn around and run back to my car. Away from this small town and sagging heap of forgotten history and back to the familiar city. *What was I thinking? Clearly, there's no story here.* But I had made the drive. I might as well take a look around.

Ida carried a flashlight and several white plastic buckets. She motioned around the Grand Hall with her flashlight. "This is what happens when you leave a building of this size shuttered for twenty years. Water damage, vandalism, mold, bats. Some people say ghosts too."

I grimaced when she mentioned bats and ghosts. "So, why are you trying to save this place, if it's in this kind of shape?" I asked, taking out my phone and pressing record. I motioned to it and asked, "You don't mind, do you?"

"You go right ahead." She took a deep breath and looked out the window. "I come from a long line of Kirkbridges in Crab Orchard. And this Oasis has been important to us all. My grandfather was on the country clinic's first board of directors. My grandmother was part of Dr. Hartman's original staff. But, more than that, it's a piece of the town. It's a piece of history. It makes us who we are." She leaned forward. "I have to say, I'm a bit surprised to have gotten a call from you. Most of the media has given up on us since demolition seems to be inevitable."

I had decided earlier I wouldn't mention my interest in Morris Hartman. Instead, I said, "We love the idea that a community group is still working to save this place."

Ida nodded. "We won't give up until the bulldozers and wrecking balls show up. Let me take you around a bit. Show you what makes this place so special. But I have to warn you, as you can see, most of the interior is crumbling and decaying." She eyed my heels warily. "Just be careful."

She led me through the entrance. The plaster on the walls had fallen off and crumpled to the floor, creating a sandy mush. With every step I took, my heels sank in.

Every twenty feet or so, Ida would stop and place a plastic bucket on the mushy floor to catch any water dripping from the ceiling. She did it with such care and love, I couldn't help but want to hug her. Didn't she know it was useless at this point?

I nodded. "Do you mind if I snap some pictures?" If there was a story here, I'd at least have pictures. Unlike the failed interview with K!ng.

"That's fine," she said. "I want to take you upstairs first. The dining area, library, and lecture hall are up there. And so is Dr. Hartman's office."

"Okay," I said, holding onto the last part about the office. I trailed behind, snapping pictures on my phone. I could see glimpses of where the charm had been years before. Suddenly, Ida put an arm out and stopped me.

"Careful, dear," she said, pointing. In front of me was a gap the size of the treadmill track in my condo's fitness center. I could see clearly into the basement. I danced around the gaping hole and followed Ida up the stairs. Despite the missing floorboards and sagging structure, the staircase was beautiful. Detailed and unique ironwork remained intact and sturdy. I snapped a few more pictures as we ascended to the second floor.

Nonchalantly I asked, "Do you know much about the late Dr. Hartman?"

"I knew him better than most people in town," she replied. "And to be honest, that's not saying much. He was gone much of the time, traveling to Europe where he did much of his research," she paused. "I only knew so much because of my grandmother."

I nodded. "Wasn't he originally from out east?"

Ida nodded. "He was. Educated in New York City. But he had heard that there was a need for doctors on the isolated prairies of the Midwest. Moved here with the hopes of helping people who had no access to health care. He opened a small country clinic. That's when my grandmother started working for him. She told me he used to make house calls on his horse, Wilson." Ida chuckled. "Actually, I think there's a picture still hanging in the lecture hall of her and Dr. Hartman at their clinic. Should we see if we can find it?" I nodded and followed her.

Ida held out a hand as we ventured down a long hallway. "Oh dear, watch your step."

There, on the floor in front of me, was a dead bat. I gasped, then hurried along with Ida. Paint was peeling off the walls. Moisture damage and mold were on parts of the crumbling ceiling. Though the wall on the south side of the building was made up of a dozen floor-to-ceiling windows, the room felt dark and dank with the backdrop of clouds and rain outside. Ida clicked on her flashlight and slowly scanned the large space.

"This was the lecture space. Dr. Hartman called it the Auditorium. He brought in experts for weekly presentations." Ida shined the flashlight on a column. "I think this room also doubled for an indoor gymnasium. You can still see a bit of padding here." She walked slowly along the plastered wall.

"Ah, here it is," she said, carefully taking a small, framed black-and-white photograph off the wall. She brought it over to me. Three figures stood in front of a one-room, one-story, clapboard building. The young woman, who I assumed was Ida's grandmother, looked like she couldn't be much older than a teenager. She wore a long, white apron and black blouse. Her hair was pinned on top of her head and covered in a small white cap. She didn't smile but wore a determined look. Her piercing eyes stared back at me. The man, I assumed to be Dr. Hartman, wore knee-high boots. Above his upper lip was a thin mustache. He was staring off in the distance. Beside him stood a huge, smiling man wearing a cap on his head. A horse—Wilson, I figured— stood near the doctor.

"That's my grandmother." Ida pointed. "That's Dr. Hartman. And he's an Irishman Dr. Hartman hired to help with the cooking and cleaning," Ida said, pointing to each of the three figures. "Mr. O'Brien, I think."

"That's his horse, Wilson?"

Ida nodded. "My grandmother said Dr. Hartman loved managing

his small country clinic. But he also loved research. He wanted to bring top-notch health care to these rural areas." She hung the picture back on the wall. "But then, the tornado hit, demolishing his beloved clinic."

"What happened?" I asked.

"My grandmother used to tell us about that day," she shuddered, "she said the sky turned a nasty green color. Apparently, Dr. Hartman got the call that a woman out on the prairie was in labor and was having trouble. He wasn't about to ignore a call for help. Grabbed Wilson and they started off. That's when my grandmother said she heard something that sounded like a freight train right outside the clinic. She went to look and saw Doc riding back yelling at her and the Irishman to get to the cellar." Ida shook her head. "She said the clinic was demolished. The town, wiped out."

"How did they rebuild to create…this?"

"The way my grandmother tells it, Dr. Hartman intended to rebuild his clinic just the way it was. But then some businessmen—I think they were fellow researchers from New York—offered to help him out. Soon, famous architects were taking the train out here to talk to Dr. Hartman. And in a few years, this," she gestured to the Grand Hall, "was built."

"What did those businessmen get out of helping a small country doctor?" I frowned.

Ida's cell phone rang. She clumsily dug through her bag before grasping for her phone. "Hello? This is Ida." She gestured at me to give her a moment.

I decided that it wouldn't hurt if I investigated a bit on my own. I wandered through the lecture hall until I found a hallway, lined with closed doors with rusty hinges. At the end of the hallway, one door was open. I walked carefully, keeping an eye out for more bats. The open door led to a large office. A decaying and rotting desk sat near a large window. On the wall were framed diplomas and dusty black-and-white photographs, most of the glass cracked or broken. Massive bookshelves holding moth-eaten and musty books lined two of the walls.

I grabbed one of the books and began flipping through it. The faded pages were brittle and torn. I returned it and grabbed another book. That's when I noticed a brick wall behind the bookshelf.

I could still hear Ida talking, so I quickly removed a few more books and set them on the desk. The empty shelf revealed that there was, in fact, a brick wall where the back panel of the bookshelf should have been.

"There you are!" Ida exclaimed, surprising me.

"I'm sorry," I said quickly, turning around. "I just thought I'd have a look around." Ida stood at the door with her arms crossed. I took that as my cue to grab my bag and follow her out of the office.

"I'm so sorry, but I'll have to cut our tour short," Ida said as we walked down the hallway back to the main entrance. "That was my mother's care center. She needs my help."

"Sure, I understand. Do you mind if I stay and look around a bit more?" I asked, hopeful to sneak back inside the office.

She shook her head. "No. I'm sorry. Legally, I can't let you stay."

"Well, maybe I could come back out another time?" I asked.

Ida, clearly distracted after the phone call, dug through her purse. "Sure. Here's my card." I grabbed it and turned it over in my hands. *Ida Kirkbridge, Friends of the Oasis co-founder.*

I followed Ida down the decaying stairwell and back through the Grand Hall. I squinted as we walked outside, letting my eyes adjust to the natural light.

"Well, thanks for meeting me," I said to Ida.

"I'm sorry I can't stay longer," she lamented, pausing before getting into a green Toyota. "There's a city council meeting tomorrow night. It's a sort of last-ditch effort to propose redevelopment ideas. Come if you want. Seven p.m. at the courthouse."

"Great. I'll try to make it. Thanks." As I climbed into my car, my phone buzzed.

"Hello?" I said.

"Sophie, it's Kase. Where are you?" He sounded irritated. "I've been trying to get a hold of you for the last twenty minutes."

Damnit. I must not get service in the Oasis. "I, um, am investigating the Hartman story."

"Ok," he said, drawing out the 'k.' "But, *where* are you?"

"I followed a lead. I'm in Crab Orchard."

"What? I encouraged you to work on the story. I didn't say you should skip town right when a huge political story is breaking," he said.

My stomach dropped to my nude heel shoes where my toes curled in shame; I felt like a kid being scolded.

"I'm sorry. I had a chance to get an inside look at—"

"I don't care. Just get back here. This story is blowing up and I need you on it." He hung up.

Tears stung my eyes. I threw my phone back in my bag and jerked my car in reverse, kicking myself and this fruitless mission. I tore through town, barely pausing at the two stop signs I encountered. Once on the highway, I set my speedometer for seventy-five and cursed myself for following a stupid lead.

An hour later, I rushed back into the office with my head hung low, hoping no one would notice. Unfortunately, the entire team was meeting in the back for an afternoon huddle. They all stopped their meeting and stared at me. My cheeks burned. Taking a deep breath, I set my bag on my desk and forced myself to walk over to join the huddle. Kase glowered at me. After a dramatic pause, he continued.

"Barry, where are you with our victim? Will she talk to us?"

"No. I called her lawyer again and all I get is 'no comment.'"

"Ok, let's have you switch gears," Kase said. "Let's summarize the other political figures who have been accused of sexual assault. See which of them got an ethics case, who resigned because of it, that sort of thing. Maybe call Al Franken's former press secretary."

Barry nodded.

"Ok, guys. Good work. Let's huddle again at five." Everyone got up and started back to their desks, including me. "Sophie, stay for a minute."

I pursed my lips and sat on the edge of the futon. Kase faced me, sitting in an orange, mesh chair.

"I get that you followed your gut on this Hartman deal. But when there's breaking news—breaking, *political* news—I need you. Here." Kase looked me square in the eyes. "First the K!ng story and now this?" He shook his head. "There are one hundred other talented and hungry journalists who would gladly step into your shoes. Got it?"

"Yes. I'm sorry," I mumbled. I didn't trust myself to say anymore without bursting into tears. He got up and walked to his office, leaving me sitting there alone, feeling like a complete idiot. At that moment, sitting in a dark production booth at ten-thirty at night producing the news didn't sound so terrible.

Jen immediately appeared and placed a comforting hand on my shoulder.

"Don't worry. He's a hard ass in the beginning to us all," she said, reassuringly. "But, seriously, where were you?"

I buried my face in my hands and shook my head. "I thought I found something that might turn up more for my Hartman story. I was so wrong."

Jen peered at me. "In Crab Orchard?"

"Yeah. Hartman's grandfather's Oasis is out there. And I thought—"

Jen stopped me. "A word to the wise. He doesn't like to talk about his grandfather." She shrugged. "I never could figure out why."

I nodded. "I feel like such an idiot.

Jen squeezed my arm. "I remember my first botched story here." She closed her eyes, shook her head, and shuddered. "I can still remember the scathing lecture I got from Kase after that one."

"Okay, now I'm curious. What was the story?"

"I couldn't find a quote from a DFL senator, so I snagged one from a competitor's piece."

My eyes bulged. "Really?"

Jen nodded. "I didn't think anyone would notice or fact-check. I was wrong. See? You're not the only one who makes mistakes. Let this one roll off your shoulders." Then she added in a teasing tone, "But you should probably answer your phone when your boss calls."

I didn't leave the office until eight that night, proving to Kase that I could—and would—hack it as a real reporter. Instead of cooking, I decided to trek north to a fantastic Middle Eastern deli that served the most amazing hummus and falafel. Ordering my usual, I waited at the counter while the chef, Halil, made my food.

"Here you go, love," he said, handing me a plastic bag. "I stuck an extra piece of baklava in there. You seem a bit sad today."

"It was a long day," I said, pointing to the bag. "But this makes it better."

Halil patted my hand and smiled. "I'm glad to hear that. You take care."

The second I walked into my apartment, I dropped my keys and purse at the door, kicked off my heels, whipped off my bra, and flipped on *Outlander*. I grabbed a bottle of moscato from the fridge and poured a glass. Then, I pulled out my comfort food. The homemade garlic hummus almost made me forget about my day. Before plopping into my buttery Egyptian cotton sheets—a splurge from Macy's when I got my first promotion at KOMO-TV—I reached for my phone to scroll through my Instagram feed. Instead, though, I accidentally clicked on my own photos. I flipped through the pictures from the Oasis, trying out different filters. What was it about that place—or this story—that I couldn't let go of? Was it just my determination to turn in a decent copy? Or was there truly something at the Oasis tugging at me? Something about the staircase in black and white was both haunting and beautiful. I posted that on Instagram, set my alarm, and fell asleep.

Chapter 8

BIZZIE

BIZZIE DIDN'T WALK OUT of The Minneapolis Journal building—she floated. She felt like crying and laughing all at the same time. Being immersed in the city reminded her of last Christmas when Mamma Maria came to visit from Norway. Papa had told Bizzie stories about a treat Mamma Maria made for him growing up: Julekake. He described it in such detail, Bizzie could almost smell the cardamom filling the kitchen. Bizzie's mother refused to make Julekake. A waste of fine ingredients, she'd say. But that didn't stop Papa from telling his stories. Bizzie's mouth watered just thinking about the spiced bread.

"Mamma would bake it, and oh! The house smelled delicious for days. But we couldn't eat it right away," he chuckled and shook his head. "It would sit near the fireplace in a special chest all season—a special decoration for Christmas. Finally, when spring harvest started, Mamma would take out the bread and drizzle it with sweet, white icing. She'd always let me lick off the icing spoon." His eyes sparkled. "It was delicious."

Mamma Maria visited when Bizzie was twelve. Together, they made the special treat Bizzie grew up dreaming about. Mother stayed in her bedroom. Bizzie got to sprinkle in the red candied fruits, each one looking like a sparkling ruby. Bursts of cinnamon, cardamom, and ginger scented every inch of the house. As soon as it was done baking, Mamma Maria whisked together the white icing and gave the spoon to Bizzie, who licked it clean. Mamma Maria drizzled the icing over the bread, letting it trickle down onto the lucky, white plate

50 | THE MUCKRAKER

beneath it. She sliced a piece for Bizzie, then gently set it on a small, dainty plate—one that was usually hidden away in the china cabinet that Mother never used—and slid it over to her. Bizzie grabbed the bread between her thumb and pointer finger and lifted it to her lips. It melted in her mouth and the icing stuck to her lips and fingers.

"Look out!" Bizzie heard someone call out. She looked up to see a huge wooden cart drawn by four massive, bulky horses lumbering toward her. A milkman, pouring thick, clotted cream into a dusty jug, hollered again.

"Girlie, look out!"

Breathless, Bizzie skipped across the cobblestones and joined the milkman and his pushcart.

"You have to be more careful," he scolded. Then, he smiled and handed her a glass of the cold, fresh milk. "For you."

Bizzie noticed the thick, accented vowels, a sign of his European heritage. He wore a ragged black-and-white striped apron that hung down to his ankles. A careful hand clasped a battered, black satchel that fell to his side.

"Thank you," Bizzie said, reaching into her handbag that was carefully tucked under her arm. She handed the milkman a nickel. He shook his head and refused to take her money.

"New to town?" he asked.

Bizzie shyly smiled. "Yes. You could tell?"

He laughed, then took off his peaked cap and scratched his forehead. "We all new here at one time."

Bizzie smiled. "I wonder if you could help me," she began. "I am planning to stay in the city for a bit." At this, Bizzie paused and gnawed on her lip. How long would she stay? A week or a month? Two months? The excitement and the energy of the city had awakened something inside of her. A dream that in Hibbing had remained silent and pleading was—maybe, finally—becoming a reality. And now that she'd had a taste of what this reality could be, she never wanted to return to a life without it. "I'm looking for a place to stay. Do you know of any boarding houses?"

The milkman scratched his chin. "Uh…is lodging house on Washington." He pointed in the opposite direction. "Nasty place, but cheap. You stay a few nights before you find something more better," he said slowly, as if trying to find the right words.

Bizzie thanked the milkman and walked in the direction he had pointed. As she approached the structure he'd pointed to, she scrunched her nose. The once-stately colonial house must have been beautiful years ago, but not anymore. The cement stairs leading to the entrance were crumbled and deteriorating. Four columns, chipped and graying, met her before she reached the front door which was off its hinges and rusty. Not sure whether to knock or just go inside, she hesitantly pulled the door open and peeked her head in. It was dark and smelled musty. A large woman with greasy brown hair sat behind a small, wooden desk and accompanied her faded, dirty white dress with an impressive frown.

"Whaddya want?" the woman barked. The milkman had been so kind and gentle. The woman's brusqueness surprised her.

"Hello," Bizzie began. "I'm new in town and looking for a place to stay." Then, she quickly added, "Just until I find more permanent quarters."

The woman let out a loud humph and hoisted her huge frame out of her chair.

"Wait here," she grunted and gestured toward a hard bench in front of Bizzie before stomping away heavily. Bizzie sat, holding her handbag and small travel bag.

A minute later, she heard slight, nimble footsteps. Around the corner peered a young woman, maybe seventeen years old.

"Hello," whispered the girl. She wore a soft gray, box-pleated dress that fit her small frame perfectly. The edges were scalloped and looked hand embroidered. A tumble of red, curly hair fell to her shoulders. Freckles dotted her face, and despite the squalid appearance of the lodging house, her green eyes sparkled.

Bizzie smiled.

"I'm staying in the first room on the right," the girl whispered and pointed upstairs. "Don't let grumpy, old Miss Chambers put you in the basement. It's drafty and cold. The other girls tell me there's rats down there." Bizzie felt a shiver run up her spine. The girl smiled. "If Miss Chambers tries to take you down there, just tell her you can bunk with me."

Upon hearing tromping footsteps, the girl turned to hurry back upstairs. But before she disappeared, she whispered, "I'm Emma."

"I'm Bizzie," Bizzie whispered back, forgetting momentarily that in this new city, she was supposed to be Elizabeth.

"Alright. Come with me." Miss Chambers waddled along down the hallway with Bizzie following close behind. To her relief, Miss Chambers unlocked a room on the main floor. Bizzie peeked inside.

52 | THE MUCKRAKER

It was cold and cheerless, the walls stained and dirty. No books, no pictures, no curtains at the windows. The only piece of furniture in the room was a rusty bed frame and flat mattress covered in a tattered, dirty sheet.

"Well, whaddya want, a welcoming committee?" Miss Chambers shoved Bizzie into the dusty room, cackling at her own joke. "Forty cents a night. Fifty if you want supper."

Bizzie nodded. "Alright."

"Well," Miss Chambers said, tapping her foot on the grimy, wooden floor. "Pay up, girl."

Bizzie set down her bag and pulled out a few coins. Papa had given her fifteen dollars from a little pouch he'd kept hidden underneath his chair. Mother never knew about his secret savings fund. That, paired with the twenty dollars of her teaching salary she'd managed to squirrel away from her mother's watchful eye, gave her a comfortable cushion.

She held out the fifty cents, which Miss Chambers snatched from her hand. "Dinner's at six. If you're late, you don't eat." She slammed the door, causing Bizzie to jump. She pulled her journal and a thin, green blanket out of her satchel. The blanket wasn't cozy or warm, but it was clean and added a bit of color to the dreary room. She spread it across the rickety bed and sat down, pulling out two pictures: one of Papa and one of Collin. She carefully set them on the floor by the bed, then pulled out her journal and flipped to an empty page. She couldn't wait to tell Collin about Minneapolis. She imagined him scoffing, reading about the dusty streets and clomping horses, wondering why anyone would actually choose to live in a place like that.

Dear Collin,

Well, you were right. E. Johansen did the trick. I got the job! Well, at least a chance to prove I can write a story. I will report to The Journal tomorrow for my first assignment! Can you believe it? My dream is coming true. And it's all because of you, Collin. Thank you. Minneapolis is quite a sight. I fear you would hate it. Too much noise, too many people. I miss you. Tell Sloane I say hi.

Until next time,
Bizzie

She tore the piece of paper out of her journal and stuck it in one of the envelopes she'd taken from her classroom stash. She'd mail it tomorrow. Then, she yawned and stretched and decided to close her eyes—just for a moment. Though she wanted to fit in and acclimate to her new surroundings, she had to admit that the noisy, dusty city had exhausted her.

Loud knocking startled Bizzie and she jumped out of bed, momentarily forgetting where she was. She stumbled across the small room and opened the door. Thankful it was Emma and not Miss Chambers, she relaxed a bit.

"It's nearly six! Are you coming to dinner?"

Bizzie nodded and rubbed her eyes. She closed the door to her room and followed Emma.

"The food here is terrible," Emma whispered, looping her arm through Bizzie's. "But it's the only time of the day we all gather together. And learning about the other floozies here is fascinating."

"How long have you been staying?" Bizzie asked.

"Just four days. And that's four days too long," Emma laughed, leading Bizzie into the dining room. A broken chandelier hung from the spotted ceiling. A huge dining table took up most of the space. "I'm planning to rent a room at a more upscale boarding house, but I need the money first. I'm going to get a job."

"What kind of job?" Bizzie asked.

Emma smiled. "Well, I want to work for Elizabeth Quinlan." She paused, waiting for Bizzie's response. Bizzie, who had never heard of Elizabeth Quinlan, furrowed her brow.

"Who's that?" Bizzie responded.

Emma clucked her tongue. "Who's Elizabeth Quinlan?" She patted an empty spot on the hard, wooden bench next to her. "Come sit."

Bizzie slid next to her.

"I want to be a cash girl at her store. You see, she's the only lady clothing buyer in the whole darn country! And she's here—in Minneapolis!" Again, she waited to see Bizzie's reaction.

Bizzie, who was quickly catching on, raised her eyebrows and let out an impressed "Oooh."

Emma grabbed the sleeve of Bizzie's dress. "Where'd ya get this dress from?"

Bizzie thought for a moment. "I made this one."

"I made this too, with fabric I bought at the dry goods store back in Sioux Falls. But at Young Quinlan Company, you can buy clothes already made. Think of it, Bizzie! You can walk into the shiny, sparkling

54 | **THE MUCKRAKER**

store and pick out any dress you'd like. And bam! Wear it that very day." Emma grabbed Bizzie's arm excitedly. "Just think of it! And I'm going to work there."

Bizzie thought back to Dayton's and the women holding up the luxurious dresses and sweaters. "How? What must you do to get a job there?" Bizzie asked, genuinely interested.

"Well, I haven't figured that out yet. But I have a plan. I'm going to walk into the store and ask to see Miss Quinlan herself. Then I'll say to her, Miss Quinlan, my name is Emma Jones, and I came all the way from Sioux Falls, South Dakota to be a cash girl in your store. I know I'm young, but I'm a hard worker. I was born to do this job." She let out a deep breath and plopped her hands in her lap.

"That sounds dreamy," Bizzie breathed. Finding an ally who had similar dreams was not something she had expected in this sad, falling-down house. "I understand how it feels to be young and have a dream."

"Well, ain't this a tender show of emotion," Miss Chambers spoke out.

Emma rolled her eyes at Bizzie and whispered, "Plus, unlike this one," she jerked her head at Miss Chambers, "I heard Miss Quinlan's a real humanitarian. Apparently, she rescued a bunch of kids from a falling-down orphanage in Chicago and found them all homes."

Bizzie smiled. "Well, I think she'd be a fool not to give you the job."

Emma shined. "I know I'll be fabulous. I just know it."

In front of each plate was a slice of stale-looking bread. A saucer of prunes and a platter of stringy, greasy meat with blobs of yellow fat on it sat in the center of the table. Emma motioned to the meat and made a gagging face at Bizzie. A group of four girls, each with long brown hair and dark brown eyes, came into the room and sat down. They whispered to each other so quietly that Bizzie couldn't hear.

"Those are the Frenchies," Emma whispered. "They just came to America from France. Don't speak a lick of English."

A girl no older than fourteen sauntered in the room and plopped down next to Bizzie. She wore a pale pink dress with a ruffled skirt and lace sleeves. Bizzie nearly drooled over the dress, which must have cost a fortune and was probably specially ordered from New York City or Paris.

"That there's Harriet," Emma whispered.

Bizzie smiled at her. Harriet scowled in return. Her gray, icy eyes looked Bizzie up and down in one swift movement. Bizzie hugged herself, wishing she was wearing something other than her faded gingham dress.

Emma cupped her hand around her mouth and whispered in Bizzie's ear, "Harriet's Miss Chambers niece. *Rich* niece. I heard she just moved here from New York City. Apparently, her parents died in a fire and Miss Chambers was her only next of kin. Imagine that. She's gotta trade in her hoity-toity lifestyle for this dump."

Bizzie snuck another glance at Harriet and felt a pang of empathy. The young girl again scowled at Bizzie, who quickly looked away.

Miss Chambers lunged for the greasy meat. She scooped a mound of it on her tin plate then greedily slurped it into her mouth with a bent, tin fork.

"Pass the prunes!" Miss Chambers demanded, meat and saliva spewing from her mouth. Bizzie stared in disbelief as she watched dinner unfold. She took her cues from Emma, who kept giving her small, inconspicuous signals. Emma pointed to the prunes and meat and quickly shook her head. Instead, Bizzie picked at her stale piece of bread, to which Emma had given a nod of approval.

"Ladies, this here is Bizzie," Emma said, jutting a thumb in Bizzie's direction. "She's new to Minneapolis. Never even heard of Elizabeth Quinlan."

The French girls didn't say anything, just kept their heads down. Harriet scoffed loudly. Miss Chambers snickered. "Got a lot to learn," she said between bites.

Chapter 9

SOPHIE

WHEN I WALKED INTO THE OFFICE at seven-thirty the next morning, it was already buzzing. No one looked my way or seemed to care that I had arrived except for Jen. Thank goodness for Jen. I set my bag at my desk and joined her in the kitchenette for some coffee. Reaching for a teal mug, I grabbed a Keurig pod and brewed a cup of hazelnut-flavored coffee.

"So, does everyone get in at the crack of dawn?" I asked Jen sarcastically.

She grinned. "Annoying, right? No, not usually this early. We're all just psyched about the Jansrud story."

I nodded. "Of course."

As I waited for my coffee, I scrolled through Instagram. The picture I had posted the night before garnered more than a hundred likes and twenty comments. Curious, I read them all. Turns out, my Instagram followers were quite intrigued about my Crab Orchard exploration and the ironwork. I looked at the photograph again. It was stunning. The detailed spindles twisted and wound elegantly.

"Wait a second," I breathed to myself. I grabbed my coffee and walked back to my desk. I pulled up my notes from my interview with Morris Hartman. The ironwork on the stairwell in the Oasis looked oddly similar to that on Hartman's desk in his office. I scanned my notes.

L-shaped desk. Dark iron legs. Reclaimed wood from grandfather's farm. Had to tear down.

Just then, Kase called out, "Okay guys. Let's huddle up."

I shut my laptop and hurried to the corner couch, coffee in hand. Kase had wheeled out a massive whiteboard that was already filled with names of possible victims associated with Jansrud. So far, we—well, actually my team—gathered that our victim was a woman who had interned for Jansrud within the last five years. I was charged with calling all of the past interns and asking for information. My first call went something like this:

"Hi, I'm Sophie McHale from News Now Online. We're investigating a possible sexual misconduct case regarding DFL-candidate Jim Jansrud. We understand that you interned for Mr. Jansrud four years ago. Do you mind talking with me for a moment?"

I heard responses like, "No, thank you," or "That wasn't me," or "I never worked for Jansrud." Some just hung up on me.

"Sophie, have you made any progress with the former interns?" Kase asked me.

"Not yet." I looked down at my notes. "I've called about a dozen of them."

Kase nodded. "Barry, how about you?"

Barry, who sat on a nearby couch, gave us the low-down on the latest Jansrud press conference he attended. "No mention of resigning yet. But it sounds like there will be an ethics committee."

Kase continued asking for details from each member of the team. When we broke away from our huddle, I was already bored with my assignment to continue calling more former interns and former employees. Now, we were extending our investigation to include the last ten years, hoping other misconduct cases might come up. At five o'clock, still without any on-the-record comments, I was frustrated. I had spent the entire day getting nowhere. Jansrud's record was nearly spotless. Until this Twitter allegation, that is.

As other writers and journalists filed out the door for the day, I took that as my cue to leave too. As I stood up, Kase walked by.

"Hey, send me that Morris piece by tomorrow, k?" He said, looking down at his phone.

Shit. I still didn't have the gritty details I was hoping to find. "Yep," I managed, grabbing my bag, wondering how I'd avoid another lukewarm story attempt. I sighed. I was hoping to go home, take off my bra, and watch last week's episode of *The Bachelor*. I threw my laptop into my tote. Guess I'd be working instead. I waved to Jen who was on the phone and I left the office. As I was walking down the concrete stairwell, my cell phone rang. It was Ida from Friends of the Oasis.

"Hey Ida," I answered.

"Hi there! Just checking to see if you're coming tonight," Ida said.

I racked my brain. *Tonight…tonight…City council.*

"Remind me of the time of the meeting?"

"Seven o'clock. At the courthouse. I'll be there," she said. Then added, "I think you might find it interesting."

I cringed, feeling the weight of a deadline on my shoulders.

I was about to tell her no when she said, "Perhaps we can take another look around the Oasis after the meeting."

This piqued my interest. Maybe I could look at that brick wall behind the bookshelf. Besides, pictures of the city council meeting and the possible demolition aspect could prove to be an added element that Kase might like.

"I'll be there."

At ten to seven, I pulled into Crab Orchard. I didn't notice the river on the west side of town the last time I drove through. Tonight, though, I saw kids fishing off a small, stone bridge. A few blocks away, the brick, four-story Crab Orchard Courthouse, stately and elegant, stood on Main Street. From the parking lot, I could see the Oasis on the hill above town. I walked in and found Ida sitting in a black, folded-up chair. Half the chairs were taken. Most people there were wearing yellow shirts with black lettering that read, "Save the Oasis."

"Hi," I said as I sat down.

"Oh, I'm so glad you came," Ida said and patted my hand. "This is my husband, Greg." She turned to Greg. "Honey, this is that Minneapolis reporter I was telling you about. She's trying to help us spread the word about the Oasis." We shook hands. I got the feeling that saving the Oasis wasn't as important to Greg as it was to Ida. He seemed bored already.

A minute later, the mayor called the meeting to order. Short, overweight, and balding, the mayor didn't exactly look like a picture of health—nor did he conjure up a picture of an ideal mayor. Despite this, I crossed my legs and listened. After discussing last month's notes, the councilors opened up the meeting to the community members. Ida and a few others clad in yellow shirts nodded to each other, stood, and walked to the front of the room. They handed out a stapled packet of paper to each councilor.

Ida spoke first. "Councilors, we know demolition seems like the easier option. But we," she gestured to those around her all wearing yellow shirts, "just can't let that happen. You see, the Oasis helped build Crab Orchard. It's part of our history. Tonight, we come to you with an idea that we believe could help boost Crab Orchard's tourism as well as preserve the Oasis."

She took a deep breath. "We want to recommend a three-step process to saving the Oasis. The first step includes preserving the Grand Hall as a historic landmark. Then, we'd like to convert the three cottages into luxury apartments. And lastly, we would update the grounds and gardens for a community green space."

Another woman next to Ida with a name tag that read "Heidi" took over, discussing in detail the three-step plan. I half-listened until I heard her say, "The surrounding land is owned by MH Manufacturing, a chapter of Midwest Steel Group."

My head popped up. Midwest Steel... That was one of Morris Hartman's businesses.

A few minutes later, the group wrapped up and received meager applause. The mayor stifled a yawn. "Thank you for your presentation," he muttered. "We'll hold a special meeting next month where councilors will vote on demolition or preservation of the Oasis."

Ida came over to me.

"Well," she whispered. "We gave it our best shot."

"You did great, Ida," I whispered back, patting her on the shoulder.

The mayor added a few more remarks about the city pool opening in June and the new pool hours. Then, he adjourned the meeting. Ida huddled around a group of Oasis supporters, chatting about their presentation. I sat next to Greg, who yawned and scratched his graying beard. He pulled out his phone and began scrolling.

To make conversation, I said, "How did you get involved with this preservation project?"

Greg stuck his phone in his pocket, rolled his eyes slightly, and jerked his head towards his wife. "Ida dragged me in." He laughed. "How about you? What interests you?"

"I love the fact that a community group is trying to preserve this piece of history," I replied, using the same half-truth I'd told Ida. "It sounds like the Oasis is really important to the town."

Greg nodded. "It's a huge piece of our history. Folks sure are passionate about making sure it's not turned into a steel mill."

I frowned. "What do you mean?"

"Like Heidi said, MH Manufacturing owns the land surrounding the campus. They're looking for a spot to plop their next plant. The town's divided. Some want the plant because of the jobs it would bring in. Some are completely against the idea. Scared the town would be turned into nothing more than a steel town. And some just don't care."

Just then, Ida came over and joined us.

"Honey, mom's nurse just called," she told Greg. She looked worried. "Sounds like she's having another hard night." She and Greg exchanged looks. Then, she turned to me. "I'm sorry, Sophie. Looks like I won't be able to go over to the Oasis tonight after all. But you have my card. Call me anytime." Greg and Ida shook my hand before they left.

Disappointed about the change in plans and worried about turning in another dud of a story, I decided to head to the Oasis alone to get a closer look. My mind was still spinning from the fact that Hartman owned the land in Crab Orchard and wanted to replace his grandfather's original clinic with a steel plant. And that he mentioned none of this when we spoke.

I started up the hill to the Oasis but stopped just before a "No Trespassing" sign. When I came last night, the chain was already unhooked and out of the way. I stepped out of my car, looking for any security cameras. Rusty and crumbling, a note in permanent marker read, "For entry, call Doug," with a phone number.

I looked once more over my shoulder before fiddling with the iron chain that was strung across the drive. It came unhooked easily and fell to the gravel drive with a clang. I hopped back in my car and drove toward the Grand Hall, shuddering as I got closer. In the dusk, it was haunting. Shadows danced across the trees, and the wind howled and hissed. I parked the car and crunched up the path.

The structure seemed larger than life. I couldn't understand how a building this massive could fall into such disrepair. The splintering front door was equipped with a keyless lock. Despite that, I jammed my shoulder against it, hoping I could force it open. No luck. Hesitantly, I wound my way around the building, looking for an open window or second entrance. A faded, wooden door at the back of the house proved to be the answer. Sweat trickled down the back of my neck. The door beckoned for someone to open it, as if its hinges had sat too long, unable to share their hideous secrets.

Chapter 10

BIZZIE

AFTER NAVIGATING MISS CHAMBERS' DINNER with Emma's help, Bizzie said goodnight and crawled into bed. She was anxious for the next day—her first day as a real reporter. She gingerly took off her gingham dress and carefully tucked it into her suitcase. She pulled out the other dress she'd packed. It was maroon with buttons down the front and had a drop-waist and long sleeves. It was her favorite and it showed. Bizzie remembered when she first walked into J.F. Gage Dry Goods in Duluth two years ago and spotted the jewel-toned fabric. Papa and her mother had driven her to the northern port city as she prepared for teachers' college. When they stopped to buy good tobacco for Papa, the speckled pattern with tiny white ovals caught her eye.

Because she hadn't started teaching yet, she'd had to plead with her mother to buy it. When Bizzie's mother shook her head no because it was "much too expensive for something so frivolous," the clerk took pity on them and offered a discount. That did the trick. Her mother, not wanting to appear poor or needy, proudly paid the full amount and Bizzie walked out with four yards of new fabric.

Now, as she sat alone in an unfriendly room in an unknown city, she lifted the dress to her face and rested her cheek against it. It smelled of woodsmoke and pine, Papa's tobacco smoke, and Collin's farm. It smelled like home, and suddenly she was homesick. She fought back tears, wiping them away with the back of her hand and looking around at the cheerless room.

"This is what I fought for!" she whispered, almost scolding herself.

For a moment, she let herself daydream about what life would be like back home. Now that school was out for the summer, she wouldn't be teaching. But she'd have to do something to get away from her mother. She'd probably disappear to Collin's farm and pal around with Sloane for the day. Collin's mother would ask if she would stay for dinner and, of course, she'd accept. They'd have pot roast and mashed potatoes, or golden chicken fresh from the farm with glazed carrots. And for dessert, a huge slice of strawberry pie with a dollop of homemade ice cream. As she lay on her lonely bed in the dreary room in the awful lodging house, she let the tears fall. Tears of homesickness. Tears of doubt. Clutching her green blanket for comfort, she curled up into a ball and fell asleep.

Bizzie rolled over and felt the sunshine on her eyelids. She rubbed her eyes groggily, then noticed the maroon dress folded neatly on the floor beside her bed. She jolted awake, remembering where she was— the big city! She threw the green blanket off and staggered into the hallway and down to the shared bathroom. Splashing some water on her face, she tried her best to calm her nerves.

"You're up early," a voice startled her. Bizzie turned quickly, then relaxed when she saw a familiar face: Emma. She was combing her mess of red curls.

"Yes, I start my new—" she paused, not sure how much information she should divulge. "I start teaching today. Er, summer courses." She fiddled with the button on her nightshirt. "Well, I'll be off. See you later, Emma." She rushed out of the bathroom before Emma could ask anything else.

Bizzie tiptoed back to her room, hoping to avoid interacting with anyone else. She understood herself well enough to know that a glimpse of doubt or skepticism on another's face would corrode the small amount of confidence she could muster that morning. She slipped on the drop-waist dress and stepped into a pair of worn, black, lace-up boots. She brushed her brown hair, combing through any knots as it cascaded past her shoulders. Then, she pinned it up on top of her head and slipped downstairs. Bizzie let out an audible sigh of relief when she turned the corner and saw Miss Chambers' torn chair was empty. She opened the door and hurried outside.

A step out of the silent, dreary lodging house and Bizzie felt excitement again in her chest. Though it was still early, the streets were filled with wooden carts and streetcars. Hawkers were standing on the corners selling buttons and potatoes. Newsboys cried out, waving the early edition.

She joined the crowds, all of them hustling somewhere, and felt proud to be among them.

"Girlie!" Bizzie heard a man call from across the street. She held a hand over her eyes to block the sunlight and caught a glimpse of what looked like her friend, the milkman.

Looking both ways before running across the street, she jumped up on the cedarwood sidewalk and stood before him smiling.

"Hello again!" Bizzie said, slightly out of breath.

"Hello to you," he said in his thick accent. Like last time, he handed her a glass bottle of cold milk.

"Thank you." Bizzie took it and tried to pay him, but just like last time, he waved her hand away. She took a sip. Her empty belly welcomed the fresh, thick milk.

"You find lodging house ok?" he asked.

"Yes, I did."

"You like?"

Bizzie hesitated. "It was—er—a bit dreary."

The milk man laughed. His laugh was deep and rich, coming from his belly. "A bit. More like much, much dreary." They laughed together. He wiped his hand against his apron and held it out for Bizzie. "I'm Engelbert Kaller." His hands were rough and calloused. His fingers were twice—maybe three times—the size of Bizzie's. He pointed in the opposite direction. "My wife and me, we find room for rent from nice people. They live first floor, we live second. The man in top floor is leaving at the end of the month. You stop by and look?"

"Yes," Bizzie said. "That would be wonderful." She thought of Emma. "I'll bring a friend." She added, "And my name is Elizabeth."

Engelbert nodded and smiled. "I see you later, Elizabeth." He continued pushing his cart down the street.

Bizzie walked the four blocks to Fourth Street—Newspaper Row. She smiled with excitement but tried to remain stalwart and straight-faced to blend in with the crowd walking the street. This was Minneapolis! She was here!

She walked past The Penny Press and Leighton Brothers Printing. Then The Minneapolis Tribune. And just a mere hundred yards past, The Minneapolis Journal.

Bizzie pulled open the heavy, wooden door and was smacked in the face with the smell of tobacco and ink. The same front desk receptionist she'd encountered the day before, the one with the thin mustache, greeted her behind a counter.

"Morning, ma'am. How can I help you?" He asked.

"I work here," Bizzie said, standing tall.

He looked at her quizzically. "You? Here?"

"Mr. Kavanaugh hired me himself," she said, pursing her lips.

He threw his head back and laughed. Bizzie had been prepared for questions and doubt and skepticism. But she hadn't readied herself for this. The anger started in her fingers. It shot through her body— first a tingle, then a ripple down her spine. Her knees shook and she grabbed the counter to steady herself.

With a clenched jaw, she spit out, "I said, Mr. Kavanaugh hired me. Feel free to check with him." She crossed her arms. "I'll wait."

The man scowled at Bizzie, then disappeared down the hall.

Bizzie's anger surprised her. Any doubt she had in her mind that she belonged at The Journal faded away. It was clear: she'd never belong. She felt a burning desire to prove to this imbecile and her mother and Miss Chambers and anyone else who doubted her that she could in fact do this job. And do it well. As well as any man.

It took every ounce of strength Bizzie could muster to stand up straight and hold her head high while men pushed passed her, all of them mumbling. A few minutes later, she heard loud, arguing voices.

"Miss Johansen," Mr. Kavanaugh said, entering the lobby. He shook his head at the receptionist, whose own head hung low. "I'm sorry. There's a reason he's working here," he jutted a thumb in the direction of the receptionist, "and you're my new reporter."

Bizzie sniffed and politely nodded at Mr. Kavanaugh. She eyed the receptionist as she left the lobby, smugly noticing his pink cheeks.

Mr. Kavanaugh led her up to the newsroom on the third floor where a handful of reporters sat at battered desks.

"Here is your desk, Miss Johansen." Mr. Kavanaugh proudly gestured to a small, wooden desk in the corner. A leather notebook and three black pencils sat neatly on top.

"Thank you," Bizzie said, sliding into the scrubbed, brown chair.

"Reporters' meeting in five minutes," Mr. Kavanaugh said.

Bizzie noticed the stares and whispers surrounding her from other reporters. She pretended to be writing notes for the day ahead while scribbling different versions of her name—Bizzie J, Elizabeth Jo, Bizz—while trying not to cry.

"Alright, gather 'round!" Mr. Kavanaugh called a few minutes later. Reporters slowly got to their feet and circled around their editor.

Bizzie walked over quickly and wedged her way into the circle.

"Fellas, this is Miss Elizabeth Johansen. She'll be writing for our little paper. I know she'll do a fine job," Mr. Kavanaugh said. And then, almost as an afterthought, he added, "I hear of anyone giving her a hard time and you'll be working in the composing room on the fifth floor for a month." Spit flew out of his mouth at the word "month."

He went on. "Remember those hundred-and-five-degree days last summer? Those poor bastards—ah, sorry Miss Johansen—those poor saps found out real quick how roasting on a spit felt."

The reporters groaned and nodded and said phrases like "Oh yeah" and "Poor saps." She shuddered and hoped to never have to visit the fifth floor in the summer.

"Alright then," Mr. Kavanaugh said and clapped his hands together. "Let's get started." There was an excitement—a spark in him that hadn't been present at their initial meeting.

"William, I want you to cover the Purley McKeown Saloon fire. The whole damn...er, darn thing is burned and charred. I'll send Floyd to take some photographs." Mr. Kavanaugh looked around. "Where is Floyd?"

"Maybe he heard about the saloon fire and decided to stay home," one man said and got a laugh.

Another said, "Or maybe he heard about the fire and went down to the saloon to see if they were giving away free pints." That got an even bigger laugh.

"Sorry I'm late." A short, skinny man wearing a suit that was two-sizes too big rushed in. He bumped into a chair and knocked it over.

"Floyd, old buddy. We were just talking about you!" someone hollered. The room erupted in laughter and cheers.

"I just stumbled across a murder on my way in off the streetcar!" Floyd said excitedly. "A lady killed her husband, no joke. Just as I was walking by, the police showed up. Got a photograph of the murderer waiting for the wagon to show up and haul her away."

The room erupted in cheers again. Everyone tried to get a hand on Floyd, slapping him on the back, congratulating him.

"Alright, alright, settle down," Mr. Kavanaugh finally said. "Floyd, good work. Get that negative developed right away. And Peterson!" He pointed to a lanky man wearing one brown sock and one black one. "Get the address from Floyd and head over there for a story. Floyd, I want you to go with Joe to Purley McKeown's Saloon. Make sure to get a photograph of Purley outside the burned joint. Word

66 | **THE MUCKRAKER**

has it the poor bastard—er, poor fella—hasn't left the saloon since the fire."

Mr. Kavanaugh doled out a few other assignments before turning to Bizzie.

"Miss Johansen, what do you think about doing a piece on a poor farm out in Clara City? It's about thirty miles east of the city. Talk to the manager there. Find out who stays there, what happens at a poor farm…that kind of thing." Then, in a quieter voice directed just at her, he said, "Let's see what you got, kid."

Bizzie nodded excitedly. She swelled at the thought of her first assignment.

"But it looks like I can't send Floyd," he noted, a bit louder.

"Floyd's a busy boy," one reporter shouted.

"Are you comfortable going alone?" Mr. Kavanaugh asked her. "There's a bus that can take you directly to Clara City."

Bizzie nodded. She thought for a moment. Without a photographer, she could pose as a young woman in search of a temporary home. She could get details most people wouldn't tell a reporter. She could actually live it—or pretend to—and then write from a real perspective. Another female reporter, Nellie Bly, did the same thing in New York. Except she pretended to be insane and was admitted into the asylum for ten days. Bizzie shuddered, remembering how Nellie had described the screams and moans she'd heard.

"Yes, sir," she said, feeling almost dizzy with excitement.

"Alright gentlemen—er, and lady—let's get to work." Mr. Kavanaugh walked back into his office.

Bizzie waited until her fellow reporters had gone back to their desks before approaching her editor's office. She knocked on the open door and peeked her head in.

"Come in, Miss Johansen." Mr. Kavanaugh motioned for her to sit down.

"Thank you, sir," she said, sitting. "I have an idea. About the county poor farm." She launched into her plan of visiting the farm as a potential lodger. She explained, in detail, how she could pretend to be new in town and desperate for a place to stay, not unlike her real experience yesterday of arriving in Minneapolis. "Think of how a first-hand account, with vivid detail about the smells and sounds, would make this story come alive," she added, getting more excited by the minute.

Mr. Kavanaugh thought about it and scratched his chin. "I'll give you a full day."

"Two," Bizzie said firmly. Then she quickly added, "Please." She would need more than just a day to get to know the residents well enough so they'd share their stories. Mr. Kavanaugh sat back in his chair and put his hands behind his head.

"A day and a half."

"Deal," Bizzie replied. "I'll be back in the office at one o'clock on Monday. I'll have the story ready for you the following morning."

"But what if you find yourself in trouble?" Mr. Kavanaugh said. "The paper won't be responsible, you know."

Bizzie nodded. "I understand. I can handle myself." She sat up a little straighter, as if to prove she was up for the task. She thought about Nellie Bly. If she could withstand ten days, surely Bizzie could make it through a day and a half. Mr. Kavanaugh smiled briefly and jerked his head toward his office door. "Good luck, then."

Bizzie hurried to her desk, tossed a notebook and pencil into her satchel, and headed out. She had her first assignment.

Chapter 11

SOPHIE

USING THE FLASHLIGHT APP on my phone, I scanned the room. My heart pounded as I took a tentative step inside. The space looked different at night. While creepy and haunting during the day, there seemed to be something terrifying lurking in every corner at night. I shuddered, forcing myself to take another step.

Kase's disappointed face flashed through my mind—both from after the K!ng interview fiasco and then when I disappeared to follow my reporter instincts. I was oh-for-two. I wanted his approval and praise when I turned in the Morris Hartman piece. I needed to find something—anything—to make this story interesting. If something was hidden in this building, I wanted to find it before it was demolished.

I took in a deep breath of damp and musty air and made my way to the stairs. Remembering to watch my step for the gigantic hole in the floor, I creaked my way up the decaying stairwell and felt my way down the hall towards the office with the concealed brick wall. Suddenly, I collided with something so cold and sharp that I lost both my balance and my phone as I fell. My flurry of curse words ended with the resounding thud as I hit the floor. Without my flashlight, I was enveloped in complete darkness. I felt around and grasped something solid and cold.

"Is someone there?" I heard a deep voice call from somewhere within the building. I fell backwards. Too terrified to even scream, I crawled away, pressed myself against the wall, and tried to become as small as possible. I could see the beam of a flashlight heading toward me. Tears pricked my eyes, and I desperately felt my way down the hall as quickly and quietly as I could. Meanwhile, the light coming toward me grew brighter. At the last second, I lunged into an open door. My heart pounded and my breathing was quick, almost hiccup-like. Cautiously, I peeked around the corner from my crouch with my breath held. A beam of bright light blinded me. I gasped and ducked back.

"I see you. Just come out," a voice said. Then a gentler, "Are you okay?"

"I'm sorry," I stuttered, breathless. I crawled toward the flashlight. I wasn't sure I could even stand on my shaky legs.

"What the hell—" He spotted my heels and squinted. "Who are you? What the hell are you doing here?"

"I could ask you the same thing," I sniffed, my heart rate beginning to slow to a semi-normal pace.

He sighed. "Come with me."

He grabbed my arm lightly and helped me to my feet. I gathered my purse and phone. Then, he guided me down the hall, pausing and shining his light on a rusty, iron, cushion-less chaise lounge chair in the middle of the hallway.

"I believe you tripped over this?"

"Yeah," I said, embarrassed. "You heard that?"

He snorted. "Yep, I heard it."

I followed the stranger down the stairwell to the entrance of the Grand Hall. He led me out the door and into the fresh, spring air. I took a big gulp and exhaled, letting my shoulders drop. The moon sparkled, lighting up the parking lot.

"So, are you going to call the cops on me?" I asked, cringing as I imagined the look on Kase's face if he found out I was arrested for trespassing.

He stifled a laugh. "Call the cops on you?" He shook his head. "But I am curious. What the hell were you doing in there?" Relieved that I wasn't going to jail, or worse, possibly fired, I took a moment to collect my thoughts and take in this stranger. He had disheveled brown hair that he'd tied up on top of his head. He was wearing a red flannel shirt, khaki Carhartt pants, and worn leather boots. Despite his rumpled lumberjack look, he smelled good—like coffee and woodsmoke.

"I'm a reporter and I'm investigating—er, covering—a story about this place." I gestured at the decaying building.

He raised his eyebrows and tilted his head. "Again, I'll ask…*what* were you doing in there?

I sighed. "I came here for a tour yesterday but didn't get to see everything. I was in town for the city council meeting tonight and decided to take a look around." I dug the toe of my shoe into the gravel.

"Didn't get to see everything?" he asked. "There's…not much to see."

"So, you know the place well?" I asked, a bit too excitedly.

He rolled his eyes. "I'm a photographer. I'm working on a project here—with permission," he added. "The moon tonight gave me the perfect light to capture a couple shots. I'm Aaron Cooper, by the way."

"Sophie McHale," I said. "I'd love to take another look around. Any chance you could take me?"

He laughed. "You must be really into this story. But really, there's nothing special inside. Just an old building."

"Please?" I begged. "It won't take long." Then, thinking back to my early production assistant days working at KOMO, I added, "I'm not bad with a camera. I can block for you."

He shrugged. "That would be helpful," he scratched his scruffy beard before continuing, "I'm almost done for the night. But I could take you around next week. How's Monday?"

Monday? I thought. I needed to give Kase a draft before Monday.

"Any chance tomorrow could work? I'll be in Minneapolis during the day, but I could—"

"Minneapolis? I thought you were local, writing for the *Tribune*. No…I don't like working with people from the city. I—I'm sorry," Aaron said and started walking toward a pickup truck parked around the side of the building. He opened the tailgate and heaved a duffel bag inside. "I have to run back and grab my camera. Take care, Sophie."

"Aaron, please!" I said, hurrying to catch up to him. "I promise I won't bother you. Just one quick peek inside." When he turned to face me, I noticed his left ear was pierced.

"I'm sorry," he said again. "But it was good to meet you. And one tip…if you plan to explore again, wear some different shoes." He winked at me and walked back into the Grand Hall.

"Damnit," I mumbled and walked to my car. My cell phone buzzed, lighting up the night.

"Hello?"

"Hi Sophie. It's Kase," he said. "Sorry for calling so late. I just got word that Hartman is holding a press conference tomorrow morning. Eight a.m. He'll be giving his response to Jansrud's sexual misconduct allegations. And, rumor has it, officially announcing his candidacy for governor. I need you there."

"Of course," I said, happy to avoid another day investigating an anonymous Twitter account. "Where is it?"

He gave me the details and we hung up. Before I got in my car, I jogged over to Aaron's truck. As a last-ditch effort, I stuck one of my heels, along with one of my shiny new business cards, on his windshield. I limped awkwardly to my car, hopeful I'd get my other shoe back soon. In my gut, I knew there was something going on with Hartman and the Oasis. I just needed another chance to prove it.

Chapter 12

BIZZIE

BIZZIE RUSHED BACK TO THE LODGING HOUSE, happy to be leaving, if only for a place much the same. But this time, she'd only be *pretending* to stay at the poor farm; it was different, she told herself. Miss Chambers was nowhere to be seen; Bizzie raced upstairs, anxious to get her belongings and get out. With her satchel in one hand and journal in the other, Bizzie stopped outside Emma's room and knocked twice.

Soft footsteps and then the door swung open. The smiling redhead stood before her, a piece of sapphire-colored fabric in her hands.

"Bizzie!" she exclaimed.

"I'm off to an assignment—er, work—but I think I found a place to stay." While the thought of living in Minneapolis thrilled her, being away from Collin and Papa made her heart ache. In a softer voice, she whispered, "Away from here." She raised her eyebrows at Emma. "Would you come look at it with me? I can cover the first month's rent."

Emma beamed. "Fantastic! When should we go?"

Bizzie bit her lip. "I'm off for about three days. Uh, teachers' conference. I'll stop by here when I'm back."

"Whatcha doing up here?" Bizzie whirled around to see Miss Chambers standing over her. Still wearing her faded and dirty white house dress from the day before, she stood with her sausage-like hands on her hips. Bizzie caught a scent of pungent body odor mixed with rotten milk.

Bizzie stuttered. "Excuse me, Miss Chambers. I was just telling Emma good-bye."

Emma smiled and winked, and Bizzie backed away and left the house without another word.

Because the county poor farm was miles away from Minneapolis, Bizzie had to take a bus. Although she had seen one in Duluth, she'd never actually ridden on it. During college, she walked everywhere.

"Excuse me, ma'am," she stopped a woman on the sidewalk. A little boy clung to the woman's long, gray skirt. Bizzie smiled at him. "I'm trying to find a bus that will take me to Clara City. Could you help me?"

The woman smiled. "Sure thing, doll. You need the Minneapolis-Clara City line. It stops just over there," she pointed across the street.

Bizzie thanked the woman, smiled at the little boy who was now peeking out at her, and hurried across the street. A group of men, all of them looking at their pocket watches intently, stood waiting together.

"Do you know if the Minneapolis-Clara City line stops here?" Bizzie asked one of the men.

"That's what we're all waiting for," he said, then he stared down at his watch. "But it's running behind. Should've been here two minutes ago."

Bizzie inched her way to the back of the group and waited. One of the men brushed past her and she caught a familiar scent of his aftershave, a mix of pine trees, fresh morning breeze and crisp, clean bedsheets. It was the same scent her Papa wore.

In an instant, she became so homesick she felt like she'd been kicked in the stomach. She could picture him sitting in his chair listening to the birds, waiting for Bizzie to get home from teaching. And her body ached to be back there—living a simple, albeit boring, life. Again, she questioned herself: *What am I doing here?!* Anxious tears ran down her cheeks, and she was glad the men surrounding her were busy inspecting their pocket watches. Her stomach churned at what Papa and Collin would say if they heard she was considering renting a room in this strange, new city.

Suddenly, all the men pointed toward an approaching bus and nodded to each other, saying things like, "Finally," "Four minutes behind," and "I could've walked to Clara City faster."

Bizzie wiped away the tears with the back of her hand. Putting one foot in front of the other was all she could manage. She feared that if she dwelled on the sadness and doubt, she might turn into a puddle of grief and collapse right there on the wooden planks. She silently followed the men up the stairs and onto the bus. She was so intent on not crying that she forgot to insert the necessary five cents to ride.

74 | THE MUCKRAKER

The bus driver furiously rang a bell and frowned at Bizzie.

"I ain't giving out no free rides," he said brusquely.

"Oh! I'm sorry." Bizzie, her cheeks hot, quickly rooted around in her satchel for the money. She pulled out five cents and dropped it in the bucket hanging near the door. Then, she scanned the crowded bus, desperate for a spot to sit.

A woman near the back of the bus gestured toward an empty spot near her. Bizzie quickly made her way toward her.

"Thank you," Bizzie said, sitting down. The woman smiled. She was impeccably dressed in a long, blue dress with lace sleeves. Her hair was pinned up, not a strand out of place, and her lips were painted a fiery red. She smelled of apples and freesia.

"You seem a bit out of place," the woman said gently. "Are you new to Minneapolis?"

"Yes," Bizzie sniffed. "I just moved here yesterday. I didn't expect the city to be so big. So busy." The woman nodded. Bizzie felt so relieved to unload her heavy emotions, she kept talking.

"I moved here to be a reporter," Bizzie said, waiting for the shock on the woman's face. But instead of raised eyebrows and doubt, she saw a smile and a nod.

"And?" the woman prompted.

"Well, I got the job. Now I'm on my first assignment. For *The Journal.*"

"Well done," she said, patting Bizzie's knee. "I love meeting other driven women. We're a rare breed, you know."

Bizzie smiled. She felt the sadness and homesickness that had nearly crippled her just moments ago slowly fade away. In its place, Bizzie felt a stirring of renewed hope.

The bus lurched and stopped. The driver hollered, "Pembroke Avenue!"

"This is my stop," the woman said, standing up gracefully. "Good luck to you—" she paused, holding out a hand.

Bizzie jutted out her hand and shook it heartily.

"Elizabeth Johansen," Bizzie said, proud that she'd remembered to use her reporter name.

"What a lovely name. Good luck to you, Elizabeth," the woman said. "And if you ever need anything, here's where you can find me." She handed Bizzie a small, white business card and walked toward the bus door. Bizzie looked down and gasped. In clean, neat print, the card read:

Elizabeth Quinlan
Young Quinlan Company
513 Nicollet, Minneapolis

Bizzie scrambled to the window and watched Ms. Quinlan float out of the bus. She didn't have to worry about bicyclists or horse-drawn carriages entering her path; everyone stopped for her. She wore a slight smile as she marched down Pembroke—almost as if she knew a secret that the rest of the world didn't. As the bus lurched forward and rocked slowly along the street, Bizzie sat back and held the business card to her chest.

As the bus left Minneapolis and bumped south toward Clara City, the hustle and bustle of the city was soon replaced with fields and farms. At the sight, Bizzie's heart settled calmly in her chest.

"Clara City!" the conductor hollered. Bizzie grabbed her bag and hustled off the bus.

She was surprised to hear…nothing. No newsboys hollering from the street corners. No streetcars carting pocket watch-wearing men and well-dressed women to the theater. No Newspaper Row. No throngs of people. The babel of languages and the crowded streets were replaced with green fields and rolling hills. She inhaled the sweet smell of tall grasses, wildflowers, and manure. It smelled like home.

Bizzie had grown surprisingly comfortable asking strangers for directions, but here, there was no milkman, no kind woman on the bus, no newsboy to ask. Amidst the distant green fields, she spotted a red, brick building. Hopeful that it was the county poor farm, she started walking.

As she approached, she could hear the cows mooing before she saw them. Bizzie remembered the first time she milked a cow. It was summertime, and she'd ridden her bicycle to Collin's farm to help Mrs. Walsh with baking and Sloane with arithmetic. Mrs. Walsh sent Collin off to the barn for milking with an egg-and-cheese biscuit wrapped in brown paper and tied with twine. An hour later, and halfway into making homemade bread, Mrs. Walsh poured a glass of fresh lemonade into a glass jar and handed it to Bizzie.

"Run this out to Collin, would you dear?" she asked. "That barn gets mighty hot in the summer."

Bizzie took the jar and floated through the pasture, happy for any excuse to see Collin. The round barn's foundation was stone, some of which was crumbling. Collin's grandfather had built the barn by hand when he emigrated from Ireland to Hibbing nearly sixty years earlier. She peeked her head inside and was overwhelmed by the smells of cow manure and hay.

"Collin?" she called.

"Over here!" he hollered back. "Careful. Some of 'em might kick ya."

Three dozen cows were harnessed to a feed bin in the center of the barn. Most didn't seem to mind being stuck in one place, but just to be safe, Bizzie tiptoed around, making sure not to upset any of them. She found Collin sitting on a stool, low to the ground.

"This," she handed him the cold, now-sweating glass of lemonade, "is for you."

Collin grabbed it gratefully and drank it all down in a couple quick gulps.

"I think it's time you learned how to milk a cow, Miss Johansen," Collin said.

"Ha! I know my way around a classroom, but farming? I'll leave that to you," Bizzie replied.

"It's a skill. A skill that every person should know," Collin said. Then he pulled up another wooden, dirt-crusted stool and said, "Come sit by me."

Bizzie sighed, knowing the argument was lost and she'd be spending the afternoon milking cows rather than in the kitchen baking bread. She sat on the low stool next to Collin.

"Now, spread your legs apart like this," Collin demonstrated, his knees pointed out. "And then you talk to this beauty, nice and sweet. Like this." He patted the cow's head. "How're you doin' today, little lady?" He looked at Bizzie. "You try."

Bizzie smiled and bit her lip. "I'm not too good at talking to cows."

"Ah, you're good at talking to me. And I'm just a step up from a cow," Collin laughed, his eyes twinkling.

Bizzie took a deep breath. "Alright." She slowly rubbed her hand against the cow's cheek. "Hi there, Miss. Thanks for letting me train on you today. I promise I'll do my best." The cow, as if understanding, nuzzled Bizzie's hand.

"You're a natural! She likes you already," Collin commended. "That's step one. You have to earn the cow's trust. Now for the next part."

With confidence and ease, he balled his rough, calloused hand and grabbed the cow's engorged, pink teat. He gently squeezed, pulling down towards the silver bucket placed underneath the cow. Within seconds, a thin stream of milk fell into the bucket with a plunk. Collin turned to Bizzie.

"Your turn," he said.

She gingerly grabbed the udder between her thumb and forefinger and weakly pulled it towards the bucket. The cow let out a grunt and rolled her head.

"No, no. You have to take command. Do it with confidence." Collin showed Bizzie again how to make a fist with her hand and grab the teat firmly. She tried again, this time balling her fist and pulling down toward the bucket just as Collin had done. Soon, a stream of milk began flowing into the bucket.

"I did it!" she squealed. Collin patted her shoulder.

"You keep working on her. I'll be right here." He edged his stool towards the next cow. They sat in tandem like that for an hour, milking together.

Bizzie smiled at the memory. She walked up the gravel path toward the red, brick building. A man in a straw hat was tending a small garden that was filled with more weeds than anything else.

"Excuse me, sir," she said. He jumped at hearing her voice.

"Startled me," he mumbled, looking at her slowly with eyes the color of a muddy swamp. Dark circles hung under them. He took his time standing up and then put a hand to his lower back, stretching. He wore a pair of threadbare, brown trousers that had been patched several times. A cotton shirt two sizes too big hung over his bony frame. In a heartbeat, Bizzie was back at her student Leon's log cabin, *Palmer Method Handwriting* clutched in her hands. She remembered the look of despair on his mother's face when she opened the door. It was the same look the gardener wore now.

"Is there room here?" Bizzie asked.

The gardener jerked his head back, signaling Bizzie to follow him. He limped from the garden to the entrance of the red, brick building—the one Bizzie had seen from the road. Without a word, he flicked a thumb toward the door. Then, with his head slumped, he shuffled back to the garden.

Bizzie hesitated, noticing the heaviness that hung in the air. She pulled on the metal handle to open the wooden door. She choked on a stench so repulsive, she instinctively pulled out her handkerchief and held it to her nose. It was a mix of feces, urine, and unwashed bodies. If pitiful could be bottled, she was sure this would be it. A man in black trousers and a starched white shirt walked briskly through the foyer. He paused when Bizzie walked in.

"Can I help you?" he said, furrowing his brow as he sharply looked her up and down.

She gulped, swallowing the fear brewing in her stomach. "I'd like—I'd like to stay here," she stammered.

"You?" He looked her up and down, eyeing her satchel and dress that, albeit faded, lacked any rips, tears, or patches. But Bizzie had time on the bus to develop her story. "I just found out I'm—I'm pregnant," she said, shamefully hanging her head. "Once I told him—Christopher—the news, he left me. And my mother and father threw me out. I have nowhere to go," she whined, maybe a little too pitifully.

The man took a deep breath. "Well, come in."

Bizzie smiled to herself. She hadn't expected requesting a place to stay to be that easy.

"Let me get a key," the man said gruffly. "Stay here."

Bizzie, anxious to start collecting details right away, peeked around. A mousy, young girl with straw-like hair the color of dirty dishwater poked around the corner. Bizzie smiled and waved. The girl smiled back. Her face looked older—or maybe it was just her eyes.

"Disa!" a voice hissed. The girl smiled and put a finger to her lips. "Disa!" Bizzie heard again.

A woman appeared and gripped the girl's arm, yanking her away from the door. At the same time, the man returned with a key. He cleared his throat, and Bizzie whirled around.

"Follow me," the man said. Bizzie grabbed her satchel and followed. The structure was set up much like her Aunt Maebel's house in Duluth. Never married, Aunt Maebel—her father's sister—ran a lodging house that welcomed big, burly men who all had calloused hands from working in the Superior Forest all day. Bizzie had stayed with her when on break from teachers' college. Maebel's life—much like Bizzie's mother's—didn't turn out as planned.

Maebel, however, hadn't turned bitter the way Bizzie's mother had. Whenever Bizzie had visited her, she'd offer Bizzie a steaming bowl of vegetable soup and, with a twinkle in her eye, say, "It's a beautiful day, isn't it?"

"I said, how long do you think you'll be staying with us?" the man snapped, reminding Bizzie of where she was.

"Oh, I'm sorry," Bizzie said, forcing her thoughts back to the present. "Just a few days, I hope—I mean, I think. I have an aunt in northern Minnesota who is sending a carriage for me. I'll be living with her until the baby comes."

"Alright. Then this room should do fine." He motioned for Bizzie to enter through the wooden door with rusty hinges. A splintered hole the size of a baseball was in the place of a doorknob. "You'll be sharing with another woman and her daughter," the man said. Bizzie wondered if it was the young girl she'd met in the front of the house.

She peeked into the room. It was the size of the closet in her schoolhouse—which was hardly big enough to hold the coats and boots of her students.

"Three of us in this tiny space?" The room contained two small, twin beds and one rickety dresser. "Where am I supposed to sleep?"

The man chuckled. "I don't get in the way of broads and their sleeping arrangements. I just provide the beds. Now, if you live here, eat here, and sleep here, you're expected to work here. All inmates meet in the back of the house to get their assigned jobs at eight a.m. sharp." He nodded his head at the last word, making sure Bizzie understood.

He grabbed Bizzie's arm and yanked her back out into the hallway. "Follow me, I'll show you where you'll be working."

Chapter 13

SOPHIE

THE NEXT MORNING, I pulled on a pair of my favorite high-rise skinny jeans, a white, frayed-edge camisole, and cropped black blazer and headed for Hartman's headquarters.

I dialed Freya's number.

"Hey, girl," she answered on the third ring.

"Freya!" I breathed, relieved to hear her voice. "I need your advice about a story I'm working on."

"Let's see if I still got the chops," she said. "Lucy, here are your pancakes!"

I merged onto the highway and explained that, while I was working on the Morris Hartman case, I came across a detail that seemed odd: the Oasis Dr. Hartman built could be slated for demolition. And Morris Hartman didn't seem to care. I told her I had taken a tour of the Oasis and may have stumbled upon something strange.

"Okay, don't laugh," I said, suddenly feeling silly, like a girl playing Nancy Drew. "I found a brick wall that is, like, hidden or something. Gah, now I'm doubting myself." I shook my head. "Never mind. It's stupid."

"Hold on," Freya said. "Remember that time we snagged that exclusive interview from the whistleblower from…oh, what was that company…"

I nodded. "Smythe Group Worldwide."

"Yes! That was it. Everyone thought we were crazy. And what did you say when I doubted whether we should do the interview?"

"Um, I think I said, 'What's the worst that could happen?'"

"Well, yes, that. But you also said, 'You're following your journalistic hunch.' And what happened? An incriminating conversation that led to Jaxon Smythe's arrest."

I nodded, thinking back to that day. Everyone in the newsroom thought Freya was crazy. Jaxon Smythe hit colossal success when he created a series of investment funds. Then, he bought the state's first professional rugby team, which won the USA Sevens its first year. When Gina Miller, Smythe's assistant, emailed one of KOMO's reporters, telling him that something was wrong with the financial numbers, he'd dismissed it. But Freya dug deeper. She had to convince a junior reporter to do the interview. The result? An on-camera conversation with Gina, who told KOMO that Smythe had never had any real, actual money. He would just send statements to investors, showing them how much they "earned."

By then, our senior reporters were intrigued and began digging in. They uncovered a massive Ponzi scheme for which Jaxon Smythe is currently serving a forty-year prison sentence.

"So, you're saying maybe I'm not completely off-base?" I ventured.

"I'm saying you've always had a keen sense. Trust that," Freya replied.

I let out a deep breath as I pulled into the parking lot. "Thanks, Freya." We hung up, and I walked inside Hartman's Headquarters, showing my media badge and finding an open seat. A podium near the window was plastered with Hartman's logo.

A minute later, Hines appeared, beads of sweat on his pink forehead.

"Alright, folks. GOP-candidate Morris Hartman will be addressing the allegations of sexual misconduct facing DFL-candidate Jim Jansrud. Afterwards, he'll have time for a few questions."

Hartman stood nearby, relaxed, with his hands in his trouser pockets. He smiled and walked to the podium, his bright eyes twinkling.

"Thanks, Hines," he said. Then he looked at us. "And thanks to all of you. Has anyone told you that you're doing a great job? You show up and tell the stories that need to be told. You make the time. You meet your deadlines. And I want to be the first to tell you thanks. A genuine, authentic thank you."

A couple of us exchanged glances, not used to hearing praises from political figures. Usually, we're on opposite teams.

"I'm trying to do my job. And it's a time like this when I'm reminded of how important that job is." He paused and stepped aside from the podium. A microphone wasn't needed in such a small room.

"I've spent the last three decades creating, growing, and leading businesses across this great state. And, throughout that time, I've learned there's one thing all of us have in common. You know what that is? We are darn proud to be Minnesotans."

A group of reporters in the back cheered and whooped.

"I mean, right? You've gotta be tough to live in a state that dishes up ice storms and snowstorms and below zero temps all in one week. That's why I am officially announcing I will be running for governor of Minnesota next year. I would be honored to lead the strong, tenacious, and bold citizens of this great state."

Immediately, hands shot up in the air. Hartman held up a hand and nodded. "Thank you. I will answer your questions, but first, I'd like to take a moment to discuss the recent news about Jim Jansrud… When I first heard about Jim, I have to admit I was shocked. I've known him for a long time."

He paused, frowning as looked around at each of us.

"Jim and I rub elbows with the same people. I've always thought of him as a friend. No, a mentor. But these allegations remind me of something. That we're all human. We all make mistakes. So, I want to be absolutely transparent… As many of you know, I own several manufacturing operations."

I remembered my conversation with Greg, Ida's husband, and the potential plans for a steel mill in Crab Orchard.

"I have decided to file disclosure forms with the Office of Government Ethics. Of course, I don't have to do this until I'm elected." He waved a humble hand at us like a teacher might do after telling her students they got an extra twenty minutes of recess. "But I want to make sure I'm being absolutely scrupulous with all three of my businesses. It's the right thing to do and it's what Minnesota deserves. Together, let's advocate for a stronger Minnesota. Let's shape our future together."

He paused and smiled. "Alright, who's first?" He pointed to a reporter in the front row.

She stood up and asked, "What policy changes or preventative measures would you consider to keep our schools safe from gun violence?"

Hartman folded his hands and brought them to his chin. "I appreciate you bringing this up. Ensuring our students' safety will be one of my top priorities. I can assure you that I will have a task force in place—*on day one*—to address this issue, keep us moving forward, and keep our kids safe."

A reporter behind me raised his hand and asked what Hartman

thought an appropriate step in Jansrud's case would be. Hartman went on about an ethics committee looking into the allegations as I mentally prepared myself for my question. I took a deep breath and raised my hand. Hartman pointed at me. I inhaled sharply and noticed the sickly-sweet smell of fresh donuts from next door.

"Congratulations on your candidacy," I said, my mouth bone-dry and my heart pounding. "I just wondered if you have a comment about the Oasis…the original clinic your grandfather built," I paused and added, "the one that could be facing demolition. The land is owned by MH Manufacturing, right?"

The room was silent. Hartman stared at me. A beat later, his charming smile returned but his eyes had frosted over. "I do have a comment. Thank you, Ms. McHale," he added, his jaw clenched.

I glanced over at Hines who was glowering at me.

"My grandfather was not only a fantastic businessman, he was also an incredible, visionary physician. I am so incredibly proud that he paved the way for all of us. Because of his efforts, you, me, all of us," he gestured around the room, "can live without fear of dying from a very curable disease." He paused, then shrugged and raised his hands. "That's his legacy. That's what's important."

He stepped away from the podium again. "Am I sad that the building might be demolished? Of course. But his clinics remain in nearly every small town across the state. That is what he would have wanted."

After a moment, he stepped back behind the podium. Damn, he was a good public speaker.

"On that note, let's start shaping our future…together. Oh, and Hines bought out the donut shop next door this morning. Make sure to take one—or two—on your way out."

Am I losing my mind? I wondered. *Maybe it really is no big deal that the Oasis is slated for demolition and Hartman owns the land.*

"Thanks for coming today," Hines said to the group, meeting my eyes with a dark glare. Any appetite I had for a donut melted away. I shivered. "I'll send out a press release summing up Mr. Hartman's comments and his official candidacy announcement later this morning." Hines finally tore his frown away from me.

As I left the building, I made a mental note to ask Jen if she'd ever encountered a strange reaction like that from Hartman. When I got into my car, my phone buzzed and an unfamiliar number popped up on the screen.

"Hello?" I answered.

"Pretty clever, leaving your shoe behind. Are you some kind of Cinderella?" a male voice asked.

"Aaron?" I said, after a minute.

"The one and only," he replied.

"Thanks for calling," I said, merging onto the freeway and heading back to News Now Online. "I didn't think you would."

"I figured you might need your shoe back," he chuckled.

"It is my favorite pair," I replied.

"Well, if you want to trek out here to the sticks again, maybe I'll return it."

My heart skipped a beat. "Yes! Absolutely!" Then, I added a calmer, more put together, "I mean, sure. That could work."

"Great. Come out on Saturday afternoon. Let's meet at The Coffee Fox. It's on Main Street in Crab Orchard," he paused. "You'll see a sign with a big fox on it."

I smiled, remembering the coffee shop from my drive through town. "A big fox. Got it."

Chapter 14

BIZZIE

THE MAN IN THE BLACK TROUSERS didn't let go of Bizzie's arm; instead, he pulled her along like a child. They walked through the foyer and out the front door. Bizzie caught sight of the gardener who appeared so weak and weary he could barely stand.

The man pulled Bizzie toward the back of the house where a group of women worked in a small field. Their faces, full of misery and fear, captivated Bizzie. For a moment, her journalist instincts kicked in and she forgot the role she was playing. She lagged behind, staring at the women, a thousand questions running through her mind: Who were these women? Why did they look so hopeless? The man jerked her arm forward, causing Bizzie to stumble.

He grabbed Bizzie's shoulder and, with clenched teeth, breathed into her face. "When I tell you to follow me, you follow." His teeth were yellowed and breaking, and his breath smelled stale. He shoved her into a small garden. "You'll work here," he spat. Then, he walked away, attending to matters further afield.

The women were wearing faded dresses that neither fit well nor covered them properly. They were bending over or crouched down, tending to the fields. Bizzie looked around frantically, unsure of what to do next.

"Just do what I do," a girl beside her whispered. She was kneeling down in the garden, her fingers black from the soil. Her face was white; the thin bones of her shoulder blades seemed sharp enough to pierce her skin. She smiled and handed Bizzie a rusty shovel. "We're planting herbs in this lot."

Bizzie gratefully grabbed the shovel and began doing exactly as the girl did. She dug a small hole, then gently placed a small grouping of seeds inside and patted dirt all around it.

The man trumped back toward Bizzie and the girl, glaring at them both. Bizzie took a deep breath, trying not to let her shaky hands give her away. With a scoff, he marched away toward the house. Bizzie exhaled loudly.

"Thanks for your help," Bizzie said. "I didn't expect the manager to be so harsh."

"He's not the manager. He's the superintendent," the girl said, punching each syllable. "And he won't let you forget it."

Bizzie wanted to gain this girl's trust right away. Wrinkles prematurely adorned the sides of her pale blue eyes even though she looked to be Bizzie's age.

The other women who had been working in the fields gathered around Bizzie and the girl.

"What's your name, honey?" one of them asked. The dress she was wearing clung to her thin frame. Her cheekbones stood out, and her wispy hair blew in the welcomed breeze.

"Bizz—Beth," Bizzie said, relieved she remembered her alibi. "Beth Johnson."

"Beth, welcome to the worst place on earth," another woman chimed in with a sad laugh. They now sat beside Bizzie—six in total. One offered her a sip of water. Bizzie, her throat dry as dust, reached for the skin. She took a swig, then immediately spat it into the dirt. She poured a bit into her hand for inspection; brown water the color of dung sloshed around her cupped palm.

"Sorry," the woman said genuinely, reaching back for the water. "That's all we've got."

"How can you stand to live in a place so awful?" Bizzie asked, genuinely curious. Grit and sand stuck in her teeth.

"We ain't got no other choice," the woman who had given her a drink of water said. She wasn't as thin as the others. Her graying hair was tied in a knot at the back of her head. She was beautiful; the lines on her face and her twinkling blue eyes were stunning. "I was married to a nasty man who nearly drank himself to death. Wish he had. He'd come home every night and whip me. Believe it or not, I'd choose this place over living with that bastard."

Then, she looked at the other women and winked. "Plus, if he ever comes looking for me, I know me and my sisters would take care of him."

The other women laughed and nodded.

"Name's Ruth," she offered a hand to Bizzie, who shook it. Although Ruth's hand was calloused and dry, her handshake was firm and friendly.

"But to live here," Bizzie waved her hand at the decrepit house, "with a nasty man and dirty water—"

"Don't say that so loud," Ruth hissed, looking around. "Mr. Hendry ain't that bad. You just gotta stay outta his way. He don't whip us if we do what he says."

"So did all of you," Bizzie gestured to the other women in the group, "come here seeking safety from your husbands?"

"Is that why you're here, sweetie?" a thin woman with mousy brown hair said, placing a hand on Bizzie's shoulder.

"No, no," Bizzie said a bit too quickly. She noticed a flicker in Ruth's eyes. "I mean, no. But I did come here seeking protection. For my baby." She cradled her stomach. "I got pregnant, and my mother kicked me out."

No one said anything for a moment, and it seemed like the women were waiting for Ruth to speak. Ruth settled to the ground and started planting seeds. As she tamped down the dirt and started another row, she said dryly, "I was pregnant once."

Bizzie saw surprised looks from the other women which said they didn't know this about Ruth.

"I knew I would love that baby more than anything." She stopped her digging, and looked off at something miles away, a soft smile on her face. "I would finally have the family I'd always wanted. But Mister came home raging mad. He'd heard from someone that I was pregnant. He was going on that I was cheating on him, that the baby was someone else's. He demanded I tell him who I'd been with."

Ruth quickly wiped away a tear that had trickled out of her eye. Bizzie and the women listened in complete stillness. "Even though he was a nasty man, I wouldn't ever cheat on him. I take my marriage vows to heart. But he beat me bad that night." Ruth bit her lip and shook her head, returning to her work in the dirt. "I lost the baby," she said quietly.

The other women remained still. Bizzie was captivated. Ruth looked up at Bizzie so intently that she felt herself fall out of her fake persona and back in a single breath.

"How far along you think you are?" Ruth asked.

"About twelve weeks," Bizzie said, her voice dusty.

After a minute, Ruth gestured to the herb plot and said, "Ladies, let's finish up here before Mr. Hendry comes back out. Dinner'll be ready soon and he'll be ringing the bell."

"Tonight's bread, tea, and boiled rice," one woman chimed in. "Ruth loves boiled rice."

Ruth rolled her eyes. "Would it kill Mrs. Boller to put a dash of salt on the rice? It's barely cooked as it is. Nearly choked on a mouthful last week."

Ruth pulled Bizzie aside so the other women wouldn't hear. "We'll talk to Mr. Hendry's wife." She pointed to a two-story, blue house surrounded by tall, barbed wire a few hundred feet away. "I think she'll help us."

Bizzie nodded. She worked silently side-by-side with the other women in the garden, surprised to feel a sense of acceptance already. She listened to their conversations, mostly small talk. All the while, she captured notes and pictures in her head, mentally imprinting them until she could transcribe them into her journal later that night. She wasted no time. While she dug holes in the dirt for herbs, she memorized the tattered dresses, wispy hair, and thin frames. She etched the landscape surrounding the poor farm in her memory: several acres of farmland containing corn and soybeans.

Ms. Sally Salter, her journalist friend and mentor from Duluth, told her to always pay attention to the scene in front of her.

"You never know what details you might need to recall later," she'd said on one of their walks with Daisy.

Beyond the farmland were fields of wheat and tall grasses. A small pond sat back behind the house. As for other lodgers—or "inmates," as Mr. Hendry had called them—the only other man she had seen was the gardener. She was curious about the small girl she had seen when she first arrived—Disa.

She looked around before asking the girl working beside her in the garden.

"When I arrived, I saw a small girl. I think her name was Disa. Does she live here too?"

The girl smiled. "We all love her. She and her mother live in a room on the second floor."

Bizzie pushed for more details. "Does she go to school of any kind? She looks so young."

"No, no," the girl replied. "Mr. Hendry doesn't believe in educating women. Although..." she trailed off.

"What is it?"

The girl shrugged. "I heard that Mrs. Hendry used to be a teacher.

But Mr. Hendry never lets her out of that house."

"Why?" Bizzie pushed for more details.

"Mr. Hendry thinks of us as inmates. Criminals. Beneath society. And he definitely sees him and his wife as above the likes of us," the girl sniffed. "Notice the barbed wire protecting their house?"

The dinner bell clanged, startling Bizzie. The women stood, stretching as they gathered their tools and shovels. Ruth held a dirty, white bucket out for each one. Bizzie's back ached from only a few hours of field work. She couldn't understand how these women did this every day.

"Well done, today," Ruth would say as each woman dropped their tool in the bucket with a plunk.

"You," she said when Bizzie dropped her shovel in. She lifted Bizzie's chin with her wrinkled, calloused forefinger. Then with a smile said, "You're a tough one, you. You'll be just fine. You stick with me." She put her arm around Bizzie and snuggled her in beside her. Ruth's cotton dress was damp with sweat, but Bizzie didn't mind. She felt nurtured. For a moment, she forgot she was on assignment. Her heart tugged at the thought of deceiving them.

"Remember what I said about the rice," Ruth whispered to Bizzie. "It's hard as little pebbles. Chew carefully." She winked at Bizzie.

Silently, everyone filed into the dining room. Disa, the small girl she had seen earlier, bounced into the room, accompanied by a slight woman with blonde hair and porcelain skin. Her mother?

Everyone sat at a long, oak table covered by a faded, see-through white tablecloth. Everyone, that is, except for Mr. Hendry. Bizzie waited anxiously for him to appear. The walls were dusty and covered in cobwebs.

A round woman with thinning hair on her head and coarse, black hairs on her upper lip stomped in carrying two bowls. With a humph, she set them down on the table. The infamous Mrs. Boller, Bizzie thought.

Just then, a woman Bizzie hadn't yet seen or met walked in. She wasn't dressed like the others. Her hair was combed neatly and pinned on top of her head. Around her neck was a string of pearls. Her sleeves were trimmed with lace and her skirt was the color of sapphires. She caught Bizzie staring. Instead of a growl or frown, she offered a gentle smile. *Mrs. Hendry?*

"Tea?" Mrs. Boller said, returning. Everyone at the table nodded yes and she started pouring hot water into the mismatched and chipped porcelain teacups. Although the tea was weak and there was no mention of milk or sugar, the water was clear without any trace of dirt or grime. The bread, however, was hard as rock. Bizzie watched Ruth dip her torn piece into her tea to soften it. She did the same. Living up to its reputation, the rice was nearly inedible. But Bizzie was starving, so she carefully and slowly chewed it.

Once Mrs. Hendry finished eating, and not until then, did Mrs. Boller come back to the dining room to clear away the dishes. Ruth stood up first, followed by the other lodgers. Bizzie scrambled to her feet. She stole one more glance at the woman in the sapphire-colored skirt. Then she hurried off with the others, wondering why Mr. Hendry hadn't joined them.

"This is your room, then?" Ruth said, pointing towards the room Mr. Hendry had shown her earlier. Bizzie nodded. The little girl, Disa, squeezed her way through Bizzie and Ruth and jumped on one of the beds.

"Disa!" the woman, who Bizzie presumed to be her mother, hissed and followed her. She mumbled something Bizzie couldn't understand.

"This is Disa." Ruth motioned to the girl. "And her mother, Asta."

At the mention of her name, Asta looked up. A perpetual worried look was plastered upon her pretty face.

"Came from Norway this spring," Ruth said, smiling at Asta. Then, in a hushed voice said, "Don't understand a lick of English. Poor thing. No mention of the girl's father, neither."

"My grandmother was from Norway," Bizzie said, forgetting her alibi momentarily. "She made the best Julekake."

At the mention of the familiar pastry, Asta looked curiously at Bizzie and smiled. For a moment, Asta's anxiety left her face. "Julekake?"

"My grandmother," Bizzie said, speaking loud and clear, "made Julekake."

At this, Asta beamed. She rushed over to Bizzie, words jumbling out that neither Ruth nor Bizzie could understand. But they politely smiled and stood there.

"This is the most I've ever heard Asta say," Ruth whispered. "Just wish I could understand what she was saying."

Bizzie smiled. Even though she couldn't speak Norwegian, she understood. Asta must have felt—for a brief moment—reconnected to a thread of home that was lost.

"Lights out in five minutes, ladies!" a voice hollered from downstairs.

"That'll be our nightly warning from Mrs. Boller," Ruth said.

Asta turned from Bizzie and Ruth to help Disa into her thin slip.

Bizzie sat down on the unclaimed bed in the corner.

"Ouch!" Something poked Bizzie and she jumped up. "This—this can't be my bed. There must be some mistake." Bizzie lifted up the thin blanket to reveal a straw tick mattress.

"It ain't too bad," Ruth came over and shook the mattress. "Just needs a good shake. Mr. Hendry thinks straw tick mattresses are more sanitary than regular ones. And no quilts allowed," she held up a thin blanket. "Just one of these."

"But what about the dust? And fleas?" Bizzie eyed the mattress.

"That's what our weekly bath is for," Ruth said with a shrug.

"Wait…weekly bath?"

"Mrs. Boller fills the basin, and we line up, each assigned to scrub each other," Ruth said. "Ain't pleasant, I'll give you that."

Bizzie was shaking with rage. "You have a right to be treated better than that. We all do. You ought to be given privacy and a proper bath."

Ruth nodded, a knowing look on her face. "Try telling that to Mr. Hendry."

"Well, speaking of a bath, I need to use the bathroom. Is it down the hall?" Bizzie asked.

Ruth stifled a laugh. "Yes. It's down the hall—down the stairs and out the door. But watch for spiders and snakes out there. You can't see very well in the dark."

Bizzie's mouth dropped open. *Spiders and snakes?* She took a deep breath and pinched the bridge of her nose.

Ruth must have read her mind because she said, "You get used to it." Then, as Asta tucked Disa into bed, Ruth pulled Bizzie aside. "After the lights-out call, meet me downstairs. We'll sneak over and talk to Mrs. Hendry about your little situation." She pointed to Bizzie's stomach.

Bizzie squinted at Ruth. "But, what about—"

"It's Tuesday. Mr. Hendry goes into Clara City to play poker on Tuesday. Mrs. Hendry'll be all alone."

"But won't we get into—"

"Trouble?" It was like Ruth could read Bizzie's thoughts. "Nah. Mrs. Hendry and I…we, well, we've gotten to know each other."

Bizzie was intrigued and wanted to ask more, but she heard Mrs. Boller holler, "Lights out!"

"Five minutes!" Ruth hissed and disappeared out the door.

Chapter 15

SOPHIE

I LEFT MY APARTMENT around two p.m. Saturday wearing a pair of black joggers, a t-shirt that said *Up North*, and camo sneakers. I texted Aaron before I left, telling him I'd meet him at The Coffee Fox in about an hour and a half. I headed west, weaving through surprisingly heavy traffic for a Saturday. Suddenly, the cars in front of me hit their brakes.

"Are you kidding me?" I muttered, shaking my head. I crawled along, following a semi that kept spitting out smelly exhaust. After twenty minutes, I had barely crawled a mile. Then, I saw it. Orange cones, neon vests, and blinking lights. Construction. Miles of it. Cursing and rolling my eyes, I texted Aaron that I'd be late. Finally, after forty-five minutes, I zoomed around the semi and sped west on the highway. When I pulled up to The Coffee Fox a half hour late, my hands were clenched tight on the steering wheel.

Taking a deep breath, I stepped out of my maroon Kia and stretched. Aaron was right. The sign—a two-foot, wooden circle with an orange-colored fox face painted on it—couldn't be missed. It caught my eye when I first drove through town. I pulled open the glass door to find cement floors, shiny wooden tables, and globe string lights that made the café feel both modern and cozy. Despite it being May and sixty degrees outside, a stone fireplace crackled in the back where a couple snuggled up to each other, both holding ceramic mugs. Photos of exotic-looking locations covered the walls.

"Hey there, Cinderella."

I turned to see Aaron behind the coffee bar. "Aaron," I said, smiling.

"I'm so sorry I'm late. Honestly. The construction. You wouldn't believe it. Wait," I paused, noticing for the first time that Aaron was behind the counter. "You—you work here?" I set my bag down on the counter.

"Nope," he replied. "I own it."

I laughed. "Why am I not surprised? The Coffee Fox. I have to admit, this is great," I said, gesturing at the coffee shop. "You did a really nice job. I love it."

He smiled and leaned against the bar. "I'm just full of surprises. What can I get you?"

"Um, how about a decaf latte?" I said, a bit flustered. I took out my wallet, but he held out his hand.

"On the house," he said. "I'll make it and be right over. Sit anywhere you want."

I nodded and found a table by the window. Three boys rode by on their bikes while a silver-haired couple walked arm-in-arm. A family poured out of a diner across the street. Aaron came over with two mugs.

"Thanks," I said, taking a sip. "This actually is a cute little town." Right after the words tumbled out of my mouth, I realized how I sounded. Seeing Aaron's hurt face made me want to swallow my words right back in.

He grimaced and ran a hand through his tangled, brown hair, which was again pulled up into a bun. "Says the girl from Minneapolis."

"Sorry, sorry," I said, reaching out across the table to him. "I'm an idiot. That's not what I meant."

"I know what you meant." He waved his hand dismissively. "You're all the same. You think anything or anyone outside the city doesn't really count. Doesn't matter."

I bit my lip. I had to admit, he was partly right. I didn't exactly go looking for life outside my four-block radius. "I'm sorry, Aaron," I said, genuine. "Can we try again?"

After a pause, he nodded. "So, you want to tell me what you were doing at the Oasis the other night?" he asked. The charm had left his voice. "You're a political correspondent. Why do you care about some crumbling building sixty miles west of," he put his hands on his heart, "Minneapolis?" He drew out the name of the city. He flicked my business card between two of his fingers. "You left this—with your shoe. Which," he dug around in his tattered green backpack that he'd brought over with the coffee mugs, "I have right here." He handed it over to me.

"Don't you want to make sure it fits first?" I winked at him, setting the shoe on the ground beside me.

Despite my attempt to lighten the mood, Aaron sat back in his chair, took a sip of his coffee, and raised his eyebrows at me. "So?" he asked again.

I sighed. "I might be making something out of nothing." I told him about Hartman's reaction to my phone call when I questioned the demolition of the Oasis. Then, I told him about the city council meeting with Ida. I added the details about Hartman's company owning the land surrounding the Oasis, and the proposed steel mill. Lastly, I told him about Hartman's reaction to my question at the press conference. I sighed, exasperated after my long explanation, and held my head in my hands. "At this point though, I wonder if I'm just desperate for a compelling story."

I was about to launch into the K!ng debacle when an apron-clad teenager in a black hoodie and converse sneakers came over to our table. A small gold hoop looped through the side of her nose.

"Do you mind if I go?"

Aaron checked his phone. "You go ahead, Claire. I'll close up in a bit." He turned to me. "We usually close at four on Saturdays. Do you mind sticking around for a few minutes?"

I nodded. "I'm happy to help. What can I do?"

"Wait." He held up his hand and looked at my camo sneakers. "Those are a bit better. But you need to invest in a good work boot. See these?" He proudly pointed at his worn boots, a similar pair to the ones he had been wearing the other night. "Can't fail you."

He led me behind the bar and handed me an apron. "Mind helping me wash dishes?" He tossed me a towel.

"Tell me about Crab Orchard," I said. "How did you end up here?" Worried he might take that as an insult, I quickly added, "In this adorable town?"

"I caught that," Aaron raised his eyebrows at me, sliding a rack of dirty mugs into the commercial-sized dishwasher. He took a deep breath. "How did I end up here," he repeated back to me. "Hmm. Well, I studied biology in college. Took a job working for the U.S. Forest Service in the Boundary Waters. Lived up there for about four years," he paused as he lifted the dishwasher after the cleaning cycle. A puff of steam filled the air.

I waited a beat, then yanked the rack out and began drying off the leftover hot water.

"Then I moved to Minneapolis," he choked out.

"You lived in Minneapolis?" I asked, surprised. "I thought you hated—"

"I did." Aaron nodded. "But I followed a girl."

I wanted to make a joke, but his face told me he was still hurting. "Didn't work out?" I asked instead.

"In every possible way," he said, sliding in another rack. A moment later, he shrugged. "So, I started over. My uncle owns a landscaping business here in Crab Orchard, so I moved home to help him."

"So, you pretty much do it all," I joked. "A naturalist, a landscaper, a coffee shop owner? Oh, and a photographer?"

Aaron smiled. He had a nice smile. The lines around his eyes looked sexy when he smiled. *I wish he would smile again*, I thought.

"That's just a hobby," he replied. He flung a towel over his shoulder, and I noticed his broad, strong shoulders. "Last one," he said, sliding in one more rack of mugs. I continued drying the clean dishes and setting them carefully on a metal shelf. When the mugs were cleaned and coffee pots turned off, I went to untie my apron. But, because my hands were still wet, I couldn't unfasten the knot.

"Um, I think I'm stuck," I pointed to my apron.

"Newbie," he joked, coming over to where I stood. He placed one hand on my lower back and the other on my side. My spine tingled and my mouth went dry. In a second, he had the knot untied. He squeezed my side and lifted the apron over my head.

"Thanks," I stammered, a bit breathlessly.

"Let's take my truck," he said, as he tossed my apron in a laundry basket with dirty towels. "The entire campus is under surveillance. Doug—he's the guy who lets me in—has my license plates. I can come and go whenever."

"You're some kind of big shot, huh?" I joked.

He smirked. "Something like that."

When we got to the gravel road leading to the Oasis, Aaron hopped out and unhooked the iron chain blocking the entrance. I noticed something I hadn't seen before: a small structure hidden by overgrown trees and brush. Only the roof was visible. I craned my neck to see more.

"What's that?" I asked Aaron when he got back in the car. He ducked his head and looked to where I pointed.

"Cottage for groundskeepers," he said, driving up the gravel path. "So, I've heard. They lived on the property back when this place was up and running."

Aaron parked his truck and grabbed a flashlight from the middle console. He punched in the four-digit code on the keyless lock and a green light flashed. He pushed open the door and shined the flashlight into the Grand Hall. Although the sun was still high, the flashlight helped illuminate the dark shadows. This time, I remembered how to navigate my way to the staircase. I pointed to the dead bat as we walked past, warning Aaron.

"Can I ask what happened to the girl you followed to Minneapolis?" I ventured as we walked through the crumbling hallway. Aaron was silent and I feared that I overstepped.

"Well," he started. "Like I said, we met working together in the Boundary Waters." There was a liveliness in his voice I hadn't heard before now. "Being outside, cutting trails, maintaining campsites." He paused and looked at me. "You ever been?"

I shrugged and shook my head. "Sadly, no. And I've lived in this state my whole life."

Mockingly, he grabbed his heart. Then, in a serious tone, he said, "It really is one of the most beautiful and peaceful places. Just miles and miles of natural beauty." He looked at me. "And no construction."

"Well, that part sounds wonderful. Sign me up!" I laughed.

"I could've stayed up there—and would've—if it wasn't for Tiffany." At the mention of her name, he seemed to wince. At the same time, we approached the office at the end of the second-floor hallway. He pushed open the door. "Is this the office you were looking for?"

I was intrigued about his past, but more intrigued, at least right at the moment, about the brick wall behind the bookshelf. I followed him in and chose not to ask any more questions about his love life. I went right to the spot where I had been earlier, when Ida was talking to her mother on the phone. Moving a few books aside, I again found the brick wall. I motioned for Aaron to shine his light.

"See?" I asked. He squinted and rubbed a callused hand against the brick.

"Strange," he muttered. He handed me the flashlight and began shoving books aside and piling them up on the floor. Once the shelf was empty, he started pushing and jabbing bricks at random. After a few minutes, he shrugged. "Must just be a wall."

My shoulders sank. I felt like a complete idiot. Now, I was sure I was grasping at straws for a story. Aaron must have sensed this because he rubbed my shoulder. Again, sparks flew up and down my spine. "Hey, you were just following your journalistic instincts," he said, smiling at me. "Or something like that."

I smirked, noting that Freya had given me the same advice. "Yeah, something like that." We crept back down the hall, avoiding the giant hole in the floor and the dead bat. But, before we left through the main door, Aaron grabbed my elbow and gestured straight ahead.

"I want to show you something." He shined his flashlight down the corridor. He led me into a room I hadn't noticed before that faced the woods instead of the parking lot. Even with Aaron standing beside me shining his heavy-duty flashlight, I couldn't swallow the fear in my stomach. At any moment, I was pretty sure someone—or something—was going to jump out at us.

He shined his light on a rickety-looking bed with a thin mattress. Near the bed was a tray filled with tools—including an archaic-looking stethoscope. "Pretty cool, huh?" he said, walking around the bed, flashing the light around it. I reached out for the stethoscope.

"Don't touch it!" he barked. Then, gentler, "Sorry. Doug loaned these items to photograph. Then they'll be donated to the university."

I pulled back my hand. "Did these belong to Doctor—"

"Hartman, yes. Dr. Hartman," Aaron finished, walking back towards me. "Cool, huh?"

"Yes," I said thoughtfully. An idea popped into my head. "Hey, what if I asked Morris Hartman to pose here—in this room—for a photograph? Might be cool to get him standing beside where his grandfather used to practice." Bonus, I thought. It'd be a feature on News Now Online no one else would have.

Aaron scratched his scruffy chin. "You think he'd do it?"

"I think it'd be great PR. And what politician turns down PR?" I shrugged. "It's worth a try."

He nodded. "Okay," he said. "If you can get him here, I'll snap the photos."

We left the Oasis and Aaron punched in the code again, locking the door behind us.

"You hungry?" Aaron asked.

"Um," I thought back to the granola bar I'd scarfed for lunch. My stomach rumbled. "Actually, yeah," I said, expecting him to suggest a local bar for dinner.

"Mind if I make you dinner?" he suggested.

I raised my eyebrows. "Really?" I cringed, thinking back to the last time a man made me dinner.

He took in my surprise and laughed. "I can cook, you know."

I shook my head. "Of course. It's just…that's so nice. I'd love that." I'd only known Aaron for a couple of days, but there was a level of comfort with him I couldn't explain. As we left the Oasis and walked to the parking lot, I rubbed my arms, wishing I would've grabbed a sweatshirt.

"Here," Aaron said, unzipping his brown Carhartt jacket. Gently, he wrapped it around me. It felt warm and heavy and smelled of coffee. As we got in his truck and left the Oasis, I felt a little silly. I mean, what real reporter investigates what she thought was a hidden wall. I closed my eyes and shook my head, silently scolding myself.

As if he could read my thoughts, Aaron said, "Hey, good job in there. To be honest, most everyone else has forgotten about this place."

I gave him a weak smile.

"I mean it," he pushed on. "It was refreshing to hear that someone still cares. Hey, you might not have found what you were looking for tonight, but don't stop digging." He winked at me as he turned down a gravel road.

The sun was beginning to set, and the sky was illuminated with bright pinks, oranges, and blues.

"It's beautiful out here," I murmured.

Aaron glanced over. "The sunset?"

I nodded. "That, yes. But...there's space to breathe. There's...space."

Aaron nodded. "See what happens when you leave the city?"

I laughed as he turned down another long, gravel drive.

"This is my driveway," he said. "You'll see the house in a minute. It's hidden down in the valley."

"Wow..." I breathed, thinking back to my high-rise, nestled between two other apartment buildings. And I thought my three-foot, outdoor, suspended deck was nice.

A minute later, we pulled up his cedar log home. Two turquoise-colored Adirondack chairs sat on a wraparound front porch. An exposed stone chimney ran along one side of the house.

"This is gorgeous," I said. "Let me guess...you built it?"

Aaron looked at me and shrugged. "You were the one who said I do a little bit of everything. I didn't build it alone, though. My uncle and cousin helped."

Aaron took me in through the front door where I saw a combination of slate and oak hardwood floors. Large windows lined the wall so I could see straight through to the back where a massive deck held a patio table and chairs. Beyond that, a lush, green valley dotted with trees dipped deep into the earthy distance before it blended into the colorful sky. The view took my breath away.

"Like it?" Aaron said, noticing my reaction. I handed him back his Carhartt jacket and nodded. "It's home," he said with a nod.

He led me into the kitchen and our footsteps padded soundlessly across sleek slate tiles.

Aaron tapped thoughtfully on the smooth granite counter. "Pasta okay?" he asked.

My stomach growled. "Sounds delicious."

He pointed to the deck. "I have some herbs growing out there. Mind grabbing me some basil?"

I must have made a face because he tilted his head back and laughed. "Please tell me you know what basil is," he teased.

"Hey, I can tell you where to find any street in Minneapolis," I joked. "But I'm not great with plants."

He grabbed my hand and led me out to the deck. He pulled me over to a group of green plants, leaned over, and plucked a leaf. Then, he held it up to my nose.

"This is basil. It's an herb," he said. I took in a whiff. It smelled like licorice and flowers. "Yum," I said.

"You're ridiculous," he joked, walking back inside. I followed, hopping on a tall stool tucked under the granite-covered island.

Effortlessly, he moved around his kitchen, boiling water, dropping in spaghetti noodles, and warming a garlicky red sauce. In a few minutes, he had a large bowl full of pasta and a dish of toasted garlic bread. He handed me a plate.

"Thank you," I said, spooning a hefty portion of noodles on my plate. "It's been a long time since I've had a meal like this."

He raised his eyebrows. "Like pasta? It's nothing special."

"I know," I said, slurping a bite. "It's just, when I produced the ten p.m. news, I worked straight through dinner. I would have a late breakfast—maybe around eleven—and head to work and munch on a snack there." I shrugged. "I guess that schedule kind of stuck."

"That sounds like a terrible schedule," Aaron agreed, taking a bite of garlic bread.

I laughed. "Yeah, it was." I thought back to my daily Diet Coke and granola bar I'd have around four o'clock in the afternoon. Then, I took another bite of pasta. "This is good. Really good." We ate together in a comfortable silence.

"Hey," I said after a minute. "What if we put together some kind of fundraiser? Like a last-ditch effort to save the Oasis? Or at least show Ida and those sweet folks I met at the city council meeting that someone is listening to them. Someone cares." I thought back to the apathetic and bored-looking mayor. "That's why I became a reporter...

or at least, why I'm trying to be one. I want to tell stories that matter. And this forgotten place in this small town has real significance to people like you and Ida and her team of preservationists.

Aaron smirked, taking one last bite of pasta. "Aren't you too busy with the election in the Cities to care about an old crumbling building in a small town?"

"That's fair," I chuckled. "But…the history of the Oasis…the meaning it has here. We have to do *something*."

Aaron scratched his chin. "A fundraiser," he muttered to himself. He snapped his fingers. "We could do it at the coffee shop. Maybe have some local musicians play."

My eyes widened. "Really? That would be awesome." Then, in a more serious tone, I added, "Aaron, thank you."

He cleared our plates. Then, for the second time that day, we did the dishes, washing the pots and pans he'd used.

"I suppose I should bring you back to your car in town," Aaron said.

I nodded, thinking about the Hartman story I still needed to write. Now that he had officially announced he was running for governor, Hartman was trending. Kase wanted something on his desk soon. "I do have some work I need to do."

We hopped in his truck and he drove us back through the valley on the dusty, gravel road.

"I grew up just down there," he said, pointing to a white farmhouse. "Parents still live there. I help my dad with farm chores a few days a week."

I smiled. "That's awesome." I wondered what Aaron would think when I told him I grew up in a church parsonage next door to Central Lutheran in downtown Minneapolis. I decided to wait on that detail. Minutes later, we pulled up to The Coffee Fox. He killed the ignition in his truck and walked me to my Kia. I opened the backdoor and plopped my purse and green leather tote bag on the seat. Then, I turned and faced Aaron.

"Well, thanks again," I said. "Dinner was delicious."

"It was fun," Aaron said. "Let's talk more about the fundraiser soon." He raised his eyebrows at me and pointed a callused finger in my direction. "You're doing most of the work. I'll just provide the space."

"Of course," I nodded. "You won't have to lift a finger."

Then, he opened his arms wide. "Up for a hug?"

I smiled and stepped into his arms, smelling coffee and woodsmoke.

"See you soon, Aaron." I hopped in my car and drove away, waving good-bye as I left him standing outside his truck and coffee shop.

Chapter 16

BIZZIE

BIZZIE WAITED UNTIL ASTA AND DISA were both snoring quietly before she slipped out the bedroom door and padded down the creaky stairs. Squinting in the dark, she strained to see Ruth. Suddenly, someone grabbed her arm and put a hand over her mouth. Arms flailing, she tried to scream, but her assailant's hand clamped hard.

"It's me," Ruth whispered. "It's just me." Ruth slowly let go.

Bizzie's eyes began to adjust to the darkness. "Scare me to death, why don't you," Bizzie hissed.

"Sorry. But I couldn't have you waking the whole house," Ruth whispered. "Come on. Let's go out the back door. Don't creak so bad."

Together, they tiptoed through the house and out the door. Once outside, Bizzie took a deep breath. The air tasted clean and crisp.

"Have you done this before?" Bizzie asked, no longer whispering. The moon, high and bright in the sky, draped the yard in a warm light.

"Once," Ruth said, looking at Bizzie, her eyes wide and illuminated by the moon. "The other girl never made it out alive."

Bizzie gasped. Ruth burst into laughter.

"Girl! Lighten up." Ruth wrapped her arm around Bizzie. "Mrs. Hendry and I have become...friends. Sort of." She didn't offer any more information. "Just follow my lead."

About a quarter mile east stood the two-story house with the white wraparound front porch. The moonlight gave Bizzie just enough light to see that flowers were neatly planted across the yard. Bizzie wondered if that had been the work of the weary gardener.

"The Hendry's house is surrounded by barbed wire," Ruth explained.

"But, like I said, me and her...we've been working together. So, she cut a small hole in the wire for me to get through. Or her to get out."

"Wait...can't Mrs. Hendry just walk out the front door?"

Ruth scoffed. "You'd think so, right? But Mr. Hendry don't want her to go anywhere. He don't want any of us getting over here, neither."

Bizzie wanted to push with more questions, but Ruth gave her a shove through the fence.

Ruth knocked twice on the back door. In a moment, the door opened just a crack. There was the woman Bizzie had seen at dinner, the one with the sapphire skirt. She looked too lovely and kind to be married to a horrible man like Mr. Hendry. Her hair fell over her shoulders, a ripple of brown curls. She was wearing a flowery, cotton nightgown.

"Ruth," Mrs. Hendry said, giving her a quizzical look before noticing Bizzie. "Is something wrong?"

"We've had a bit of a—" she paused and looked at Bizzie. "Situation. Might we come in?"

Mrs. Hendry raised her eyebrows. But, to Bizzie's surprise, she opened the door for them and stepped aside. Bizzie caught a faint scent of lilacs and grapefruit as she walked past Mrs. Hendry.

"Come into the kitchen. I'll put the kettle on," Mrs. Hendry said. She grabbed her robe that had been sitting on the stairway railing and led them through the hallway to the large kitchen.

Painted sky-blue, the kitchen felt airy and roomy and smelled of gardenias and vanilla. A white teapot sat on the kitchen stove. Though Bizzie's palms were still sweaty, and her heart raced, she began to relax.

Mrs. Hendry started water for tea. "Mrs. Boller has turned in for the night, but I don't mind." She smiled at them and added, "I like three cubes of sugar in mine, and I know she thinks that's too much."

Bizzie smiled. She felt warm and welcome here. The house was beautiful and tidy, yes, but Mrs. Hendry's smile and demeanor calmed her. Once they had their tea—and sugar—the three women sat down at the oak table.

"So, what's this about?" Mrs. Hendry asked, taking a sip of her tea.

"This is Beth," Ruth said, gesturing to Bizzie. "She's our new girl." For a minute, Bizzie forgot her alibi. She covered up her confused glance with a sharp nod.

"Yes, I saw you at dinner," Mrs. Hendry said.

"Well, Beth is in a pickle. She's pregnant and alone. And once her mother found out, she threw her out of the house."

Mrs. Hendry frowned. "I'm sorry to hear that."

"Mother fears my pregnancy outside of wedlock would bring judgment on our family, ma'am," Bizzie said, navigating this chapter of her story. "My aunt is planning to send a carriage for me, but I need a place to stay while I wait."

Mrs. Hendry nodded. "I see. Well, I'm not sure how I can help. Again, I'm sorry you're in this situation, dear—"

Ruth stepped in. "Beth hasn't seen a doctor yet. And she's figuring she's twelve weeks along."

"I see. Well, you know I'm no midwife," Mrs. Hendry said, looking confused.

"But you do have access to the midwife in town. I reckon Mr. Hendry won't help us set up an appointment with her. We were hoping..." Ruth's words drifted off. "We were hoping maybe you can help us schedule a visit?"

Bizzie expected Mrs. Hendry to shake her head and ask them both to leave. Instead, she took a sip of her tea and looked at Bizzie intently. "How old are you, dear?"

"I'm eighteen," Bizzie said, telling the truth about that.

"Eighteen," Mrs. Hendry said to herself, drumming her fingers on the table. "And what happened to the father of your child?"

Bizzie jumped into her prepared answer.

"He works in the mines like his daddy. And he isn't ready to become a daddy himself. When I told him the news, he just...shut down. Didn't offer any support." Bizzie shook her head. "Should've known. But he's my high school sweetheart." She shrugged and looked away.

Mrs. Hendry nodded and said, "I remember my high school sweetheart." She looked at Ruth and Bizzie for a moment before continuing. "He wanted to be a teacher—like me. We wanted to stake a claim out West and build our own house." She paused, took a breath, and crossed her hands in front of her. "But, clearly, I'm not out West," she said with a sad laugh.

"I take it Mr. Hendry isn't that man?" Ruth ventured. By the way Ruth said this, Bizzie could tell the two had formed some kind of bond, maybe even a friendship.

Mrs. Hendry smiled and shook her head.

"He met someone else. He wrote to say life out there was hard and the woman he'd met was better suited for it than me."

Mrs. Hendry kept her eyes downcast, her lips sealed tightly. Ruth reached out and gently took her hand. Bizzie did the same, taking her other hand. Mrs. Hendry sniffed and finally lifted her head, a slight smile on her face.

"I married Lester out of spite." Her sparkling eyes had hardened. "I thought to myself, I'll show that son of a bitch that I can endure a frontier," she laughed wickedly. "Stupid, right?"

Bizzie waited to speak.

"Not stupid." Ruth patted Mrs. Hendry's hand. "Normal. Any woman in your place would've been heartbroken and unsure of what to do. You were dealt a rotten situation, and you found a way to move forward."

"Yes," Mrs. Hendry snorted. "To this." She gestured around her. "Lester never even lets me leave the house. He's terrified that the—" she rolled her eyes, "— 'inmates' will attack me."

She looked at Bizzie and Ruth, and the three of them started laughing.

Suddenly, heavy footsteps dragged outside on the gravel. Mrs. Hendry hushed them. She went to the window and peered outside frantically, then looked back at Ruth and Bizzie.

"He shouldn't be home yet," she said, wringing her hands. "He's usually out much later than this."

Then, the sound of jingling keys at the front door. Bizzie's heart pounded.

Mrs. Hendry's eyes were as wide as saucers.

"Come with me!" she hissed. Ruth and Bizzie flew off their chairs and followed Mrs. Hendry through the kitchen to a small door the size of an overstuffed pillow. Mrs. Hendry made eye contact with Ruth and Bizzie, then pointed to the door. Bizzie nearly laughed, sure they wouldn't fit through the small opening.

"Abigail!" they heard Mr. Hendry slur. They had no choice. Ruth grabbed a handful of Bizzie's dress and pushed her through the small opening, leading into the dark, musty cellar. Ruth then contorted herself to crawl into the small space.

From the small space, Bizzie saw Mrs. Hendry brush off her dress and call out, "I'm here, Lester!" Her voice was strong and even. "A bat got into the house again. I let him out."

Bizzie heard Mr. Hendry holler something in reply but couldn't make out the words. Then, something crashed and shattered. A teacup? Their teacups that they'd left on the table!

Ruth took a deep breath and closed her eyes, saying nothing.

A scream from Mrs. Hendry pierced the air. Then another crash.

Bizzie scrunched her body into a ball against the field stone-lined wall and realized that their fate rested in Mrs. Hendry's hands. If her husband decided to check beds, he would see that the two women were missing. If Mr. Hendry asked about the teacups, Mrs. Hendry could tell him the truth—that she'd had visitors. She was the only one who could stop him. There was no escaping the cellar. There was one way in and one way out. Bizzie shut her eyes tight and muttered a short, silent prayer. At the same time, she heard a soft jangle. Ruth shoved a chain of small, wooden beads into her hands.

"I always carry around an extra rosary," she said. "Praying it will keep our minds off being stuck in here."

Bizzie didn't want to admit she didn't know how to pray the rosary for fear she'd disappoint Ruth. But her friend didn't seem to mind or care. She whispered prayers for both of them.

"Glory be to the Father, the Son, and the Holy Spirit. Amen..." she murmured.

Bizzie heard another scream and pressed her shoulder against Ruth's. She clutched the rosary beads between her thumb and forefinger. She could hardly believe that just days earlier she was in her schoolhouse teaching arithmetic. Never in a million years could she have predicted that telling stories would mean huddling with a woman she hardly knew in a dirty, dark cellar. But she reminded herself, these are the stories that matter. Women like Ruth and Mrs. Hendry and Disa and Asta...their stories needed to be told. And Bizzie would be the one to tell them.

Bizzie heard another scream. A sickening thud. Then, she heard nothing at all.

Chapter 17

SOPHIE

On Sunday morning, I had three pressing notes on my to-do list: call Morris Hartman and get him to agree to do a photo shoot, call Ida to talk with her about a fundraiser idea, and write the damn Hartman story. Kase had given me an extension until Monday morning.

Even though I'd gotten home from Aaron's after ten the night before, I was too energized to sleep. I spent three hours working on the article, finally finishing up and sending it to Kase around one a.m. I hoped when I told him my idea of a photo shoot, he'd approve.

Sitting in my black sweats on my couch, I dialed Ida's number. I explained the idea of a fundraiser at The Coffee Fox. She was overjoyed. I think she actually started crying. I definitely heard sniffles. I left a message for Hartman, asking him to call me back.

Instead of popping a freezer-burned veggie burger into the microwave for lunch, I decided to try a salad. I smiled, knowing Aaron would be proud. At the thought of him, I felt a flutter in my stomach. I opened the fridge and realized I didn't have much to make a salad—at least not one that's actually edible. I bought a bunch of romaine during my last trip to the grocery store, but that was at least three weeks ago. Most of it was mushy and slimy. I managed to pull off a couple pieces that were still greenish. In the pantry, I found a can of tuna that hadn't expired. I mixed the romaine and tuna together in a bowl and sprinkled on some olive oil. It wasn't perfect, but it was at least fresh. Sort of. My cell phone rang.

"Hello, this is Sophie from News Now Online," I said brightly, swallowing a bit of tuna.

"Sophie, Morris Hartman here," I heard on the other line.

"Mr. Hartman, hello!" I replied.

"If you were calling to ask me to comment about my grandfather's—" I stopped him mid-sentence. "No, no, it's not that." I explained that I'd met a photographer from Crab Orchard who was interested in documenting him, standing inside his grandfather's clinic. After several questions and stipulations, we had a date. But I was told there would be no questions; "This is no press conference, Ms. McHale," he told me, his demeanor still cool toward me. Although, he did say I could feature the photos and story on News Now Online. I hung up and immediately texted Aaron.

Good news! Hartman in for the photo shoot.

I typed, *Thanks again for making me dinner.*

As I finished my salad, he responded.

Awesome. Dinner was fun. We should do it again sometime.

My heart flip-flopped in my chest. What was this feeling? It had been years since I'd been on a proper date. My life was consumed by all things KOMO and producing the news. There wasn't time for much else. That is, except for that time with the production assistant, Dan. I cringed at the memory. I debated texting Freya and telling her about Aaron but decided to wait. *Maybe I'm reading into this,* I thought. *Maybe it's nothing.*

On Monday morning, I came to the team huddle with a new sense of confidence. I even spoke up.

"I had an idea that might be cool for our Instagram account," I said, noticing a couple of my coworkers exchanging glances. Nevertheless, I plowed forward, explaining my idea of photographing Hartman in his grandfather's clinic. Kase leaned back in his chair and gave me his full attention. "I'm impressed," he said. "That's a great idea." I was flattered that he thought my idea was good. No, great. After our meeting, I skipped back to my desk.

"Got your article," Kase said, stopping at my desk. "Great work. I love that you added in the potential demolition of his grandfather's original clinic. I hadn't heard that." He knocked twice on my desk. "And really like your photo shoot idea. Good work."

I beamed, shooting a quick text to Freya. *Actually having a good day at work! Finally did something right!*

"You seem happy," Jen said, perching herself on the corner of my desk.

I offered her a wide grin. In a singsong voice, I said, "Because Hartman agreed to do a photo shoot."

"I heard," Jen said, scrunching her eyebrows.

"You don't think it's a good idea?" I shot back immediately, my confidence faltering.

"No, no. I'm just surprised," Jen said, shaking her head. She smiled at me. "He just must like you better. In our four years working together, he never divulged a whole lot about his past to me." She playfully punched my shoulder. "No fair."

The following week, I bypassed the office and drove west to Crab Orchard. I had told Kase I'd update him later that day. Aaron and I were going to meet at the Oasis a few minutes before the Hartman caravan was slated to arrive. I had teeny butterflies fluttering around my insides. Even though we had been texting, I hadn't seen Aaron since he made me pasta in his kitchen.

"Hey," he said when I pulled up. He was leaning up against his truck wearing faded jeans, his scratched brown boots, and a blue flannel. His auburn hair was tied up in a bun.

"Hey!" I said, grabbing my green tote. "It's good to see you."

"You too," he said. Several cars were parked in the lot, including one that looked to be Ida's Toyota. Once she found out that Aaron and I were putting together the photo shoot, she insisted on being there too. The front door was propped open, and the lobby had been swept and straightened. It looked halfway decent. A table was set up with a coffee carafe, Styrofoam cups, and little packets of powdered creamer. Ida's doing, probably. A cardboard box of donuts sat beside the coffee.

"You get a politician in here and folks roll out the red carpet," I said with a laugh.

"Well, he is entering the building completely legally. Not trespassing at night like some criminal," Aaron chuckled.

I nodded. "True. I am guilty of trespassing."

"Sophie!" I turned to see Ida wearing her bright yellow 'Save the Oasis' shirt. She gave me a tight hug.

"How are you, Ida?" I greeted her, genuinely excited and relieved to see her. I felt a bit frazzled, hopeful that the photo shoot—which looked to be turning into a full-fledged event—went over well. Kase told me that once the other news markets heard about this, they'd be all over it, figuring out how they could run the pictures on their ten p.m. broadcast. I nodded, knowing that during my time as a producer, I would've scrambled to find a way to share photos of a governor candidate in his grandfather's old clinic.

"You are just the sweetest reporter I think I've ever met," Ida said, taking my arm. I felt a tinge of guilt burn deep in my chest. Of course I wanted to help Ida and Crab Orchard and the preservationists, but in the end, I was really looking for answers for my hunch—that, and validation that I had what it took to do more than just produce a show. A putter of fear crept up my spine at the thought of being on camera or going live, but I swept it away. "I mean, you're really making an effort to get this place preserved," she added.

I nodded and muttered, "Something like that." At that moment, a black Range Rover pulled up just outside the front door. Hartman climbed out with Hines in close tow behind. They walked through the front doors, taking off their sunglasses at the exact same time. Hines immediately pulled out his phone. Aaron, Ida, and I approached them.

"Hello, Mr. Hartman," I said, holding out a hand. "Good to see you again."

He was guarded and standoffish; not at all the same friendly, open man I'd met a few weeks before. I introduced Aaron as the photographer for the day. When I turned to Ida, I stopped. Hartman was staring at her yellow shirt with "Save the Oasis" plastered across the front in black letters.

"Er, this is Ida Kirkbridge," I started. "She's here representing Crab Orchard." I added quietly, "and the Save the Oasis committee."

Hartman glared at me.

Ida didn't seem to notice my hesitation. Nor did she notice Hartman's glare. She immediately and aggressively shook his hand with both of hers. "Hello, Mr. Hartman. It is so good to meet you. I am honored to be working to preserve this beautiful building. Your grandfather was a visionary," her words tumbled out.

Hartman seemed to be listening to Ida, but his eyes pierced through me.

After Ida had finished gushing over him and his grandfather, he smiled broadly and seemed to put his politician hat back on. He replied, "Well, thank you. I appreciate that. And I thank you for your efforts to preserve the building. No matter what, his legacy will live on."

Ida smiled and nodded, then offered him coffee and a donut. Aaron's camera was slung around his neck.

"Mr. Hartman, I think we're ready," he said.

"I'll let Aaron take you down to the room where we believe your grandfather used to practice," I told Hartman.

Hartman stiffened. "What? What room?"

Aaron and I exchanged glances. "Uh, it's just over here," I said, pointing to an open door behind us.

Hartman visibly relaxed. "Oh. Of course," he stammered and followed Aaron.

I grabbed a steaming mug of coffee and a chocolate-covered donut. A car door slammed outside and a moment later, the front door was yanked open. I recognized the man walking toward us but couldn't place him.

Ida walked over. "Mr. Mayor!" she exclaimed. Yes, that's it. The mayor from the city council meeting. Ida introduced me.

"Mayor Palmer, this is Sophie McHale. She's the one who put this whole thing together," Ida said proudly, touching my elbow.

"Ah, yes," the mayor said, shaking my hand. He looked to be about fifty. Tufts of brown hair shot up in different directions like he'd just rolled out of bed. His khaki pants were two sizes too big; his wire-rimmed glasses sat a bit crooked on his face, and his breath smelled stale. "I remember you from the city council meeting." He looked past me, his eyes scanning the room. "I hear you're holding a photo shoot today. Is Morris around?"

I was a bit taken aback. The mayor of rural Crab Orchard and gubernatorial candidate, Morris Hartman, knew each other? On a first name basis?

"Well, yes, he's back with Aaron, the photographer," I replied.

"Ah, Aaron, of course," the mayor said, nodding. When I didn't say anything, he stuck his head forward. "I need to see Morris. Just for a minute."

"Oh!" I stammered. "Oh, okay. Well, sure, right this way." I shrugged slightly at Ida and led the mayor down the hall.

I could hear Aaron's voice, then the clicking of a camera. I gestured towards an open door, "He's right in here."

"Perfect, thanks Sarah," he said, absent-mindedly.

"Uh, Sophie," I replied. But he had already pushed past me.

"Excuse me, this will only take a minute," he said, walking into the room. Aaron frowned and stopped clicking.

"Jed!" Morris smiled at the mayor.

"Morris, my man," the mayor said. The two clapped each other on their backs.

Hartman looked at Aaron, then me. "Give us just a second, okay guys?"

Aaron and I exchanged glances before walking out together.

Aaron muttered something I couldn't understand.

"What?" I asked. "What did you say?"

Aaron shook his head. "Nothing. Just," he placed a hand on my lower back and led me further down the hall into an empty room with crumbled walls and shredded, dusty floors. A chill ran down my back and I wrapped my arms around myself.

"Mayor Palmer is, um, not the most ethical man," Aaron whispered, standing close to me. I smelled coffee on his breath.

I frowned.

"Remember I told you I moved back to Crab Orchard to help with my uncle's landscaping business?"

I nodded.

"This is off the record, right?" he asked.

"Of course," I nodded, curiosity stirring my thoughts recklessly.

"Well, one of my first jobs was at Mayor Palmer's house. He lives out on Sand Prairie Drive, west of town a bit." Aaron swallowed. "Big house. Lots of acreage. His wife had big plans for their backyard garden, but spent most of her time in California, helping their daughter with her newborn. So, we'd Skype, and she'd tell me what she wanted." Aaron paused and looked in the direction of Mayor Palmer and Hartman. "Each day I was there, I would see a black sedan pull up in the drive around the same time. A blonde woman would climb out, go inside the house, and about an hour later, leave."

I recoiled. "What? Ew. You don't think—"

"I didn't want to make any assumptions. I mean, his life, his choices. But, when I was getting ready to wrap up the job, I knocked on the door. She answered wearing his t-shirt. Nothing else. He came to the door, shooed his mistress away and wrote me the check. As he handed it to me, he said, 'I added an extra thousand. What you see here, stays here.'" Aaron shrugged. "That was it. I left and never told anyone about what I saw." He scratched his chin. "But it's weird that he shows up here…and knows your Mr. Hartman."

Just then, Hines appeared in the doorway. He looked up from his phone for half of a second to tell us that Hartman was ready for us. I rolled my eyes at Aaron, and we walked back down the hall.

"Sorry about that," Morris said, smiling at us. "An old college friend." Aaron nodded and began to work the lens of his camera. I wandered out and found Ida pouring a cup of now-lukewarm coffee for Hines.

"So, is your committee on board with the fundraiser?" I asked her.

"Oh yes, everyone is so excited," she said, grabbing my arm. "I'm just so grateful. I mean, for so long, we thought we were fighting a lost cause. Now, we have hope again." She squeezed my arm.

Again, that guilt burned like a fire in my belly.

Ida held out the coffee to Hines who mumbled a "no thanks" without looking up from his phone.

Minutes later, Hartman and Aaron joined us in the foyer. "All done," Aaron said, winking at me. Morris clapped his hands together.

"Great, thanks for setting this up, guys," he said. He looked at me. "You'll send me the photos before sharing them online, right?"

I nodded.

Ida rushed over to him. "Mr. Hartman, I hope you'll come to the fundraiser we're having," she said, looking up at him as she brushed her bangs out of her eyes. I gnawed on my lip, worried Hartman would see this as a set-up. Ida pushed on. "It's at The Coffee Fox next Saturday." Hartman glanced at me for a beat, then back to Ida.

He smiled. "I'll try to make it." With that, he and Hines left the Oasis.

Chapter 18

BIZZIE

BIZZIE FELT A NUDGE as someone whispered her name. She opened her eyes but saw only blackness.

"Bizzie," a woman whispered again.

"Ruth?" her voice sounded gravelly.

Ruth felt around for Bizzie's hand and grasped it tight. "It's okay, I'm here."

"So am I," she heard another woman's voice—Mrs. Hendry.

"Where is—" Bizzie started.

"He's—he's sleeping." Mrs. Hendry's voice sounded different. Stronger? Clearer? Bizzie couldn't tell.

Bizzie crawled on all fours through the small, dark hole. Mrs. Hendry waited with two helping arms to pull her out. Ruth followed behind. Bizzie dusted off her dress.

The moon, high in the sky now, shone through the kitchen window. "How long were we in there?" she asked the women beside her.

"A couple of hours," Mrs. Hendry replied, guiding the women back to the hole in the fence. "Lester was adamant about making sure there weren't any more bats in the house." She sighed. "Too bad there never was a bat in the house in the first place. But it was funny watching him stumble around with a baseball bat and tennis racket."

Bizzie shuddered at the thought of Mr. Hendry walking around with a baseball bat.

"I'm sorry about him," Mrs. Hendry said, prying open the barbed wire. She dug the tip of her shoe in the grass. That's when Bizzie noticed Mrs. Hendry was wearing lace-up boots—the kind reserved for cold, snowy Minnesota winter mornings. Not only that, but she was wearing dirty overalls and a man's button-down shirt. Bizzie cocked her head to the side. Mrs. Hendry had been barefoot and wearing a nightgown the last time she saw her.

"Mrs. Hendry," Bizzie said, following the women toward the run-down house reserved for Ruth, Asta, and the other poor farm residents. "I can't help but wonder why you're wearing those boots? And those dirty overalls?"

Ruth and Mrs. Hendry looked down. Then, Mrs. Hendry looked up at Ruth with piercing eyes and pinched lips. That's when Bizzie noticed one of Mrs. Hendry's eyes was swollen shut. Mrs. Hendry and Ruth glanced at one another, silently communicating something.

"Where is he?" Ruth finally asked as if she were inquiring where Mrs. Hendry kept her spare bed linens.

Mrs. Hendry just stared at Ruth.

"Abigail?" Ruth asked again.

Bizzie thought back to the screams and crashes and then that thud. Bizzie's eyes grew wide. Mrs. Hendry had just murdered her husband. Bizzie let out a gasp.

"Bizzie, why don't you go back inside the house and get some sleep? It's been a long night," Ruth told Bizzie without taking her eyes off Mrs. Hendry.

Bizzie nodded and slipped into the shadows to gather her thoughts and refocus.

She heard Mrs. Hendry whisper, "He kept saying, 'Who you been screwing? Who you been screwing? Who you been screwing in the back of the house?' I was terrified!"

Ruth spoke up. "Okay, okay. You're alright now." After a few more muffled consolations, she added, "Let's go clean up the mess."

Bizzie let out the breath she'd been holding in. Her legs gave out and she slid to the ground, wrapping her arms tightly around herself. She sat like that for a few minutes before a thought occurred to her: this could be the perfect time to escape. She was worried about leaving the poor farm under Mr. Hendry's watchful eye, but now he was…gone. Besides, she had an article to write.

Bizzie pushed herself up, walked into the inmate's house, and tiptoed upstairs. The hint of pre-dawn gave her enough light to pack up her small satchel and leather-bound journal. She glanced over at Disa and Asta who were breathing quietly. Asta formed a half-circle around her daughter and draped a protective arm across her. Bizzie paused for a moment, admiring their bond. With one last look, she skittered down the stairs. She tore a piece of paper from her notebook. It would be impossible to explain the truth about why she had visited the poor house. Instead, she kept her note simple.

Mrs. Hendry, John was wrong. You are the toughest woman I've ever met and suited for life in any climate or frontier.

Ruth, take care of your sisters.

xo, B

Bizzie folded the note and placed it gently on the teetering dining room table. She took one more deep breath of the musty house and left.

She walked to the bus station while taking in the bright sunrise. Grateful to catch an early morning bus, she finally relaxed once she was sitting on the hard bench, clomping along toward Minneapolis. As the sun came up, Bizzie watched the farmland and meadows pass before her eyes. She used her time to write two letters, one to Collin and one to Papa. Because her mother would have to read the words to Papa, she kept her stories concise, leaving out details she knew he'd love but her mother would despise. Once the letters were written, Bizzie began to work on her story. She scribbled notes about the horrible Mr. Hendry. About the smells. About the lack of bathing and privacy. Then, she wrote about Ruth and Mrs. Hendry.

Chapter 19

SOPHIE

I MET AARON AT The Coffee Fox the following Saturday morning—the day of the fundraiser. We had planned to meet early to set up before the first band arrived. Apparently, Aaron knew musicians. Lots of them. He had a full line-up of bands for the day, including Blackberry Jam, The Show Offs, and The Leftovers. I'd never heard of them, but he assured me they were crowd pleasers.

Ida pulled up with a backseat full of plastic tubs. Aaron and I helped her carry them into the coffee shop.

"I've been saving these things for years," she said, wiping off a layer of dust on the top of a tub. "My grandmother passed all this down to my mother," she paused for a minute and wiped a tear from her eye, "and she's now passing it down to me."

I squeezed Ida's arm.

"I mean, look at this!" She held up a black and white maid's uniform. Beneath that was another uniform—a starched white dress that looked like it could've belonged to a nurse. I reached out and touched the stiff fabric. In the bin, it had faded from what was probably a pearly white to a dull yellow. I was touching history, and I was desperate for more details.

"Do you think these things belonged to your grandmother?" I asked.

Ida nodded. "I'm sure." Then, she pointed to the maid's uniform. "But I'm not sure about this one." She combed through a few other items in the bin—a jangle of keys attached to a dusty, iron ring, a faded and torn map of the Oasis, and a few black and white photographs.

"These are incredible, Ida!" I said, sorting through the photos. "Do you mind if I display these on a few of the tables?"

Ida nodded and kept looking through the bin. Aaron scooted behind the counter to prep his barista bar for the day and the fundraiser. I gingerly set out the dusty uniforms on one table and a map on the other.

"This place was really something, huh?" I said, not looking up from the map. Besides the Grand Hall, there were strings of smaller cottages and even an outdoor pool. "I would have loved to see it in its heyday."

"Well, you can. Sort of. Here's an old photo album of more pictures," Ida said, handing me a book the size of my laptop. I sat down at one of the empty tables and began flipping through the pages.

"This must be Dr. Hartman?" I asked Ida, holding up one of the pictures.

Ida glanced my way as she sorted through another plastic tub. She squinted to get a good look. "Yep, that's him." He had the same dark hair and jawline as Morris, though Dr. Hartman was taller and slimmer.

Out of the corner of my eye, I saw commotion outside on the sidewalk. I heard a few shouts and then saw Morris Hartman step out of a black sedan.

"Look who decided to show up," I said, pointing outside.

Aaron scoffed beside me. "More PR?" he asked.

I shrugged and we walked to the front door.

"Hello, Mr. Hartman," I said as he walked into the coffee shop.

"Ms. McHale, hello," he said, taking in The Coffee Fox. He nodded, as if approving of what we'd done. "This looks nice." Hines was steps behind him, a phone in one hand and a cardboard cup of a Starbucks drink in the other. At that, Aaron gave me a side-eye in contempt.

"Mr. Hartman, what can I make for you?" Aaron asked, tying an apron around his waist.

Hartman looked at the menu hanging above his head. "How about a white mocha?"

While Aaron steamed the milk and Hines punched something on his phone, Hartman strolled over to me. "So, any other news media showing up today?" he asked.

"Andy Jacobs just showed up," Aaron jerked his thumb toward the front door. "He's the local reporter for the *Crab Orchard Tribune*."

I nodded at Aaron. "Well, other than the local news, we're covering it on News Now Online," I said. Kase had encouraged me to post pictures and videos on News Now Online's Instagram stories and

TikTok account. "I'm hoping other sites and stations pick it up after we share it," I said, taking a sip of my chai tea latte Aaron had made me earlier.

Kase—although happy to post pictures from today's fundraiser—made it clear that I shouldn't spend any more time on Morris Hartman. Instead, I had spent the week digging into a new healthcare nonprofit breaking into Minneapolis. Also, Congresswoman Grace Ling had held a press conference to explain why she's supporting the city council's vote to slash millions from the police budget. Whew. That story got tons of backlash once we posted it. Kase ate it up.

Hartman perused through the pictures, uniforms, and maps. I caught a glimpse of Hines setting up a small table near the front door. He laid out bumper stickers and buttons, all with Hartman's familiar logo on them—the letter "M" inside the state of Minnesota with the tagline "Advocate for a stronger Minnesota."

Beside the swag, Hines propped up a wooden frame. Inside was one of the photographs Aaron had taken inside the Oasis. It was breathtaking. I had only seen the images online, which were among News Now Online's most popular clicks throughout the past week. Our parent company, Gavett Media, had even reached out inquiring about the rights to share with other media outlets nationwide. But seeing the photo up close like this gave me chills. Aaron had captured light streaming in through the window while Hartman was somewhat hidden in the shadows. I placed the frame back on the table, just as Hines set out a neat stack of *Save the Oasis* yellow postcards. Aaron glanced up, and I jabbed a thumb in Hines' direction. We smirked at each other. I picked up a yellow postcard.

"So, you're excited about saving the Oasis, huh?" I said.

"Hmm?" he muttered, not looking up from his phone.

I shook my head and set the postcard back onto the table.

The day went according to plan; the bands all showed up and played their sets. They were all good. Really good. I made a mental note to track down when Blackberry Jam was playing next. Maybe Aaron and I could catch a show. I snuck a glance at him behind the coffee bar steaming milk and blending iced drinks. As usual, his hair was pulled back into a messy bun and his blue eyes sparkled.

"Hey, thanks again for all your help. This," I gestured around the café, "is amazing." He looked up from a latte he was making and smiled.

"It's all you, city girl," he said.

I nodded. "I might live in—and love—the city. But your small town is…hmm…it's something special."

Aaron's smile disappeared. Had I said something wrong? "What?" I asked.

Aaron shook his head. "Nothing. Just…just reminds of…" his voice drifted off. He didn't have to say it. His past girlfriend.

"Hey you!" I heard a familiar voice and looked up to see Jen.

"Jen! You came?!" I scooted out from behind the table to give her a hug.

"I couldn't miss this," she said, smiling. Her dark hair fell down below her shoulders in soft waves. In her ears were rose gold earrings that spelled out 'Love.'

"This place is awesome," she nodded in approval.

"So are your earrings!" I told her. "Are those Tiffany? I just read an article on the Huffington Post about those. They're Picasso's own handwriting, right?"

Jen flipped her hair back and smiled. "Yep. Cool, huh?"

I was slightly jealous. So cool. Instinctually, I fiddled with my gold thumbtack studs in my ears.

"Hey, seriously though, nice work here," Jen said, looking around. I beamed. She picked up one of the black and white photos Ida had placed on the table. "So, tell me more about this place," she said.

Ida was about to start in with her practiced rhetoric, but I stopped her. "Let me try this one," I said, giving Ida a shrug. I'd been listening to Ida explain why the Oasis needed to be preserved, and I was pretty sure I could now deliver her speech almost as well as she could. She nodded encouragingly.

"The Oasis is a huge part of Crab Orchard, a town I'm getting to know and, honestly, like," my eyes flicked to Aaron. "The people here—like Ida and Aaron," I jabbed my thumb towards the coffee bar, "are incredible. They would say that the Oasis built this town and made it what it is today. Because of the Oasis, Crab Orchard has this amazing legacy. Dr. Hartman was a medical innovator and chose to make his home here. He brought care and answers and vaccines to people who were previously alone on the prairie, forced to either seek care in the city or figure out a solution on their own."

I looked at Ida, who gave me a thumbs-up. Jen waited for me to continue. "Now all the buildings are in danger of being torn down. And, while Dr. Hartman's legacy lives on, the people of Crab Orchard want these structures to remain in place as a reminder for all the good he did."

"Wow," Jen murmured.

"Well done!" Ida cheered. "You *were* paying attention!"

120 | THE MUCKRAKER

I laughed. "This event is just one more way that we're trying to gain support from the public."

"Genesis?" Hartman left a group of local city council members he'd been chatting with and walked over to us. I smiled awkwardly. *Genesis?*

"Morris!" Jen said, embracing him in a hug. "Isn't this guy great? I miss working with you, I really do." Jen smiled at him. "But, hey, Sophie's pretty awesome, huh?"

"Wait, Genesis?" I looked at Jen.

She shrugged. "That's my real name. Most people call me Jen." She punched Morris lightly on the arm. "Some of the special ones call me Genesis."

"Huh," I said, taking in this new information.

Jen—Genesis—and Hartman continued chatting while I sunk my teeth into a chocolate-glazed donut Aaron had set aside for me. I closed my eyes. It was delicious. Aaron sidled up next to me.

"Good, huh?" he nodded toward the chocolate on my fingers.

"So good," I mumbled, wiping the crumbs from my lips.

"How We Roll, the bakery truck you might've seen around town, drops off a couple dozen most mornings. We usually sell out."

"I can see why," I replied.

By four o'clock, the crowd had pretty much dissipated and Hartman and Hines—along with Jen—had left. Aaron wiped down the tables as Ida and I wrapped up the photographs and maps carefully in the tissue paper she'd brought. We placed the uniforms back in the dusty bins and helped her carry them to her car.

"Great job today, guys," she said, clasping both our hands. "I think we really brought attention to the Oasis."

I squeezed Ida's hand. "We gave it our best shot."

We waved good-bye to Ida, who was off to visit her mom, and walked back into the café.

"You want another drink?" Aaron asked, untying his apron.

"Have any wine?" I asked, smiling.

Aaron disappeared for a minute and then returned with a dusty bottle of red. He closed the blinds and locked the front door. Then, he grabbed two ceramic mugs that were sitting on the drying rack. He looked at me and shrugged. "Wine, but no wine glasses. Will these work?"

I smiled. "Have wine, will drink."

We sat at a table in the back. He uncorked the bottle and poured a bit in each mug. I took a sip. I tasted a hint of blackberry. My feet ached and I took my shoes off.

Aaron laughed. "You finally wear comfortable shoes," he said, pointing to my pink tennis shoes.

"I learn from the best," I replied. We took a few sips in silence.

"Thanks for your help today," I said after a while. "I thought it was a great turn-out."

He nodded. "It was fun. And bonus—got a lot of new people in the door."

"Oh hey, look at this," I said, taking out my phone. I posted a live video on News Now Online's Instagram page. We were getting lots of attention and support from our followers. "Listen to these comments. 'Love that you're seeking out a story that really matters…Thanks for bringing attention to this important cause…A legacy that must remain in place…'" I looked up at Aaron. "Cool, huh?"

He nodded and took a sip of wine. I tucked my phone in my bag.

"So, um, earlier," I stammered. "I didn't mean to bring up any memories of your former girlfriend." I rolled my eyes. "Trust me, I have my own memories I'm trying to forget."

Aaron smirked. "Oh yeah?" He took a sip of his wine. "How about I tell you something about Tiffany and you tell me something about your past."

Chapter 20

BIZZIE

BIZZIE WANTED NOTHING MORE than a hot bath and a nap. Her body cried out for rest. But her mind tumbled through the last several hours at the poor farm. She knew she must write now while her memory was fresh and the experiences close enough to taste.

Walking into The Minneapolis Journal building and to her desk, she almost felt like she was in a dream—or that the last string of hours was a dream. A few of the other reporters looked her way. One of them sneered, one of them nodded, and one of them winked, looking her up and down. She ignored them all, hunkered down at her desk, and began to write. She wrote for hours, stopping for a brief moment to eat a handful of nuts from a stand outside and slurp down a stale, lukewarm cup of coffee. Under her pen, facts came alive, yes, but she was aware of her own anger at the injustice and heavy hopelessness that was so present at the poor farm. Her story came to fruition before her eyes.

When her pen finally came to a stop, blisters had formed on the tips of her fingers. Her back ached from sitting hunched over at her desk. When all of the reporters had left for the day, Bizzie stood outside Mr. Kavanaugh's office door.

"I believe I've finished, sir," she chewed on her lip. She handed the story to her editor, but as he reached for it, she clutched it in her fingers. He gave the papers a tug, and her fingers loosened their grip. She retreated a step, wringing her hands.

Mr. Kavanaugh smirked at her. "Relax, would you?"

Bizzie shook her head. She stammered, "Hard to relax when a

dream is at stake."

Mr. Kavanaugh paced around his office as he read Bizzie's words. He would pause to look up at her quizzically, and then his eyes would scan the story again. Bizzie's heart echoed in her chest so loud, she feared Mr. Kavanaugh would hear it. Finally, the editor walked over to his desk, sat down, and laid the story in front of him. He took off his glasses and pinched his nose. Bizzie's knees buckled, and she had to grab the side of the door so she wouldn't fall. She felt like she might vomit.

"I was expecting an interesting story," he started. "But this," he gestured to the story, "is haunting prose. I feel like I was at the poor farm with you." He grabbed the story, stood up, and shoved a finger at the paper. "This Mr. Hendry fellow. I can feel the hatred he has toward the workers there. And that poor girl from Norway!" He looked up at Bizzie. "We'll run it in three parts," he began pacing again. "We'll call it, 'Life on the County Poor Farm.'"

Bizzie's mouth fell open. Three parts? He liked it? "Sir…" she started.

"Just one thing," he added. Bizzie nodded. "What's the name of the poor farm?"

Bizzie squinted. She hadn't included the name—nor did she intend to. "Does that—does that matter?"

Mr. Kavanaugh blasted out a laugh. "Yes, it matters! Readers will want to know where this farm is. They'll want to know every detail possible. You've just taken me on a trip that transcends time. And yet, I don't even know fully where I've been."

Bizzie thought about Ruth and Mrs. Hendry, both of whom had been so kind to her. She knew that by sharing the name of the poor farm, readers would inquire about Mr. Hendry. And when he couldn't be found, the truth about what his wife had done could bring ruin upon her—and Ruth and the others. "I fear that by including the name, I would deeply injure innocent people."

Mr. Kavanaugh shook his head. "Deeply injure innocent people?"

"Besides," Bizzie continued, "by not including the name of this particular poor farm, readers will not focus so much on this one location but instead, on their own relationships. Mrs. Hendry, Ruth, Asta, Disa…they're all of us. They're your wife, daughters, nieces." Bizzie thought of Emma. "They're our friends and neighbors. They're you and me."

That was that. They would run the story—in three parts—without the name of the farm. Bizzie returned to Miss Chambers' Lodging

House to collect her few possessions and, she hoped, Emma. When she told her new friend that the floor above milkman Engelbert Kaller's was for rent, Emma was skeptical.

"You heard about this from a milkman?" she asked with her hand on her hip. "No offense, Bizzie, but you never know who you'll run into on the streets. You have to be careful who you trust."

"Oh! That reminds me," Bizzie said, pulling out a small card from her pocket. "I sat next to this woman on the streetcar." She handed it to the redhead.

Emma scanned the card, squealed with joy, and embraced Bizzie. "You know who this is, right?!" she exclaimed.

"Well, yes, thanks to you," Bizzie answered. "So, what do you say? A new job, a new place to live?" In a whisper, she added, "That's away from this dump?" Emma nodded.

Later that week, Emma and Bizzie claimed the top floor of a three-level, clapboard house on East 28th. Bizzie's favorite part was the cast iron, clawfoot tub just outside their bedroom. After a few days of normal bathing and sleeping on a mattress that wasn't rail thin or straw tick, Bizzie felt like a new person.

Meanwhile, her three-part story was quickly becoming a sensation. Because Bizzie hadn't revealed the name of the poor farm, there was plenty of speculation. Some thought it was a lodging house south of St. Paul. Others claimed it was there—in the heart of the city. Bizzie took a small amount of joy picturing Miss Chambers reading the piece and shaking, wondering if the scorching piece was about her and her terrible house. The publication rocked Minneapolis. By the end of the week, there was hardly a person who hadn't read the story or heard about it from someone else. In just days, E. Johansen the reporter was a familiar name. Papers across the country had picked up her three-part story. Bizzie mailed two copies of her published work to Hibbing—one to her parents and one to Collin. She added a note for her parents—keeping it brief, because she knew her mother would read it aloud to her father—explaining that she'd gotten a writing assignment and would be staying in the city for at least a couple of weeks.

Bizzie arrived for her second week of work feeling confident.

"Elizabeth," Mr. Kavanaugh motioned for her to join him in his office.

He ran an ink-stained hand over his balding head. Then, he gestured for her to sit.

"You've done well," he said, walking to the window facing Fourth Street.

"Thank you," she responded with her hands in her lap.

He turned and looked at her. "It may not seem like it, but this paper needed new life breathed into it. Your story may have just saved us from losing a few of our biggest backers." He stuck his hands in his pockets, paced back and forth a few steps, then stopped and scratched his chin. Bizzie was beginning to feel uneasy.

"I've just gotten a tip," he flitted back into his chair and continued, "from a small town west of here along the Minnesota River. An old friend lives there. Says something's going on with the swanky new medical center out there. The place caters to wealthy businessmen and their families from Minneapolis and Chicago." Mr. Kavanaugh pushed himself up out of his chair again and began pacing the room. Bizzie listened intently.

"I'm intrigued, Elizabeth. I want to know what's going on." He turned to her. "Here's the best part. The guy running the resort? Doc Joe Hartman."

Bizzie furrowed her brow. Dr. Joe Hartman. She'd heard of him. As if he could read her mind, Mr. Kavanaugh continued.

"You know Dr. Hartman. He moved to the Midwest from New York City a few years ago. Bought a bunch of land west of here in Crab Orchard, a little town on the prairie. He's big into research. Studied under some famous physician who used herbs instead of modern medicine. Hartman started with a small clinic and added buildings every few years. Then, he added this…" he looked down at a small notebook, "health center." He spat out the words and Bizzie stifled a laugh. Mr. Kavanaugh was the last person she could ever picture at a health center. "It's become known as the Oasis of the Midwest." He rolled his eyes and shrugged, holding up a brochure with a photograph of—just what he described—an impressive-looking building. "Hell if I know what that means."

"So, you want someone to investigate what's really going on at this Oasis," Bizzie said.

"Bingo."

"And you're asking me, because—" she trailed off.

"Isn't it obvious?" He tapped an ink-stained finger on Bizzie's article in The Journal. "This. You. You're a gem."

Bizzie nodded, understanding now. "Ah. You want me to go undercover again."

Mr. Kavanaugh nodded. "If you're up for it, of course."

Bizzie shuddered, thinking back to hiding in the root cellar with

Ruth. "Do you think I'll be safe?"

"Yes, yes, of course," he said absentmindedly. He shuffled papers around his desk, then grabbed a crumpled classified ad. "They're hiring young girls to work in the laundry service." Then he looked up at Bizzie apologetically and shrugged. "It isn't glamorous, but it'd get you in the door."

"And this source. You're sure it's legitimate?" Bizzie questioned.

"Positive. My friend has known Dr. Hartman for a long time. Something's going on. But he's not sure what." He sat back in his chair and clasped his hands behind his head. "What do you think?"

Bizzie took a deep breath. "I'll do it."

Mr. Kavanaugh jumped up and clapped his hands together. "Fantastic. I knew you would. Atta girl!" Then, he paused and cleared his throat. "I mean, great. Thank you, Ms. Johansen. I'll arrange for your transportation. Can you be ready by two?"

Chapter 21

SOPHIE

AARON TOOK A DEEP BREATH in and looked out the window at the street.

"I was a couple years out of college and working in the Boundary Waters," he started, meeting my gaze. "I told you that, I think."

I nodded.

"Tiffany had just graduated college and started working as a guide during the summer." He paused and took a sip of wine. "We hit it off right away. We dreamed of moving up north permanently and making a go of it. When we weren't working, we'd spend our time portaging these super remote inlets and bays. Places off the beaten path where the tourists never camped. It was incredible. I couldn't believe I'd found her. In the middle of nowhere. We were the perfect match."

He shrugged. "Or I thought we were. That September, the outfitter Tiffany was working for went out of business. She told me she found a temp job in the Twin Cities. She begged me to come with her, saying we'd just start a new adventure." He chuckled cynically and repeated, "A new adventure." He shook his head. "I moved to Minneapolis—quitting a job I *loved*—to follow her."

He paused and raised his eyebrows at me. "Your turn."

I sighed, not really wanting to get into my own hurts, but I was desperate to learn more about why Aaron obviously hated the city, so I began.

"I didn't start out at KOMO as a producer. I was actually hired on as a reporter. The morning show reporter—which is pretty low-ranking," I said, taking a sip of my wine. "My schedule was brutal. I would show up to the station at three a.m., get my assignment, and usually do a live shot at some obscure location at six a.m."

"What's with you and these awful schedules?" Aaron smirked.

"Chasing a dream, I guess," I sighed.

"Doesn't sound like a dream to me," he laughed.

I shook my head. "One morning, we were expecting an epic snowstorm. Conditions were already bad at five a.m. Sleet and freezing rain. It was going to be a horrible morning commute. So, the producer wanted me downtown for a live shot so we could show how backed up traffic was."

"You know where there's not traffic?" Aaron smiled.

"I know, I know. Crab Orchard. It's Mayberry!" We laughed.

I took another sip of wine. "Okay, I think it's your turn again."

Aaron scratched his chin. "Well, I started working at an outdoor sporting goods store in Minneapolis. Most of the dickheads I worked with had never even been camping. About a month into my new 'adventure,'" he lifted his fingers for air quotes, "I learned something new about Tiffany."

He took another sip of wine and I braced myself.

"She had a college boyfriend all along. And that temporary job? Turns out she had gladly accepted a full-time position without so much as mentioning it to me."

My mouth fell open. I was speechless. Who would treat another person like that? Instinctively, I reached out and grabbed his hand. "I'm so sorry, Aaron. That's awful."

He looked down at the table and swirled the swallow of wine left in his mug. "I found out about Bart—her boyfriend—when I went to pick her up for a weekend of hiking. I knocked on her apartment door and this dude opened the door," he pinched the bridge of his nose. "She told me that they'd been on a break but decided to get back together. Oh—and that he'd gotten into medical school and needed a supportive partner."

I couldn't help but blurt out a laugh. "This just keeps getting worse. Seriously! What an asshole. Both of them. Mr. and Mrs. Asshole. I hope they're super happy together." My blood was boiling. "Who does that?"

Aaron sat back and smiled. "Well, thanks. I appreciate the support." He let out a deep breath. "You can see why I don't usually talk about that...or her."

I smiled. "No wonder you hate us Minneapolis girls. But, I promise, we're not all like that."

We were both quiet for a minute.

"Your turn," Aaron clinked my glass. "You were about to report on… wait for it…traffic."

I smiled and shook my head. "My photographer and I were driving to the live shot location and got rear-ended by a pickup truck who couldn't stop on the icy roads. We weren't hurt, but I was really shaken up. And that put us behind for getting set up. So, we had to rush, and I wasn't able to fully formulate my story before I went live on-air."

"Uh-oh," Aaron said.

"Yeah," I replied. "The morning anchor, Cassie, said, 'Now let's go to Sophie who's on First and Marquette downtown. Sophie, what are the roads like? What can people expect for their morning commute?'"

I looked down at my wine glass. "I said, 'Thanks, Cassie.' And then, this feeling came over me. Like nothing I've ever experienced before. It felt like the world was closing in around me. My heart started beating so fast. I started sweating. I couldn't catch my breath. Meanwhile, my camera guy was giving me hand signals to start talking. That's when I realized I hadn't said anything else. On live TV. I was just standing there. My producer was screaming in my ear—through my earbud. But still, I couldn't speak. My legs started shaking." I stopped and sniffed.

Aaron reached out and grabbed my hand. "A panic attack?"

I nodded.

"On live TV?"

I nodded again.

"I'm so sorry," he said with such genuineness that it caught me off guard.

"It was terrifying." I felt a tear trickle down my cheek. "I thought I was dying."

"What did you do?"

"I croaked out, 'Back to you in the studio.'" I snorted. "Cassie covered for me, and they did an extra-long weather segment. But I never reported again. Not because my producer didn't want me to. Once I explained the accident, the weather conditions, and the rush we were in, my team understood. I just couldn't face being in front of a camera again. And I did try," I added.

"Like the next day? What happened?" Aaron asked.

"Try days. Every time I tried to go live, I froze up. And then I became too terrified to keep trying. Just seeing a camera became triggering. That's when my friend and producer, Freya, suggested I try producing instead." I shrugged. "And it worked out."

"Except that you stopped telling stories," Aaron said.

"Well, yeah, that," I smiled. "That's what I'm trying to do…what I'm hoping to do…" I drew designs with my finger on the table.

"At News Now Online. You want to make it right," Aaron finished for me. "Another chance."

I looked up at him and our eyes locked. I nodded. "Another chance," I repeated. I cleared my throat. "Well, I should probably head back to, er, the dreaded city." We shared a smile. "Thanks for the wine," I added.

As he closed and locked the door behind us, a black Cadillac swung into the alley across from The Coffee Fox. Another car, lights on and running, was already in the alley, apparently waiting.

"That's weird," Aaron said. When I stepped out to walk to my car, he grabbed my arm and pulled me back into the shadows of the café. "Wait, just a second." He pointed at the alley.

I looked just in time to see Morris Hartman open the door and get out of the Cadillac. At the same time, Mayor Palmer got out of the other car.

"What the hell—" I muttered. The two stood facing each other for a minute and appeared to be talking. Then, the mayor discreetly handed Hartman a file folder. He looked around to make sure no one saw. My heart skipped a beat when the mayor's gaze seemed to linger on Aaron and me hidden in the shadows. He turned slightly and clapped Hartman on the back, hopped in his car, and zoomed away. Hartman climbed into the Cadillac. I swear I saw another shadow, waiting in the back seat. But the Cadillac was gone in a second. Aaron and I looked at each other.

"Okay, that was weird," I whispered.

Aaron nodded. "You don't do business with a shady mayor in a dark alley at night if you're not up to something," Aaron replied, scratching his chin.

"Think we can follow him?" I said, my eyes widening.

Aaron looked at me intently before he said, "Let's take my truck." We raced to the truck and jumped in.

"I knew something was going on when Hartman refused to comment about the Oasis at that press conference," I said as Aaron pulled onto Main Street.

More to himself than to me, he mumbled, "The Cadillac went down Main Street. I can cut him off on Fourth." We crept along the dusky streets, neither of us saying a word. Then, a couple of blocks north, I saw the Cadillac.

"There he is!" I pointed.

"That's weird. You'd think they'd be heading to the highway toward Minneapolis. It looks like they're going—"

"West. Toward the Oasis."

Aaron followed a couple of hundred feet behind the Cadillac. Sure enough, Hartman drove up the windy path to the "Castle on the Hill." Aaron waited to follow until the Cadillac had gone around the turn. He pulled off near the groundskeeper's cottage I pointed out the other day. We could stay in the shadows but still see the Cadillac from here.

Morris got out. So did someone else. Another man I didn't recognize.

"Who's that?" I asked Aaron.

He shook his head and squinted. "He's too far away. I can't tell."

The two men began walking around to the back of the building.

I looked at Aaron. "Should we follow them?"

Aaron looked at me and nodded. "But stay in the shadows."

Chapter 22

BIZZIE

AT FOUR O'CLOCK, Bizzie stepped out of the Ford Model T that Mr. Kavanaugh had arranged for her. She thanked the driver and crunched up the driveway toward the campus. There were at least six buildings. The colossal, five-story structure in the middle of the campus was by far the largest of them. Bizzie recognized it from Mr. Kavanaugh's picture: the Grand Hall. Two long, straight wings radiated from it, forming a U-shape. Three ornate brick towers stood in the center. Bizzie had never stepped foot inside a building like this. The fanciest place she'd ever visited was the Duluthian Hotel in downtown Duluth at Christmastime.

She walked up to the main entrance in the Grand Hall and opened the door. Two Romanesque-style pillars greeted her. To her right, a grand staircase with elegant ironwork climbed majestically to the second floor. To her left was a cigar lounge filled with leather chairs and bookcases. Despite the mild May weather, a fireplace held a roaring and cracking blaze. Men sat in various chairs, smoking and laughing. A woman stood behind a tall, wooden desk, writing vigorously. She wore a button-down, gray blouse with a pointy collar paired with a white bib and apron. Her hair was tied up in a tight bun, and on top of her head sat a starched, white cap.

Bizzie cleared her throat. The woman looked up.

"Can I help you?" she sighed, making a fuss about the fact that she had to set down her pen.

"Hello, ma'am," Bizzie said, raising the newspaper article Mr. Kavanaugh had given her. "I'm here to see about getting a job in the laundromat."

"Well, you're at the wrong entrance," the woman stated, her nose in the air as she stood and walked around the tall desk.

Bizzie's cheeks grew red. Her encounter with the receptionist at *The Journal* flashed in her mind. She balled her fists and gritted her teeth. Then, she reminded herself that she was undercover on an assignment. She didn't want to blow her alibi before she'd even started.

"You need to go to the service house," the woman said, her voice dripping with disgust. She led Bizzie out the door and pointed to a smaller structure hidden in the woods behind the Grand Hall. "Go past the medical clinic and the bunkhouse." She pointed with a bony finger.

Bizzie thanked the woman through her clenched jaw and crunched her way to the service house. She was expecting to find a ramshackle lodging house, but what stood before her was a charming, albeit shabby, farmhouse. A white, wooden fence covered in vines ran around the perimeter.

She opened the creaky gate and walked up the brick path. To her right was an oak tree that was so tall Bizzie couldn't see the top. A flutter of birds flew out as Bizzie approached. To her left was a well-groomed garden. Bizzie thought back to the frail and hopeless gardener she encountered at the poor farm and shuddered.

A massive, wraparound porch greeted her. The white wooden door needed a fresh coat of paint, and a few of the wooden boards covering the house were chipped and rotting, but Bizzie immediately loved the structure. It reminded her of Papa's chair: well-loved and well-used. Bizzie knocked twice and then slowly opened the door.

A big-bellied man was limping down the hall, hollering orders in a heavy, Irish accent as he went. Two girls about Bizzie's age ran past with a pile of white, starched towels. They nodded at her, then flew out the door. A young man carrying a tray full of teacups, cream, sugar, and a teakettle approached the door.

"Mind the door, miss?" he said to her, nodding towards the door. Bizzie grabbed the knob and held it open.

"Thank you!" he hollered as he walked toward the Grand Hall without wavering.

"I'll be right with ye, filly," the large Irishman hollered over his shoulder. "Take a seat there." He nodded to a white chair in the corner, then limped away. Just before she sat down, he called, "Careful, though, lassie! It's missing one of the legs. Just like me!" Then she heard him laugh a full-bellied blast that echoed through the halls.

Bizzie couldn't help but chuckle. She checked the chair. Sure enough, one of the legs was splintered and broken. She stood instead.

A few minutes later, the Irishman limped back. Suspenders held up his black-and-white checkered pants, and a small pair of glasses were perched on his nose. His head was covered in a mass of thick, gray hair.

"Alright, filly," he said, clapping his large, calloused hands together and stopping in front of her. "What can I do for ye?"

"I'd like a job." Bizzie said, placing her hands on her hips.

"Ye would, eh?" The Irishman's eyes twinkled. He stepped back and brought a hand to his chin. "Ye look a bit small." He grabbed one of her arms and held it up. "Are ye sure these arms can bear the weight of a basket of towels?"

Bizzie swallowed the lump of embarrassment and cocked her head to the side. "Sir, I am pretty sure that I can do just about anything." She crossed her arms.

"Are ye, now?" He paused for a beat, then led Bizzie toward the dining room left of the small entryway. "Come sit, then. Let's have a cuppa."

Bizzie followed behind, smelling roasted onions and garlic wafting from the kitchen. Her mouth watered. The floorboards, though worn, were swept and clean.

The Irishman, gesturing toward the kitchen, which was to her right on the way to the dining room, said, "Preparin' for dinner." He took a deep breath in. "Pot roast." Then he turned around, smiled at Bizzie, and patted his large belly. "I love me a pot roast."

The dining room table was bare except for a small, chipped porcelain vase holding a bunch of drooping yellow and orange wildflowers. The chairs, though sturdy, were all mismatched and covered in peeling paint.

"How do ye like your tea there, filly?" the Irishman asked, standing beside a tray of pewter teacups.

"Milk and sugar, please," Bizzie replied and sat with her hands in her lap. He poured the hot water for them both, then handed Bizzie a small cup. As he sat down, the chair groaned.

"What's your name?" he asked.

Bizzie had decided beforehand that she would remain truer to her real identity than she'd done at the poor farm. "Bizzie Johnson," she said, taking a sip of her tea. It tasted minty and sweet.

"I'm Mr. O'Brien," he said, smiling. "Pleased to meet ye. So, you want a job, do ye, Miss Johnson?"

Bizzie set her cup down on the table. "Yes, sir, Mr. O'Brien."

"And what experience do ye have before this?"

"I come from a family of hard workers. Miners on the Iron Range. I taught school up there," she thought for a moment, then added, "and I farmed. Helped milk cows and prepare meals. Like pot roast."

"Ye can cook?" Mr. O'Brien scratched his chin. Then, he mumbled to himself, "We could use a kitchen maid." He looked at Bizzie again. "Let's go have a chat with Mrs. Mason." Then, quieter, he said, "Mind yourself, filly. Mrs. Mason has a temper like a heifer in heat." Bizzie's eyes grew wide, and she stifled a laugh. Mr. O'Brien turned on his heel and pushed open the kitchen door.

Chapter 23

SOPHIE

AARON AND I CREPT SILENTLY toward the Oasis, careful not to step on any twigs or branches that might snap and give us away. Aaron pointed to the back side of the building where Morris and the other figure had gone. I nodded. Together, we snuck along the massive building, huddling in the shadows. Then, a conversation broke through the silence. Aaron held out a hand, stopping me.

"—asking too many questions. Getting too close," I heard Morris say.

Another deep voice responded with something I couldn't make out. I heard Morris whisper, "— Genesis said—" and his voice cut out. Why would he be whispering about Jen?

"—want to demolish it sooner—"

It was quiet for a minute, then I heard the words "evidence" and "tunnel" and looked at Aaron. He shook his head and put a finger to his mouth.

I heard, "I'll take care of it," from the other voice.

Then, footsteps crunched in the other direction. When all was silent, I finally exhaled. Aaron and I exchanged glances.

"What the hell was that about?" I whispered, still paranoid that someone was listening—or watching.

"No idea. But I'd say your reporter instincts are dead-on," he said. "Let's get out of here before they come back."

On the drive back to The Coffee Fox, I pondered aloud what we'd heard.

"Is Jen involved in this somehow? I mean, I know she worked with Morris before me, but why would he be whispering her name in the shadows of some abandoned building?"

Just as Aaron was about to respond, I blurted out, "And when he said, 'demolish sooner,' does that mean demolish the Oasis? The city council hasn't even voted on it yet."

Aaron cleared his voice, ready to speak.

"And what about evidence?!" I exclaimed. "What evidence? What in the hell are they trying to hide?"

"Sophie!" Aaron broke in. I looked up, surprised. "Can I say something?"

"Sorry," I responded.

"Remember what I said about the mayor not always living up to the law?" he asked. "I wonder if he has something to do with this. I can't be sure, but I wouldn't be surprised." He looked over at me. "Maybe that's another place to look?"

I nodded. "Thanks, Aaron."

He pulled up to the café and turned off the ignition. I grabbed my bag and met him near my Kia. He leaned in for a hug. As he was backing away, I placed a small, quick kiss on his bristly cheek. I smiled and blushed, then looked at the ground, embarrassed.

He gently grabbed my chin and led my face to his. Our lips touched and I inhaled his sweet smell of coffee and woodsmoke. I closed my eyes and for a moment felt like I was floating. Sparks flew up and down my spine. Finally, we backed away, staring into each other's eyes. Then, we both began to laugh.

"That was...nice," I started.

"Well, you started it," he said, lightly punching my shoulder. I smiled and pecked him on the cheek once more. He opened my door for me. I hopped in, started the ignition, and rolled down my window.

"Well, thanks again for all your help today," I said, still a little dizzy from our kiss.

He leaned down and stuck his head in the window inches from mine. "Thank you," he whispered. Then his lips brushed against mine.

"I'll call you tomorrow," he said, backing away and leaning an arm on the hood of my car. "Maybe you can come back over." He gestured to the coffee shop. "I'm working tomorrow but could make you a latte. On the house."

I smiled. "I might take you up on that." I waved good-bye and watched him in my rearview mirror. Still on cloud nine, I started my favorite playlist on Spotify. As I zipped through town with my window rolled down, Lizzo sang about feeling good as hell. I drove past Kelly's Bar where dozens of patrons sat at an outdoor patio draped in light from glowing bulbs. I smelled french fries and heard bursts of laughter.

As I turned onto the highway, thoughts flooded my mind. Why was Morris in a dark alley with the mayor? And then sneaking around a decrepit Oasis talking about demolition and evidence? And how was Jen involved?

I was lost in thought when bright lights suddenly swung up behind me, blinding me.

"Shit!" Assuming the car was a police officer or emergency vehicle, I slowed to a crawl, hoping it would pass. When the vehicle stayed behind me—sans flashing lights—I got nervous and sped up. But the car was glued to mine—if I slowed, it slowed. If I swerved, it swerved. I tried to get a glimpse of the driver, but the lights were too bright. I couldn't see a thing. My heart pounded, and my palms began to sweat. My breathing got shallower. With a shaky hand, I grabbed my cell phone and dialed Aaron's number.

"Miss me already?" his calm voice answered a second later.

"Aaron," I said in a shaky voice, "I think I'm being followed. I'm on Highway 90 heading toward Minneapolis... I'm not sure what to do."

"Maybe it's just a couple of teenagers goofing off," he said.

"This...this doesn't feel like sixteen-year-olds out for a joyride," I replied. "Something's off."

Aaron paused, then said, "I'll start heading your way."

"Thanks," I said. "I'm just outside of Crab Orchard." I desperately searched for a mile marker along the highway.

"Put your blinker on and move into the other lane," he demanded. I did.

"They followed me," I cried.

"Slow your speed."

I did. I slowed my speed to forty. I didn't even have to look; the lights flooded my backseat. I knew the car following me had shifted back to the right lane and slowed as well.

"Aaron, I'm scared," I said.

"I'm on my way. Just keep going. Don't stop. Stay on the phone with me," he said. "I'm just getting onto 90 right now." In the background, I could hear his truck rev and I prayed that he would get to me soon. "I want you to tell me any details you can. The color of the car. The make. The model. Anything."

I glimpsed behind me. "It's maybe a dark color," I took a shallow breath, "can't tell for sure. And I think it's a sedan." I squinted in my rearview mirror, willing my eyes to see past the blinding headlights. At one point, my follower got so close, my bumper blocked his headlights, allowing me to see a silhouette of a person. "Looks like just one person in the car."

"Good. You're doing great, Sophie," he replied. "Just hang in there."

He stayed on the phone with me, giving me words of encouragement while I crept along at forty miles per hour and he rocketed down the highway in his truck.

It felt like hours before he caught up to me, but it was likely only ten minutes. "I'm coming up behind the car," he said. "I got his license plate. Sophie, I'm going to flash my lights behind this guy. Just keep going the same speed. I'm right here." A gush of bright light flooded the highway, and I heard Aaron's truck rev behind us.

After a beat, the sedan zoomed around me and sped off. I tried to catch a glimpse of the driver, but I couldn't see more than a shadow through the tinted windows. And just like that, the car was gone.

"You okay?" Aaron asked, still on the phone.

"Yeah," I managed. "Aaron, thank you."

"I'm going to follow you home. Just keep going. I'll be right here." Hearing his voice on the other line and knowing he was right behind me helped me regulate my breathing to almost normal.

"Are you sure? It's at least another half hour to the city," I said, sniffling.

"You kidding? I love driving into Minneapolis. Do it anytime I can," he joked.

Despite my terror, I managed a laugh. When we got to my apartment building, we circled the block to find parking spots on the street near each other. I climbed out of my Kia, ran to Aaron, and flung myself into his arms. Tears streamed down my cheeks.

"I was so scared," I whispered into his chest. He ran a rough hand through my hair, and I felt the pull of a couple of strands caught on his rough calluses. I sniffed and stepped back. "Thank you," I murmured. "Who…who do you think that was? Why were they following me?"

"Let me walk you inside," he said, putting an arm around my waist. I pointed to my apartment building, and we walked in step together, saying nothing. I led him up to the second floor and unlocked my door.

I gestured around, turning on the hallway light. "This is it." I was relieved I had scooped my dirty laundry off the floor that morning. "Do you want some wine? Or coffee?"

Aaron took off his faded boots, gently set them off to the side, and stepped into the kitchen. "How about you sit and I'll get us some wine?"

Grateful for his presence, I smiled and collapsed onto my overstuffed couch in the next room. I wrapped myself in a cream-colored, fleece throw.

"So, who do you think that was?" I asked again. "Just some kid trying to scare me?"

Aaron joined me a minute later with two glasses and a bottle of red wine. I was too tired to ask how he knew where to find everything and instead gulped two swallows.

"I texted the picture of the license plate to the sheriff," Aaron shrugged. "I was the best man at his wedding. He can tell me who the car belongs to. We'll see if that helps us."

I curled my legs up under me and buried my head in my hands. Quiet, muffled sobs escaped me. A moment later, Aaron was beside me, his strong body engulfing me. I rested my head against his chest. We sat like that in silence for several minutes. He gently rubbed my back, and I let my tears fall onto his Carhartt jacket, worrying at my bottom lip with a forefinger.

The buzzing of his phone made us both jump. Aaron checked his texts.

"The car belongs to a Walter Hollace," he said. Then he looked at me quizzically. "Walter Hollace? Does that name sound familiar?"

I shook my head. "No. Not at all."

Aaron rubbed his chin. "Walter Hollace," he whispered to himself. "I feel like I've heard that name before." He snapped his fingers. "Wait a second..." He whipped out his phone again and began punching the screen.

"What? What is it?" I asked, leaning over to see what he was doing.

"Bingo," he said, showing me his phone. "Walter Hollace is on the city council in Crab Orchard." Then, to himself, he muttered, "I *knew* I knew that name."

I racked my brain, trying to remember if I had met him the night I went to the meeting with Ida.

"Wait, does he know the mayor?" I asked.

Aaron shrugged. "I don't know Walter personally, but I'm sure he and the mayor know each other."

"Aaron, I could have sworn the mayor saw us in the shadows earlier tonight," I said, goosebumps pricking my skin. "Do you think he had Walter follow me," I swallowed, "as a threat?" Again, I ran my finger along my lip.

Aaron sat back in his chair and let out a deep breath. "What the hell is a small-town mayor doing threatening a journalist?" He rubbed his eyes and looked at me. "Hey, stop rubbing your lip. It's turning red."

"What?" I asked, then pulled my hand away from my face. "Oh, I didn't realize I was doing that." I chuckled. "I have an old scar there. Got it ice skating with my dad when I was three years old. Whenever I'm stressed, my scar gets sensitive."

"Ooh, kinda like Harry Potter?" Aaron asked, gently touching my scar. He placed his rough hands on my cheeks and led me close to him. His lips met mine for another kiss. I closed my eyes and breathed him in. He pulled me into his lap, and I wrapped my arms around his neck, playing with his hair. His hands moved from my shoulders to my back to under my shirt. He rubbed my back and found his way to my bra.

"As much as I love this," I murmured, still kissing his lips, "and trust me, I really do love this, I'd rather continue this on a night when my life wasn't threatened." I backed away, inches from his face and bit my slightly swollen lip.

Aaron smiled, giving a slight nod. He pecked me on the lips and brushed a piece of hair out of my face.

"Besides," I added, "my mind won't stop racing." I stood up and began pacing. "What are Hartman and Mayor Palmer doing that they don't want me to know about?" I paused and looked at Aaron. He smiled at me. "What?" I asked.

"I like seeing this side of you," he replied.

I sat back down next to him. "Think you could help me?" I pleaded. "I would love to take a look at some of the past city council meeting notes to see if anything comes up linking the two of them. Do you think the notes are archived online?"

Aaron chuckled. "We're not quite as modern as you city slickers, but come to The Fox tomorrow. I'll see what I can do."

Chapter 24

BIZZIE

THERE, COVERED IN FLOUR, a mess of flaming red hair falling out of a knot on top of her head, stood a frantic Mrs. Mason.

"Oh, I've done it now," she said to Mr. O'Brien, not looking up. He winked at Bizzie.

"Now, now, Mrs. Mason. Whatever it is can't be that bad. What's got your knickers in a tizzy today?"

Mrs. Mason paced back and forth behind the counter that separated her from Bizzie and Mr. O'Brien. She held up a basket of carrots. "I'm makin' chicken pudding for dinner tonight."

Mr. O'Brien whispered to Bizzie, "Ah, chicken pudding. I thought it was pot roast."

"Are you listening to me?" Mrs. Mason shrieked, looking up at him for the first time. Her fiery green eyes were wide and her cheeks pink.

Mr. O'Brien held his hands up in the air. "I'm sorry, Mrs. Mason. Ah, your carrots?"

"As I was sayin', I'm makin' chicken pudding with carrots. But, the menu says," she paused, pinched the bridge of her nose and closed her eyes, "turnips."

"Ah, Mrs. Mason," Mr. O'Brien started, holding up one of the carrots from the basket. "Haven't you heard? These are the finest carrots in the Midwest. Travelers from as far as New York and even London are flocking to our little town to have just a taste—just one tiny taste—of these golden jewels." He spoke with such heart and conviction that spittle flew from his lips. "The guests will thank you—no, praise you—for using such a delectable ingredient."

Mrs. Mason blushed and hid a sheepish grin. "You really think so?"

Mr. O'Brien shook his head. "I know so."

With that, Mrs. Mason grabbed the bundle of carrots and began washing them, humming a song as she worked.

Bizzie cocked her head at Mr. O'Brien. She whispered, "You're pretty convincing. I don't even like carrots, and I'm curious to try one."

"Don't be," he laughed quietly. "I made that whole story up."

Bizzie smiled.

"Now, let's put you to work," he winked. He waited until Mrs. Mason finished washing the carrots to deliver the news. "Ah, Mrs. Mason, I have some good news for you—other than the carrots, of course."

Mrs. Mason looked up. "Yes?"

He gave Bizzie a slight nudge. "I've hired a kitchen maid for you."

"Her?" she asked, setting down the vegetables and walking over to Bizzie. Mrs. Mason picked up one of Bizzie's arms and made a face as if she'd smelled something rotten. "She's puny," Mrs. Mason said as if Bizzie couldn't hear her. "Has she even cooked in a real kitchen?"

"Now, Mrs. Mason," Mr. O'Brien said. "Do you think I would hire someone who has never cooked in a real kitchen before? You know me better than that."

Mrs. Mason squinted at him, then at Bizzie. Finally, she nodded. "Well, if she's the best you can do, I'll take her. The kitchen *is* desperate." She reached for a tattered, faded white apron and threw it to Bizzie, who snatched it mid-air. "Put this on and help me with these carrots."

Mr. O'Brien winked at Bizzie and nodded at Mrs. Mason. Bizzie had so many questions for him—like where she would sleep and bathe—but for now, she was grateful to be knee-deep in her next assignment.

Chapter 25

SOPHIE

I SLEPT HORRIBLY. I kept dreaming that a monster with big, bright, blinding eyes was chasing me. At six o'clock, I finally threw back the covers and got up. Instead of making coffee at home, I pulled on some yoga pants and a gray sweatshirt and headed west for Crab Orchard.

I took a chance that Freya might be up feeding the baby and called her.

"What the hell are you doing up at this hour?" she answered.

I laughed. "Well, I do have a regular schedule now, remember? No more late nights for me. No more sleeping in until eleven."

"Girl, your life sounds like mine. Maybe you should move to the suburbs, too."

I scoffed. "Ew. Although, you will be shocked to learn that I've been spending time in a small town. And I kinda like it."

"You? In a small town? Ha!"

I nodded. "I know. I even met someone."

"Wait. What? Tell me more."

I could hear Freya's baby cry. Freya soothed him, sounding so loving. I loved that she could be both a badass news producer and a gentle and nurturing mother.

I launched into how I met Aaron while I was sneaking around an abandoned medical campus, searching for something that I could add to my story. Freya hung on every word.

"Who knew you were such a little investigator, huh?" she joked. "Did you find anything?"

"I don't know. Something's definitely going on." I told her about being followed last night.

"Be careful," she warned. "I know you want to prove yourself, but seriously, don't go too far."

I smiled. "Says the girl who almost literally ran down former Timberwolves forward Joshie Colms."

"Hey! He was accused of murder. And he was walking on the sidewalk right next to me! What was I supposed to do?"

Lucy screamed in the background.

"I gotta go. But keep me posted on this small-town mystery man." Freya and I hung up. I pulled up to The Coffee Fox a little after seven. I was about to open my car door when my cell phone rang. My dad. I winced. I'd been avoiding his calls.

"Hey, Dad," I answered. "Sorry I haven't called you back…I've been, er, busy working on a—"

"No need to apologize, sweetie. Mom and I know you're busy. We're just packing for our Holy Land Pilgrimage." In the background, I could hear my mom yelling something to my dad. He murmured something back. "We leave next week, you know. Taking fifty members of the church with us. Would love to have dinner with you before we go," he pushed.

"That's right. Er, yeah. I'd love to come for dinner." My parents no longer lived in the church parsonage. When my brother Hank and I left home, they bought a downtown condo within walking distance of the church.

"Your mom said she'd make pot roast," he urged, knowing that was my favorite meal. She used to make it every Sunday. After a long day at church with my dad, we'd come back to the parsonage and the whole place smelled warm and cozy. Suddenly, there was a lump in my throat. A vision of being followed last night scorched my memory, and I wondered whether being home with my parents eating pot roast was smarter—and safer—than following this lead.

"That sounds nice," I said.

"Hey, Soph, are you doing okay?" my dad asked.

"Oh, me?" I managed a quick laugh. "Yeah! Never better!" I added with a punch of enthusiasm. "Why do you ask?"

"Oh, just making sure. I know it's a big move to go from producing the news to actually delivering it. I'm always in your corner," he said. "And, if you ever need help, I'm just a call away."

A tear welled in my eye. "Thanks, Dad," I sniffed. "But I'm doing great. Really. In fact, I have to run. But thanks for calling."

"Soph, I love you," my dad added.

146 | THE MUCKRAKER

I wiped away the tear. "Love you too, Dad."

I took a deep breath and headed into The Coffee Fox. Aaron looked up from the drink he was pouring and smiled.

"You're up early," he said a bit loudly. A few of the patrons looked up from their books and newspapers at me. I smiled and watched him pour steamed milk into a ceramic mug. Then, he stirred in some espresso.

"Mind bringing this over to the guy sitting by the window?" he asked me, gesturing to a large window adjacent to the street.

"Sure," I said. "But I better get my drink on the house." I winked. I set the warm mug beside the newspaper the man had been reading. On the cover of the *Crab Orchard Tribune* was a picture of Morris Hartman at yesterday's fundraiser—smiling, sitting at the table covered in "Vote for Morris" t-shirts. The headline read, "Morris Hartman Supports Preservationists' Cause."

"Are you finished with this?" I asked him. He nodded and took a sip of his drink. I sat down at the high-backed stools facing the coffee bar and spread the paper out before me. Aaron was wiping off the counter and restocking milk in the fridge.

"Listen to this," I said. "'I have such a passion and deep appreciation for this legacy. We need to do everything in our power to save the Oasis. I've been working tirelessly, fighting for this cause.'" I looked up. "That's complete bullshit! What a liar," I said, shaking my head in disgust. "He's done nothing but pose for pictures and smile for the camera. Oh, and make sure other news agencies are watching." I folded the paper and set it beside me. "Pathetic."

Aaron slid a mug in front of me. I brought it to my lips. It smelled spicy. "A chai?" I asked. He nodded. "Thanks," I said, taking a sip.

Aaron flicked a plastic card onto the counter. "My friend from city hall stopped in this morning," he said. "The offices are closed today, but she said she left her office door unlocked. Minutes from the recent meetings are on her desk."

My eyes widened and I grabbed the key card. "Really? Gosh, you really are tapped into this community. Thank you."

"Do you think it's safe for you to keep digging around in this story, though?" Aaron asked as he draped a towel over his shoulder and planted his hands on his hips. "I mean, I get that you're invested in this story now and," he swallowed and paused, "working to overcome stuff from the past. But I…I'm worried about you. Your safety."

"You're worried about me?" I replied, smirking. "That's kinda sweet."

"I'm serious. Last night scared me. Just…be careful."

"I will. I promise. Besides, I have you nearby, right?" I winked. "Do you care if I run over there now?" I asked, standing up and grabbing both the key card and my mug.

Aaron shook his head. "You know where to find me."

He gave me directions to City Hall, which was just a few blocks away from the café. I decided to walk. The sunshine felt nice on my face. I passed Bev's Café, and the smells of bacon and cinnamon rolls wafted from the door. I was tempted to duck in but instead took a sip of my chai. A woman pushing a stroller walked by me, and we exchanged smiles.

I walked around the corner to City Hall just as Aaron had directed me. I pressed the key card against the front door, and it clicked and beeped, then unlocked. Yanking the door open, I took a left and followed the shaded hallway to the first door on the left—Wren Coleman. Aaron had said her office door would be unlocked, and it was.

Wren's office smelled like vanilla and lavender. A framed picture of a woman—I assumed Wren—doing yoga on an exotic-looking beach sat on her clean and dustless desk. There, in the middle near her desktop computer, was a manila folder. My name was scribbled on a sticky note and stuck to the front of the folder.

I sat in Wren's cushy, black office chair and scooted up to her desk. I flipped open the folder. A meeting agenda dated from a year ago—June 6th—was first. I scanned the notes. An address from the mayor. Old business. New business. The new business was nothing exciting: city pool hours, a maternity leave request for a city employee, and a vendor presenting his plan for new city streetlights.

I flipped to the next agenda. It was much the same. I was about to close the folder when something from a meeting in January caught my eye. It was listed under "Closed Door Meeting with MH Manufacturing."

MH Manufacturing—owned by Morris Hartman. I shrugged. It could be something. I made a mental note to ask Aaron what he thought. I decided to take the file folder of meeting minutes with me back to the café to review. I grabbed my chai, closed Wren's office door, and walked down the hallway toward the front door. When I passed a door with Mayor Palmer's name on it, I slowed and tried the door. Unlocked. I quickly zipped in and closed the door behind me.

His office was nearly empty. The only thing on the desk was a humming desktop computer. The space smelled like Windex. Dust floated to the floor, illuminated in the sunshine streaming through

148 | THE MUCKRAKER

the window. My heart pounded. I was terrified that someone would blast through the door to find me there. I also felt thrilled that I was actually doing this—snooping in a shady mayor's office.

I sat in his black office chair and swiveled around. For a mayor who kept the appearance of being tuned into his town, he sure didn't keep much in his office. To the left of the desk was a file cabinet. I tried all the drawers. Locked. Then, I pulled open the thin drawer beneath his keyboard. A small key. I grabbed it and tried the top cabinet again. It clicked and unlocked. Inside, I found neatly labeled file folders. Employees, finances, personnel. I closed that drawer and looked into the next one. More of the same. I was about to shut it and leave the office when I saw something near the back. "Closed meeting notes—Confidential."

I grabbed the file folder and pulled it out. The first thing I saw was a printed email conversation between MHartmanMinnesota@gmail.com and MayorPalmer@gmail.com.

> *Palmer,*
>
> *I'm calling in an old favor. You know you owe me. How many times did I save your ass in college? Besides, I know too much about you.*
>
> *I need to make something disappear. I know reporters will be digging up any skeletons and I have a big one. Can you help? There's big $$ in it for you. Keep this confidential.*
>
> *MH*

I flipped the page and read the next email.

> *Morris,*
>
> *You know I'd do anything for my old roommate. Say the word.*
>
> *Palmer*

A few more emails had been printed and saved, but nothing noteworthy. Then I found a screenshot of a text conversation the mayor had printed.

Morris Hartman: *Situation's come up. A reporter is on my case. Need to move on sooner rather than later.*

Reading that made me shiver. I knew I was the reporter. My heart pounded.

Mayor Palmer: *May have been the same one who's been at city council mtgs.*
Morris Hartman: *I know you've called on Walter before to make people disappear. Can he help? Maybe have her followed? Just want to scare her. For now.*

The hairs pricked up on my arms and I shivered reading that.

Mayor Palmer: *I'll see what I can do. Send me a picture of the girl. I'll pass it along to Hollace.*
Morris Hartman: *Don't want to send via text. Meet me and I'll give you copies Oberg has.*

The hairs on my neck stood up. They had pictures of me? I gasped. That's what they were exchanging in the alley. It must have been.

I jumped in the air when I heard the front door of the city hall office click.

Aaron?

Then, a familiar voice. Mayor Palmer. I had about two seconds to close the file drawer and duck under the mayor's desk before he barged into the office. My heart pounded. I couldn't breathe.

"I told you, Walter," the mayor scolded. "I want to know what she's up to. I know it was her in the shadows last night."

To my horror, he pulled out the office chair and plopped down. My chai! I had left my drink on his desk. Shit. I curled my arms around myself, forming a ball tighter than a coil of rubber bands. His knees were inches from my face.

"I don't care," he said into the phone. "When Morris Hartman asks you to do something, you do it." Then in a hiss, "You follow that nasty bitch. Besides," he added in a lighter tone, "it's nice to have friends in high places. You can bet your ass that I'm documenting all I'm doing for him. It'll just be a matter of time before I'll be calling on him for a favor."

I closed my eyes tight and bit my lip. I heard him open up the top desk drawer. I wanted to scream and run back to The Coffee Fox. Any minute, I was sure he was going to notice my cup on his desk.

"Well, you figure it out," he said, blessedly standing up. Then, "I'm just popping into the office to grab a couple things." Then, in a barky laugh, he said, "Tonight, Mindy is coming over." Silence, but I could hear echoes on the other line. "Yeah, *that* Mindy!" he said and let out a loud belch. I wanted to vomit. "I don't know. I've never asked her to do *that* before."

I had visions of standing up and whacking him on the back of the head with his keyboard.

"Okay, Walter," he said in now-friendly tones. "Remember what I said. You keep an eye on her."

I heard another drawer open and close. The mayor was still talking to Walter as he closed his office door. I could hear footsteps down the hallway, then the front door opened and closed. It wasn't until I heard his car zoom away that I moved.

"Holy shit," I whispered to myself. I still had the file folder and hugged it close to my chest. Before the mayor or Walter or anyone else could find me snooping, I grabbed my chai, bolted out of the office, and hurried back to The Coffee Fox.

"Holy crap," I said, collapsing on the stool across from Aaron.

He lifted an eyebrow at me. "That took you a while. Everything okay?" Then, he hollered toward the kitchen. "Lauren! I need that egg white and turkey bacon sandwich pronto!"

"No! It wasn't okay!" I said, close to tears. I told him how I had peeked into the mayor's office, and how he had almost caught me. "Wait…you didn't send him there on purpose to catch me, did you?" I asked, only sort of kidding.

Aaron hollered over his shoulder. "And another spinach quiche order coming your way!" Then he turned to me. "Yep, right after you left, I flashed the evil Mayor Palmer sign across the city. He must have seen it and jumped in his Palmer-Mobile." He rolled his eyes at me. "Of course not."

I raised my hands. "Okay, okay. Sorry." A deep breath in. "It's just… this is starting to get real. And scary. Like," I looked at my hands. "Are these scumbags worth my time?" I swallowed hard and looked at Aaron. In a quiet voice, I said, "Are they going to hurt me?"

Aaron looked into my eyes. "Hang on," he said. He motioned to Lauren to take over the coffee bar. He took off his apron and set it on the counter. Then, he walked around and sat next to me. He rubbed my back gently.

"I know this is scary," he said. "Hell, I was scared last night. But you have what it takes to bring these guys down." He clenched his teeth and grabbed my hands. "You can't stop now."

I sniffed and wiped away a tear. "You really think so?"

"Don't do this for me or for Kase, or for News Now Online, or for anyone else." He squeezed my shoulder. "Do this for you."

"Aaron," I said softly. I rested my head against his shoulder, and he brought his arm around me, hugging me. "Thank you," I murmured. Then, I pointed to the file folders I had taken from city hall. "I think I have a date with some city council meeting minutes."

"Good," Aaron said. "Oh, and hey, did I tell you I'm going to the Oasis again Monday night?"

I sat up. "No. You are? What for?"

"I was hired by *Preserve History Magazine* to take some more photos of the Oasis to use for their fall cover," he said nonchalantly, taking a sip of his coffee.

"Aaron!" I swatted his arm. "Seriously! That's great news. I'm so proud of you." Then, I added, "I'm coming with you."

Aaron smirked. "I figured you'd say that." He pulled a paper from his back pocket and smoothed it with his hand. It was a map—the same one Ida had put out on one of the tables during the fundraiser. "Ida gave me this. I thought," he said, pointing to a dot on the map, "maybe I'd investigate this."

I looked where he was pointing. I frowned and looked more closely at the map. "That hallway looks like it goes underground," I said. "That must be a mistake."

Aaron shook his head. "I don't think it's a mistake. I think it's an underground tunnel."

"A tunnel," I murmured. "I heard Morris say something about a tunnel when we followed him last night. Maybe the tunnel leads to the evidence? And," I raised a conspiratorial eyebrow and pointed to the mayor's folder, "skeletons."

Chapter 26

BIZZIE

BIZZIE DID WHATEVER Mrs. Mason told her. She ran to the chicken coop to collect eggs for the chicken pudding. She hustled to the garden to pick fresh basil and parsley for soup. She fetched Mrs. Mason some bourbon for her afternoon Old-Fashioned. By the time dinner was ready to be served, Bizzie was exhausted. Fortunately, Mrs. Mason couldn't fathom the idea of her actually serving the dinner.

"You look worse than those wilting wildflowers," she scowled, testing the chicken pudding with a wooden skewer. "Erm. Not quite set." Then, as a side note, she mumbled to Bizzie, "Go get some rest. I need you here at six a.m. sharp tomorrow morning! We're making a full breakfast."

Bizzie nodded to Mrs. Mason. But she had no idea where she was supposed to go. Were there shared rooms with straw mattresses like at the poor farm? Or would she have her own room like at the Lodging House in Minneapolis? Then, she remembered the woman in the lobby of the Grand Hall had mentioned a bunkhouse. Instead of bothering Mrs. Mason, she decided to go look for Mr. O'Brien. She hung her apron on a hook on the wall and slipped out the backdoor.

She walked along the back of the brick house, turned the corner, and smacked right into someone.

"Watch it!" the girl scowled.

"I'm so sorry," Bizzie stammered.

"Francine, she didn't mean to," another girl chimed in. She held a cigarette between two of her fingers. She brought it to her lips, took a drag, and let it hang out of her mouth. To Bizzie she said, "Don't

mind Francine. I'm Louise." She stuck a hand out and shook Bizzie's.
"I'm Bizzie."

Louise took another drag on the cigarette. "Want one?" She wore a crisp, black blouse tucked into a floor-length black skirt. On her feet were laced-up, black boots. Covering her blouse and skirt was a starched white apron. Her hair was screwed up in a tight bun on top of her head, which was covered with a small white cap.

"No!" hissed Francine. "I could only get a few. Those are for us." Francine's white blouse was stained. Her apron was dirty and covered with brown splotches. Her cheeks were rosy, and strands of hair that had escaped her loose bun were plastered to her face. Bizzie also noticed her right arm hung limp at her side.

Bizzie shuffled her feet. "No thanks. I don't smoke."

"Haven't seen you here before. You new?" Francine scrutinized.

"Yes," Bizzie replied, trying not to look at the girl's limp arm. "I was hired on as the new kitchen maid."

Francine and Louise exchanged glances, and then both burst out laughing. "Good luck working with Mrs. Misery."

"You mean Mrs. Mason?" Bizzie asked, puzzled. "She seems okay. A bit, er, frazzled maybe."

"That's one way to describe her," Francine muttered, tucking a strand of hair behind her ear.

"Well, I'm just glad to have been given a job." Bizzie smiled brightly. "Say, I wasn't assigned to a room. Could you help me?"

"Only one room for all of us girls," Louise answered. "The bunk hall." She took one last drag of her cigarette and stomped it out. "We'll take you there."

Louise and Francine led the way, Bizzie trudging along behind on the gravel path behind the Grand Hall. She gaped at the size of it, feeling so small against its immense presence. Louise noticed.

"It's something, huh?" She jerked her head towards the building.

"It's amazing," Bizzie awed.

"It's too big, in my opinion," Francine fussed. "Well, too big to clean, anyway."

"Is that your job, then? To clean?" Bizzie asked.

"We don't just clean," Francine squawked. She sniffed and raised her head. "I'm a scullery maid. Head scullery maid. I manage the laundry."

"And I'm a housemaid," Louise said. "Although I used to work for Mrs. Mason in the kitchen. That's where most of us start. She usually fires us all eventually and moves onto the new girl." Both girls eyed

154 | THE MUCKRAKER

Bizzie. Louise continued, "A piece of advice—when she asks you keep whisking, you keep whisking. Don't stop until she tells you."

"Yeah, or until your arm falls off," Francine added with a sarcastic laugh. She gestured to her limp arm. "How do you think this happened?" Both girls erupted into giggles.

Bizzie cleared her throat. "So, this place—this medical center," Bizzie started. "Why is it called the Oasis?"

Louise snorted. "This is no oasis. That is, unless you're rich and can afford to come here."

"Were you looking for some kind of vacation?" Francine mocked in a sing-song voice. "Because you're in for a wild ride with Mrs. Misery." Louise and Francine laughed again.

Bizzie ignored them. She wanted some tangible detail to clutch onto. Something to point her in the right direction for her story. Although she had a bit more time than her stint at the poor farm, she needed to learn more about Dr. Hartman—fast.

"Well, what about Dr. Hartman?" Bizzie asked. "Do you ever interact with him?"

Both girls stopped laughing immediately. Neither one said anything.

"I assume you must have some kind of contact with him," Bizzie pushed.

"We—we don't see him," Louise stammered. "Ever."

Bizzie furrowed her eyebrows. "You never see him? But doesn't he run this place?" She gestured to the grounds.

"Well, we might catch a glimpse of him," Louise uttered. Then, quieter, she added "But, we're not supposed to talk about him. And definitely never talk to him."

"You'll report to Mrs. Misery and Mr. O'Brien," Francine said, her teeth clenched. "That's all you need to know."

"Here's the bunkhouse," Louise said, gesturing to a narrow, three-story, brick structure. "Boys are on the second floor. Girls on the third." Then, she added quickly, "We've gotta finish our nightly chores. The third bunk on the left is open."

Francine snickered. "That was the last kitchen maid's bed. She lasted a whole three days."

The two girls turned, linked arms, and hustled away. Bizzie noticed them whispering to each other. She sighed and sized up the bunkhouse. It was a bed, she told herself.

She yanked the door open and headed up the narrow staircase, her shoes clicking against the concrete. A mix of sweat and tobacco filled her nose. She hesitated at the landing outside the boys' floor, putting her ear to the door. Nothing. She thought about Collin. He'd probably make some sly remark about sneaking onto the girls' floor later that night. She smiled at the thought as she climbed to the third floor.

Thirty or so beds—fifteen in each row—lined the room. Each one was covered with an itchy-looking, gray wool blanket. The space was neat and tidy. On most beds, she noticed small belongings like books, handwritten letters, and photographs. Just like Louise had said, the third bunk on the left row appeared vacant. The blanket was tucked tightly under the mattress and a crisp white pillow sat on top of it.

Even though the sun hadn't set yet, Bizzie conceded to her exhaustion. She tucked her satchel under the pillow and, without even changing out of her chicken pudding-splattered clothes, crawled under the scratchy blanket and fell asleep.

A growling noise startled her. Bizzie sat up abruptly. For a moment, she forgot where she was. The bunkhouse. The Oasis. The room was completely dark. The growling again. Then, Bizzie realized it was coming from her own stomach. She hadn't eaten anything since the prior morning—a cinnamon bun and coffee for two cents at the food stand just outside her newly rented room. When she had tried to snatch a bit of chicken pudding, Mrs. Mason smacked her hand. But now, hours later, she was famished.

She laid back down and tried to think of something other than food. No luck. Her mouth was salivating. She figured she could sneak into the kitchen and find a small snack. Everyone would be sleeping, she assumed.

She crept down the bunk bed ladder, trying to avoid any creaking. Then, she tiptoed past the other bunks, all of them occupied by a sleeping body. Opening the door to the hallway just a sliver so as not to wake anyone, she slid through. She crept past the boys' floor, down the stairs, and out into the cool night air. Grateful for the moonlight, she retraced her steps from earlier in the day.

Cupping her hand, she peeked through a dusty window into the dark kitchen. No movement. No Mrs. Mason. She slipped in through the back door. Without turning on the kitchen light, she felt her way around the pantry. Neatly organized aluminum tins and other storage jars probably held flour, sugar, spices, and tea. Giving up on the pantry, she carefully made her way to the counter, hopeful that Mrs. Mason would have left out a slice of chicken pudding or a flaky biscuit. That's when she saw the shape of a tin canister near the sink. Reaching for it, she took the cover off and happily discovered cookies inside.

As she grabbed one, she accidentally let go of the tin cover. It fell to the tile floor with a clash. Bizzie swooped down and picked it up, setting it back on the counter and rushing to the backdoor. In her panic, she ran right into one of the kitchen chairs and it fell over with a bang.

"Who's there?" she heard Mr. O'Brien holler. She was nearly to the door when a stream of candlelight stopped her in her tracks.

"What the—" Mr. O'Brien shuffled over to where Bizzie stood. "What are you doin' in here?" His voice sounded deep and raspy. His graying hair was rumpled, and he wore a cotton, long-sleeved, ankle-length nightshirt. "Aren't you the filly I just hired?" He rubbed his eyes as if to make sure he wasn't seeing things.

"Yes, sir, Mr. O'Brien," Bizzie stammered, hiding the cookie behind her back. "You see, I couldn't remember if I had cleaned up properly. And I heard how Mrs. Mason likes everything neat and tidy for the morning." Bizzie motioned to the kitchen. "I know it'll be a big breakfast and an early morning. I just wanted to be ready."

"Well, Mrs. Mason is a stickler," he scratched the top of his head. After a moment, he nodded. "I think she'll appreciate your extra care."

Bizzie exhaled.

"But next time, wait until the sun is up so you can see what you're doing," Mr. O'Brien said. "Or at least light a match for yourself."

"Yes, sir. I just didn't want to wake anyone," Bizzie replied.

"Well, now that I'm up, I could go for a snack," he said, lighting a few candles around the kitchen. "Care to join me?"

Bizzie nodded. When he turned his back, she stuck the entire cookie in her mouth. The dry pieces melted on her tongue, and she swallowed every last crumb.

"Mrs. Mason usually leaves some leftovers in the icebox," he said. He pulled out something wrapped in parchment paper, tied with a string. "Ah, she did. Cold veal and cornbread." He gestured for Bizzie to pull up a chair as he unwrapped the meat and muffins. Bizzie wasn't one for veal, let alone cold veal, but she couldn't remember a meal ever tasting so delicious. She pressed her finger on the table, collecting the crumbs dropped from the corn muffin.

"Care for some coffee?" Mr. O'Brien asked, his mouth full of food. Bizzie nodded. "Yes, please."

He stood and peeked into the black, cast-iron kettle that hung beside the coal-fired range. Seeing that there was still water inside, he set it on the stove. Then, he reached for a tin canister of coffee and set that on the counter. He lumbered back over to the table and sat down next to Bizzie. He placed his hands on the table and yawned. Bizzie, seeing this as a chance to get some answers for her story, dove in.

"Mr. O'Brien, have you been working here for a while?" she began.

"For the last twenty years," he replied proudly. "I started as Dr. Hartman's clerk."

Bingo. Bizzie tried not to show her excitement.

Mr. O'Brien walked back over to the stove. Wrapping a tea towel around the kettle handle, he poured the hot water into two pewter teacups. Then, he scooped the instant coffee into each cup.

"You like cream and sugar?" he asked, walking to the pantry to collect the sugar tin.

"Yes, please," she said.

He brought the teacups over to the table and sat down.

"Dr. Hartman," Bizzie said, feigning puzzlement. "I've heard his name."

"Heard his name, filly?" Mr. O'Brien nearly spat out his coffee. "I hope you've heard his name. He's only the best doctor in the state." He gestured to the kitchen. "And he built all this."

"How could one man build a practice—and center—like this?" Bizzie asked, taking a sip of her coffee. It tasted thick, tar-like. But she was thirsty after the veal and cornbread and slurped it down.

"Well, he was a newcomer to the Midwest—like me. He was born in New York. Went to medical college there." He took a sip of his steaming coffee. "Heard there was a shortage of doctors here in the Midwest. Moved out here and started a small country clinic. Made house calls on his trusty horse, Wilson. Then, folks from St. Paul started to hear about Dr. Hartman, the good doctor from New York. They'd travel down the Minnesota River to see him. Eventually, he had enough money saved up to build a modest building. And," he sat back in his chair proudly, "hire a few folks. That's when I started working for him."

He took another sip of coffee and scratched his whiskered chin. "Of course, back then there were no bells and whistles like there are today. It was just me and him. I helped him with the cooking and cleaning and ushering patients in the door."

"You must know him well," Bizzie noted.

"Like the back of my hand," he replied.

"How did he turn the clinic into a health center like this?"

"Well, he didn't. The tornado did."

Bizzie wasn't pretending now—she was truly curious. "A tornado?"

"Aye. A terrible day. I remember it like it was yesterday." He rubbed his eyes and took another sip of coffee. "I'm still hungry. You want more veal?"

Bizzie was anxious to hear more of the story, but she didn't want to come off as pushy. "No, thanks. Coffee is fine."

He shrugged and limped over to the icebox, pulling out another veal cut wrapped in parchment paper. Then he lumbered back to the table and sat down, the chair groaning.

"Where were we?" he asked, biting off a huge chunk of meat.

"The tornado," Bizzie said, a bit impatiently. Then, kinder, "I think you were going to tell me about that day."

"Ah, yes. It was late August. The sky was three different shades of nasty. Black, green, and a swirling gray." He shuddered. "Never saw anything like it. The whole day had been hot. At about six o'clock that night, Dr. Hartman got a call about a woman in labor. He gathered his bag and was about to ride off on Wilson. I remember looking at the sky and warning him. I said, 'Doc, I don't like the look of that sky.' Doc looked up for a minute before waving me off and riding toward town. I went back inside to tidy up from the day when I heard a noise like a freight train. I rushed back outside and saw the Doc riding towards me hollering, 'She's a twister! She's a twister!'

"Now," he paused and slurped down a swallow of coffee, "when Doc built the clinic, he didn't add anything more than a hand-dug root cellar, but boy were we grateful for that cellar then." He paused, shook his head, and closed his eyes. Bizzie thought about her time hiding in the cellar with Ruth. "Aye, I'll never forget that sound. It was a roar. A howl, even." A deep breath. "Then, just like that, it was over. I'll never forget the look on Doc's face when we crawled out of the cellar. The clinic was flattened."

Mr. O'Brien stopped talking and took a deep, heavy breath. He shook his head and stared at nothing in particular. Bizzie waited for him to continue, but when he didn't, she offered, "That must have been traumatic. For you both."

"Things started to change after that," he said, still looking away. "Businessmen from St. Paul started coming down and talking to him, offering to construct state-of-the-art buildings in exchange for his research. He stopped interacting with his staff…and me."

As if remembering where he was and who he was talking to, he smiled weakly at Bizzie. "I'm probably boring you with these old stories." He offered her a little smile and took one last swig of coffee.

Then, he stood up and gently clapped his hands together. "On that note, I think it's time I go back to bed, lassie. An early morning." He nodded at Bizzie. "Good night."

Bizzie listened to the stomp-drag, stomp-drag of his footsteps down the wooden hallway. A door opened, then closed. She sat in silence for a minute, cementing the details he'd just shared. Then, she took one more sip of her now-cold coffee and brought both teacups to the counter. With one last look around, she slipped out the back door and returned to the bunkhouse.

Chapter 27

SOPHIE

"I DON'T WANT TO WAIT until Monday. Can we go over there now?" I begged.

Aaron eyed the crowded café. "I can't take off now." Then he added, "Let's go tomorrow after you're done with work."

I looked longingly at the map and nodded.

"I gotta help Lauren." He gestured at the coffee bar. "Are you going to hang out here and look through your notes?"

"I think I'll head home where I can Google stuff," I said, standing up. Aaron reached his arms out and curled me into a hug. He smelled like coffee and bacon. "Thanks again for your help with Wren," I said, handing Aaron the key card.

He nodded. "See you soon," he murmured into my ear. I shivered.

An hour later, I was curled up on my couch with my laptop, a lemon La Croix, and my notes. I started with what I knew. Morris Hartman was somehow collaborating with Mayor Palmer. I saw them exchange what were probably pictures of me in the alley at night. Then, we heard Hartman and someone else talking about a tunnel and evidence that were apparently inside the Oasis. I was followed by Palmer's alleged personal hitman and city councilman, Walter Hollace.

Beyond that, I knew that Hartman's grandfather built the Oasis into a major medical center during its day. And now, it was set for either preservation or demolition. In public, Hartman appeared to want to save the building, but he seemed apathetic in private. A subsidiary of one of his companies, MH Manufacturing, owned the land surrounding the Oasis. And, just a few months prior, MH

Manufacturing sat in on a closed-door meeting with the mayor.

"Let's figure this out…" I whispered and opened the file folder I had taken from the mayor's office. Inside were several pieces of letterhead with the MH Manufacturing logo on top. I began reading.

February 17
Dear Morris,

You have the council's support to move forward with the demolition of the Oasis, currently owned by the town of Crab Orchard. In return, the council will receive $100,000 in tax revenue in the fiscal year. Each year following, the council expects to gain 12% of steel mill profits.

"What?" This made no sense. This letter was written in February. Four months ago. Why would Hartman come to the fundraiser, do the photo shoot, pretend to support the Oasis if all along he knew…

"No…" I shook my head. He knew all along. He and Mayor Palmer knew that none of the work Ida and the other preservationists were doing would ever come to fruition. The Oasis had been doomed all along.

"Bastard!" I said.

I pieced through the other paperwork. A tattered, yellowed, and torn newspaper clipping from The Duluth Tribune was crumpled in the back. It was dated June 10th, 1920. The headline took my breath away:

Beloved Dr. Hartman conceals hidden sanitarium; conducts experiments on real patients.

"What the hell?" I whispered. I flipped through the other papers in the file folder, searching for where this clipping might have come from. Nothing. It was like it appeared out of thin air.

I spent most of Monday following up on a libel lawsuit brought to News Now Online from Jansrud's team. All the while, I was anxious to get inside the Oasis again, especially after finding the old newspaper clipping. My mind was swirling.

"Nice work this weekend at the fundraiser," Jen said, walking by my desk and startling me.

"Thanks," I responded. "It was fun, huh? I hope we brought some attention to the preservation efforts." Even though it'll do no good, I thought bitterly.

Jen nodded, setting down her luxurious shoulder bag on my desk.

"Oh, this is yummy," I crooned, touching the leather.

Jen flashed me a smile. "You like?"

I nodded. "Is this Hermes?"

She grinned and raised her eyebrows. "You know it."

"Oh, I love this so much," I said, eyeing the smooth, chocolate-brown leather and gold clasp. *They must pay her a lot more than they pay me*, I thought, remembering her Tiffany & Co. "Love" earrings.

"So, who's that cute guy I saw you chatting with? You two seemed pretty into each other." Jen smiled and winked.

My cheeks flushed. "Oh, he's—he's a friend."

Jen raised her eyebrows. "Uh-huh. A friend. Sure," she said, drawing out the word.

"Hey, Jen," I said. "On Saturday night, I—"

"Yeah?" Jen replied. Something about her intensified gaze stopped me from continuing that sentence—that Aaron and I had seen Morris and Mayor Palmer in the alley after the fundraiser. And then later that night, I'd been followed.

"Um, on Saturday night after the fundraiser, Aaron and I shared a glass of wine. So, maybe there is something between us," I smiled and shrugged. "But who knows?"

Her relaxed expression returned, and she smiled. "Well, you guys make a cute couple." She knocked twice on my desk and added, "Good work. I had fun."

After several failed Google attempts to locate anything more about the mysterious *Duluth Tribune* clipping, I decided to spend my lunch break at the downtown public library, despite the fact that I hadn't set foot inside a library in years. I didn't even have a library card.

I walked the four blocks and breezed into a crowded lobby. A sculpture of a child reading was on my left. A floor-to-ceiling light fixture was on my right. A few teenagers hung out on the couches and chairs, reading and scrolling through their phones. I made my way to a desk with a sign hanging above it that said, "Research Desk." Behind a computer sat a woman in her fifties focusing on something. Her hair—a mix of white and blonde—was cut into a chic bob.

"Excuse me," I said, just above a whisper. She looked up and smiled, then pulled on her red-framed glasses.

"Sorry, didn't see you there," she said. "How can I help?"

I pulled out the brittle newspaper clipping and set it on the counter between us. "Yes. I am doing a bit of research and came across this clipping," I said, sliding it closer to her. "But I couldn't find any more information."

The woman gingerly lifted the clipping. "Wow," she said, looking up at me and then back to the clipping. "Where did you find this?"

"Uh, it was tucked into some other papers I've been combing through," I said. Then added, "I'm a reporter working on a story."

She nodded and scrunched her face for a moment. "Let's start over here," she said, leading me to a computer nestled inside a cubicle. She motioned for me to sit and stood behind me. I pulled the plastic chair up to the computer and followed her lead.

She scanned her card against a small box next to the computer and the screen lit up.

"Ok, this is our historical database," she said. "Start here." She pointed to a book icon with a link that said, "Library Database." I clicked on that, which led me to a menu of research options.

"I think your best option is to look here first," she said, pointing to a newspaper icon. I clicked on it and the browser quickly showed the Minnesota Digital Newspaper Hub.

"Now...," she said, taking off her glasses and letting them hang around her neck. "Click on this link—the 'Search Newspapers' link."

I followed her directions. Another menu of options. This, though, gave me specific search ranges: title, year published, month published, city.

"Click on the search bar and begin typing in dates, events, anything that could lead you to learn more about that newspaper article." She pointed at my clipping.

I typed in the exact title and a second later, the clipping that I held in my hand popped up on the screen. There weren't any other results from any other newspapers, though.

Why had no other papers—other than The Duluth Tribune—picked this story up?

I squinted to find the date the story was published: June 10th, 1920. I punched in that date plus or minus a couple weeks and hit Enter. A long list of results popped up from varying newspapers. The headlines differed a bit, but all rang out one message:

Dr. Hartman releases miracle vaccine against deadly disease.

Chapter 28

BIZZIE

THE NEXT FEW DAYS tested Bizzie's endurance and mental stability. Each morning, she'd arrive at the kitchen at six a.m. where Mrs. Mason would immediately begin barking orders. "Grab those eggs. Pour the sugar. Not like that! Like this!" She muttered flippant comments under her breath about Bizzie being only slightly more helpful than a monkey.

Mr. O'Brien popped his head into the kitchen. "Excuse me, Mrs. Mason?" he said. "There's a delivery here for you. Box loads of some clover and," he looked down at a piece of paper, "goldenseal. Not sure what you'll use that for, but no doubt it'll be delicious." He winked at me.

"Goldenseal?" Mrs. Mason shrieked. "What the dickens? I didn't order any goldenseal. That's cow's food. Lord Almighty." She handed me the whisk and told me to continue beating the egg whites while she looked at the paper Mr. O'Brien was holding.

"It says here, this needs to go to…Dr. Hartman," Mrs. Mason remarked. "Huh. The doc must be feeding cows, eh?" She cackled. Then she turned to look at Bizzie who'd taken a break from whisking.

"You can't stop whisking! Even for one second." Mrs. Mason dumped the egg whites in the garbage while glaring at Bizzie. "That's it! I've had enough." Mrs. Mason ordered her out of the kitchen immediately.

Tears in her eyes, Bizzie stumbled back to the bunkhouse. Her hands were rough and raw from scrubbing dishes in ice-cold water. The tips of her fingers were scorched and sore from grabbing boiling-hot kettles. Her arms were weak and tired from lifting massive trays filled with plates of broiled steak, mashed potatoes, baked bean salad, and rhubarb pie. As much as she wanted to comply with Mr. Kavanaugh's assignment and investigate Dr. Hartman, she wasn't sure how much more of this she could endure.

Footsteps snapped her out of her thoughts, and she looked back to see Francine. She tried to wipe away the tears.

"You look terrible," Francine said, a slight smile on her lips. "I warned you, you know."

Bizzie shook her head and sniffed. "I can see why you call her Mrs. Misery, that's for sure."

Francine chuckled and nodded. She gestured to the gravel path. "Mind if I walk with you?" Bizzie nodded. Francine continued, "When I started here at the Oasis, I was assigned to Mrs. M too."

"You were?"

"Yep," she gestured to her limp arm at her side. "But it didn't take long for us all to realize that wouldn't work out." She paused for a beat, then laughed. It was the first time Bizzie remembered seeing her smile—or laugh.

"Then you were assigned to the laundry?" Bizzie asked, wiping her tired eyes.

Francine nodded. "It's fine for now. But," she nodded in the direction of the Grand Hall, "I want to become a nurse."

Bizzie's mouth dropped open. Francine? A nurse? She was about to voice her doubts when she remembered the receptionist at *The Journal*. The other male reporters. Everyone who doubted *her*. And then she remembered Elizabeth Quinlan on the bus. That spark had boosted her confidence when she was filled with doubts.

"I think you'd make a great nurse," Bizzie said.

"I think so, too," she said quietly. "After I was thrown off a horse—I was four years old—doctors said I should be sent away to a home for injured children. They said I'd never walk the same again. But a nurse spent time with me."

The two started walking toward the bunkhouse.

"Ellen. That was her name," Francine continued. "She helped me learn how to walk again. Then use this arm," she slightly raised her right arm. "This one," she tilted her head toward her left arm, "never worked again."

After hearing Francine share something so personal, Bizzie decided to take a chance and share her own dream.

As they climbed the steps to their bunkroom, she said, "I have a dream like yours too. Not a nurse, but…" She pulled her journal out

166 | **THE MUCKRAKER**

from under her pillow. Tucked inside was the newspaper clipping headlined *Poor Farm Conditions Terrible, Lodgers Deserve Better* from *The Minneapolis Journal.* She handed the clipping to Francine. "That's me. I wrote that."

"Holy smokes! That's you?" Francine looked from the newspaper clipping to Bizzie.

"Yes, that's me," Bizzie whispered. "My last assignment was at a poor farm. It was…" Bizzie paused, thinking back to the terrifying hours hiding in the root cellar waiting for Mrs. Hendry to reappear, "…an enlightening experience."

"I'll bet," Francine said, sounding impressed. "So, this is your next assignment, huh?" She handed the clipping back to Bizzie, who placed it carefully in her journal.

"My editor got a tip that something's happening here," Bizzie said. "But, he didn't give me any details beyond that. And frankly, I'm not even sure where to begin." She looked at her hands then held them up to Francine. "And I'm not sure how much longer I can pretend I'm a cook."

Just then, the bunkroom door swung open. Francine and Bizzie jumped. They whirled around to see Louise standing there with a pile of laundry.

Francine eyed the laundry. "I have an idea."

Chapter 29

SOPHIE

"**What?**" **I whispered** to myself, more confused than ever. I shook my head. One newspaper was reporting that Dr. Hartman was experimenting on patients. Meanwhile, all the others reported that he'd found a miracle vaccine. Which one was right? I skimmed the clipping in my hand, searching for the journalist's name. I saw an 'E. Johansen' listed at the bottom.

I punched that name in the search bar and waited. One other article popped up: a three-part series about a county poor farm in rural Minnesota. I printed it off and walked back to News Now Online. On the way, my cell phone rang.

"Hey," I said, excited to see that it was Aaron. "Are you ready to explore?"

"Okay, don't be mad at me," Aaron said, sounding a bit sheepish.

"Okay…" I replied.

"I brought my stuff over—just intending to get set up. But I couldn't wait to check out that tunnel," he said.

"And?" I replied.

"I think you have to see it to believe it."

When I pulled up to the gate at the Oasis around six p.m., the chain had already been unhooked. I sped up the winding gravel, parked, and jumped out of my car.

Aaron met me outside.

"I'm dying to find out what you found."

He grabbed my hand. "Wait until you see this. It's going to blow your mind."

He led me through the front door and punched the flashlight app on his phone. I looped my arm through his and held on tight, dancing around the mushy ground. He led me upstairs, down to the end of the hall and back into the small, now-familiar office.

Aaron pulled the map out of his back jeans pocket.

"This is where the tunnel starts," he said, shining his light over the map. "You were right about this being a hidden wall." He pointed to the crack in the ceiling above us. "And I found this." He crouched down and pointed to a black statue of a collie, about the size of a fist. Aaron tilted it forward and the bookshelf swung open. It revealed a dark, brick hallway. I gasped.

"No way," I whispered, peeking my head inside. "A hidden tunnel." My jaw dropped.

"You were right," Aaron said, smiling at me. "And it gets crazier." Aaron shined his light into the dark, open space. "You want to see what's down there?"

Chapter 30

BIZZIE

BIZZIE FILLED LOUISE IN on what she was really doing at the Oasis. From there, a plan began to form. Francine and Louise approached Mr. O'Brien and persuaded him to transfer Bizzie from the kitchen to the laundry. Apparently, Mrs. Mason wouldn't stop complaining about the new kitchen recruit. Mr. O'Brien gladly complied.

Grateful for a friendlier mentor, Bizzie followed Louise from the Grand Hall to the laundry room to the kitchen. She curtsied when Louise did, smiled when Louise did, spoke when Louise did, and shut up when Louise did.

When Louise brought clean linens to the medical clinic, Bizzie followed along. The space smelled of vanilla and antiseptic—an unusual smell, but not an unpleasant one. The nurses greeted Louise by name and thanked her for the daily delivery of towels and bed sheets.

"We'll drop these towels off in the spa and then change linens in the bedrooms in the Grand Hall," Louise said, leading Bizzie out of the clinic. Then she whispered, "We could catch a glimpse of Dr. Hartman. His office is up there." She pointed to a window on the second floor of the Grand Hall. Bizzie tucked that detail away.

The girls were given a brief break for lunch of boiled chicken and crusty bread in the kitchen under Mrs. Mason's watchful eye.

"Is this work a bit easier for ya, then?" she asked with a smirk on her face.

"She's doing great," Louise jumped in.

After lunch, the girls hustled in all directions of the campus, carrying towels, changing linens, and delivering afternoon tea. That night, as they climbed into bed under their scratchy blankets, Bizzie bided her time. Her deadline was fast approaching. She needed evidence to show that Dr. Hartman was doing more than just research. She closed her eyes and retraced her steps from earlier in the day, memorizing the path she'd take as soon as she heard snoring. Within minutes, Bizzie heard quiet snores coming from the surrounding beds. She crept down from her bunk and snuck to the door. With a glance back to make sure no one heard her footsteps, she disappeared down the stairs.

She crept into the back door of the Grand Hall just like she and Louise had done earlier that day. Only this time, it was raining. She gently removed her boots so she wouldn't leave any tracks. The halls were silent. The cigar lounge was dark and shadowy. She crept along, hugging the side of the wall. Up the staircase with the ironwork and down the hall she tiptoed. Unlike earlier in the day, Dr. Hartman's office was dark. She grasped the cold, metal doorknob and turned. Locked.

"Darn," she muttered under her breath. Just then, she heard a giggle behind her. She gasped and turned around. Louise stood just a few feet away, her eyes twinkling in the dark.

"Louise," Bizzie put a hand on her beating heart. "Did you follow me here? I thought everyone was sleeping."

Louise shrugged. "You let the door slam when you left the girls' floor."

Bizzie gestured toward Dr. Hartman's door and shrugged guiltily. "I need more information about what's going on—*if* there really is *something* going on. Because so far, I haven't found anything."

"Well, then, it's a good thing I have this," she held up a cast iron skeleton key.

Bizzie's mouth dropped open. "Where did you get that?"

Louise shrugged. "I'm a housemaid, remember?" She shoved it in the lock. "I keep it in my side-lacer," she said, pointing to her chest.

Bizzie shook her head. "Of course you do."

After a beat, Louise had the door unlocked. With no light from the moon, the office was cloaked in darkness. Louise produced a candlestick, matches, and brass taper. She lit the candle, peeked in the office, and jerked her head back at Bizzie, indicating the office was clear to enter.

"Just what are you looking for?" Louise whispered, her candle flame illuminating the space. A spotless desk sat in the corner framed by a massive window that overlooked the Minnesota River. Two wooden chairs faced the desk. A crammed bookshelf lined two of the walls. The remaining wall was filled with framed diplomas and photographs.

"Not sure," Bizzie replied, her heart pounding. At any moment, she was sure someone was going to jump out of the shadows. "Some kind of evidence. Something that proves Dr. Hartman is part of something…or covering something up…" Her voice trailed off as she opened the drawers of the massive desk. Louise began looking through the books on the shelves.

"Anything?" Bizzie asked, walking toward Louise after her pursuit of the desk proved fruitless.

Louise shrugged. "Not unless you care about woodworking." She gestured to the bookshelf. "There's a whole shelf here devoted to it. Seems strange to me."

Bizzie took the candle from Louise, knelt down beside the bookshelf, and began to move some of the books around. A steel collie—no bigger than her teacup at breakfast—sat on the shelf. Bizzie didn't think much of it when she tried to move it aside. Only, the dog didn't move—it seemed bolted to the shelf. She tugged at it again, but it still didn't budge. Bizzie shrugged to herself and continued scanning the shelf.

"This is kind of cute," Louise said, tilting the collie statue forward. Suddenly, the bookshelf swung open.

Bizzie and Louise gasped and scattered to the other side of the room where they huddled together. Bizzie was both terrified and curious. Louise was shaking beside her.

"Oh my," Louise gaped. The bookshelf opened to a dark, brick tunnel. The girls gaped at each other. Bizzie tiptoed toward the opening and peeked her head through the hidden doorway. It led only to blackness.

She stared back at Louise, stunned.

"A cover up," she said, shaking her head. Then, when she caught her breath and her heartbeat slowed, she thought out loud. "A hidden door leading to…what?"

Louise was pale and stayed frozen in the corner of the office, as far away from the opening as possible. "I'm all for helping you get answers and report the truth, Bizzie, but I'm not going down there."

Bizzie had to admit, she wasn't so sure about venturing into the dark passageway herself. She shuddered, thinking about huddling in the dank root cellar with Ruth at the poor farm just days earlier.

"There's something hidden down there," Bizzie said. "I'm going to find out what it is."

"Alone?" Louise hissed. "We don't know what's down there."

"My job is on the line," Bizzie replied, still holding the candle.

"Your life could be too!" Louise urged. "Think about this for a minute. Is this really worth it?"

Bizzie thought about Hibbing. Sure, she could teach and live on the farm with Collin. But she wouldn't feel alive like this. She nodded once. "I'm going."

Louise seemed to understand. "Be careful, Bizzie." She gave her friend a quick squeeze and handed her an extra match.

Bizzie hugged the field stone-lined corridor as she carefully navigated the uneven steps. Her footsteps echoed against the walls. The air felt damp and cold. After twenty or thirty steps, the wall seemed to open to a larger space. Bizzie felt her claustrophobia ease. She held up the candle and wondered if it could be nothing more than a storage room or cellar. Then, she heard a noise like a soft whisper. She crept along the side of the room until she felt a doorknob. She turned it and creaked open the door.

Chapter 31

SOPHIE

I grabbed Aaron's arm so tightly I'm pretty sure I left marks. The dark, shadowy hallway smelled musty and felt damp. He punched the flashlight app on his phone to illuminate our way. Our footsteps echoed off the stone, brick walls. I was too enthralled to say anything. Aaron seemed to be growing more and more confident with each quickened step. I gladly let him lead the way. The tunnel opened up to a large, open room.

"I set up my camera here," Aaron said, "but a door behind me caught my eye. So, I explored further. And this is where it gets really interesting." Carefully, he pushed open a splintered, water-stained door to reveal another room. This one was completely different from the open space. It was smaller and felt cramped. The walls were crumbling and the floor buckling.

I thought back to the newspaper clipping written by E. Johansen. *The hidden sanitarium*, I thought.

There was evidence of it all around us. Rusted shells of bed frames, sans mattresses, were lined up side-by-side against one of the walls. Broken, jagged glass tubes and vials were tipped over at a dusty workstation. I stood looking around with a hand over my mouth.

"Did no one know about this?" I shook my head. "How could this have gone on, literally right under people's noses?"

"What do you think went on here?" Aaron asked.

I pulled out the newspaper clipping from *The Duluth Tribune* and held it in front of his phone light.

"What?" Aaron glanced up at me from the clipping. "But..." his

174 | **THE MUCKRAKER**

voice trailed off.

"Hartman had money. He had power. He discovered some big breakthroughs in medicine. At least, that's what everyone believes around here. And Ida's brochures seem to back that up."

I paused. "Ida. That's who we need to talk to. Her grandmother worked for Dr. Hartman. If anyone would know about this, it'd be her." I shivered again, taking one more look at the dark, shadowy room, curious and haunted about what exactly went on there. "I wonder…I wonder if Ida's grandmother knew the writer," I pointed at the clipping, "who published this story."

"This could explain why Morris wants this place torn down," Aaron offered. I nodded. "Let me just grab my tripod." He pointed up a small window in the corner of the dark room.

"Is that safe?" I squinted at Aaron as he set up a rusty ladder. "And where'd you find that ladder?"

He shrugged. "I'm good at finding stuff. Besides, I used this ladder earlier. This window leads right to the back parking lot where I parked my truck. Saves me from going through the entire building."

I laughed. "If you say so." A thought crossed my mind. "Aaron, I'm sure these photos are going to be amazing. Once they run in the magazine, you're going to get notoriety for bringing these to light. But," I stammered as I climbed up the ladder toward the parking area, "do you mind keeping this discovery between us? Just for now?"

Aaron held the ladder for me. "You think I'd want to miss all the fun you're going to bring to this? I'm just going to sit back and watch what happens next."

Together, we grabbed his tripod and climbed back down the ladder into the dark, shadowy room. I shivered as I helped Aaron adjust his lighting. I moved rickety bed frames in and out of shots. I lined up glass tubes and vials I found on the dusty counters. All the while, questions pinged through my brain. And I knew who might have the answers.

As we crawled out of the Oasis after Aaron was done shooting, I pulled out my phone and punched in Ida's number.

"Hello?" Ida answered. I explained that I had some questions and wondered if we could meet. Meanwhile, Aaron headed to the Coffee Fox to help with the dinner rush. Becoming more familiar with Crab Orchard, I didn't need my phone's GPS system to direct me to Kelly's Bar. I found a parking spot and grabbed the only open table on the patio. The sun was setting, and I was grateful I had thrown an extra sweatshirt into my car.

A minute later, a waitress wearing a black apron showed up with a glass of ice water and a worn, plastic menu.

"Hey," she said. "Just you today?"

"No, a friend is joining me," I said, smiling at her. After I ordered a glass of moscato, Ida walked in and scanned the patio for me.

"Hi!" I said, standing and giving her a quick hug. "Thanks for coming."

"How are you?" she asked, scooting her chair toward the table. She opened the menu. I chattered about work and Aaron while she looked through the options. I could barely keep in the bombshell we'd just discovered. Our waitress came back with my wine and a water for Ida. We ordered a few appetizers, and Ida ordered a glass of the house red. As soon as the waitress walked away, I nearly exploded.

"Ida, Aaron and I found something in the Oasis," I blurted out, grabbing her hand.

She tore the paper off her straw and looked at me quizzically. "Found something?" She chuckled and took a sip of her water.

"Something I don't think we were supposed to find," I said, leaning in toward her. I explained that Aaron had stumbled across what appeared to be a hidden sanitarium during his photo shoot. Then, I pulled out the newspaper clipping and pressed it against the table. "It all comes together. But why has no one discovered this before?" My words tumbled out. "I knew there was something going on. I just didn't have enough evidence to prove it."

Ida looked at me oddly. "What do you mean, you knew something was going on?"

"What?" I asked. "Oh, just that it seemed clear that…I mean, I thought Morris Hartman was…I figured that…" my words drifted off as Ida stared at me, unblinking. I bit my bottom lip.

"You used me for your story, didn't you?" Ida stiffened. She shook her head. "Oh, all this time I thought you were one of the only reporters who really cared." She closed her eyes and clenched her hand that sat atop the table. "Oh, how silly of me. Of course a reporter from Minneapolis isn't going to be concerned with our little preservation effort."

"Ida, no. That's not it at all!" I reached out for her hand, but she snatched it away. A couple sitting at the nearby table looked at us. Quieter, I said, "I mean, I'll admit, at first, I was digging a bit for my story. But then Aaron and I got involved, and we care about this. We really do."

"Are you just using that poor boy for your story too? Because I think he likes you," Ida pursed her lips.

"Aaron? No! I like him…I mean, wait, you think he likes me too?" I quickly shook my head. "Doesn't matter. Ida, you have to believe me. We want to help you. And trust me, this discovery could really help the preservation effort."

Ida shook her head and sighed. "I have to go visit my mother." She stood up, threw a twenty down, and stormed off the patio.

Chapter 32

BIZZIE

DIMLY LIT BY ONE SMALL CANDLE, Bizzie took in what she was before her: twelve beds—two rows of six beds each—lining the two walls. And in each bed was a child. Bizzie gasped. She backed away, horrified. The candlelight flickered, revealing a glint in a child's somber gaze that stopped Bizzie from running back the way she came.

"Help...help me," he groaned. He tried to sit up, but his frail body wouldn't allow that. At that moment, Bizzie knew taking a step forward toward the boy meant she couldn't back out. She'd get too involved. This is what Dr. Hartman had been hiding. This is why Mr. Kavanaugh sent her here. Bizzie swallowed her fear. She tried to ignore her racing heart. She took a step forward.

"How can I help?" she whispered, grabbing his cold and clammy hand. His skin was the color of the towels Bizzie and Louise had delivered around the campus that morning.

"Sam," he said, pointing to himself. "Trapped," he gulped. Then, he pointed to a body at the end of the row. "Ella. My sister. Needs help." He wilted into the mattress.

"What?" Bizzie prompted. "She needs what?" But he'd already closed his eyes.

Bizzie looked at the body at the end of the row. She walked softly past the rest of the sleeping children, trying to regulate her breathing and stay calm. When she approached the last bed, she peeked at the child lying on the pillow. A girl lay there—about ten years old. Immediately, Bizzie thought of Sloane and Leon, and her heart ached. The child's skin sagged on her thin frame, and dark circles hung under her closed eyes. Each time she let out a breath, a high-pitched hiss escaped from her. Bizzie reached out a hand and gently tapped her shoulder. No response. She tried again, this time with more vigor. Still nothing. Bizzie glanced back at the boy who spoke. He watched her with pleading eyes and nodded slightly. His lips moved as if he was trying to tell her something.

Bizzie looked around frantically. She walked over to a brown cabinet against the wall behind the girl. The shelves were lined with white towels and small notebooks. Bizzie reached for the top notebook. It was labeled Patient A. She looked back at the two rows of children— who she was beginning to understand weren't sleeping. They were either sedated or extremely sick. Both possibilities made her stomach churn. She swallowed hard, turned back, and flipped the notebook open. The entries were short and written neatly in black ink. Each entry had a date attached.

4/19/1920 Patient A was given one dose.

Bizzie's finger followed the entries onto the next page.

4/12/1920 Patient A was given four doses.
4/5/1920 Patient A was given six doses.
3/30/1920 Patient A was given eight doses.
3/23/1920 Patient A was given four doses.

Bizzie looked back at the boy. He nodded. Immediately, Bizzie knew who could help. She placed the notebook back on the shelf and squeezed the boy's hand. Then she turned toward the tunnel, but the boy didn't let go of her hand. Instead, he gripped it tighter, and with his other hand, tried to point to the corner of the room.

"Small door," he whispered. "Safer."

Bizzie looked to where he pointed and saw a crawl space. A ladder shot up to the open air. Bizzie glanced back at the boy, who nodded at her. She blew out her candle and crawled up the ladder. Bizzie worried for Louise who was waiting for her in the small office. But she knew who she needed to find first. After ten or so steps, Bizzie was above ground behind the Oasis. She had passed the cellar several times that day alone, but the opening was so inconspicuous that she would never have known it was there. She raced to the bunkhouse. Taking the stairs to the girls' floor two at a time, she found Francine in her bed, snoring softly.

"Francine!" Bizzie hissed, trying not to wake anyone else. "Francine! Wake up!"

Francine groaned and squinted at Bizzie, then rolled over. "Still dark out. Too early to get up."

"I need your help," Bizzie pleaded. "Francine, please."

Francine must have heard the urgency in Bizzie's voice because she rubbed her eyes and sat up.

"Okay..." she said, groggily.

Bizzie grabbed Francine's hand. "Come with me." She pulled Francine through the bunkhouse and across campus. Together, they crept along the back side of the Oasis until Bizzie found the cellar window buried beneath shrubs and bushes.

"Kids are being drugged. Or...something..." Bizzie shivered, remembering the look on the frail girl's face. "But I don't have the knowledge...I don't know why those kids are there."

Francine gaped and shook her head. "What?"

"Something is wrong. These kids...they don't look normal."

Francine shook her head, confused. "Kids are being drugged?" Bizzie pulled her arm, hoping Francine would follow her down the ladder.

"But wait," Francine stopped. "What if someone checks at night... or a night nurse..."

Bizzie hadn't stopped to think about that. She shook her head, brushing the fear away. Brushing even her story away too, for now. Lives were at stake.

"These kids need our—your—help," Bizzie gulped. "Please, Francine."

Francine nodded once and silently followed Bizzie down the ladder. Once inside the sanitarium, Bizzie used the extra match Louise had given her to light the candle.

After a moment, Bizzie said, "What do you think? What is going on here?"

Francine pinched her lips together and walked to the shelves of notebooks. "Patient A?" Francine said incredulously. She looked at the children lying in the beds. Then, she opened one of the cupboards. Syringes and needles neatly lined the shelves. Without missing a beat, she reached for one and examined it. Then she opened another cupboard and began inspecting the contents.

Bizzie couldn't stand the wait any longer. "What are you looking for?"

Francine was quiet for a few moments. Then, she said, "I heard a rumor when I first started here. A rumor that Dr. Hartman was experimenting on children. But," she turned to face Bizzie, "I just assumed that's what they told all the new girls." She motioned to her arm. "Especially girls with an arm that doesn't work." She paused and chewed on her lip. "But this…seeing this…" Her voice trailed off. She took a jar out of the cupboard. It was filled with a green substance that looked like paint. Francine unscrewed the cover and took a sniff. Bizzie held her breath, expecting Francine to recoil in response to the green goo. But she bit the corner of her lip and squinted, as if trying to remember something. Then, she sniffed again.

Bizzie peered at her. "What? What is it?"

Francine shook her head. "I don't know. It smells like clover. It's some kind of plant, I think." She held it up for Bizzie, who breathed it in. Francine was right. It did smell like clover. Bizzie envisioned cows munching on a meadow of clover. Then, she stopped and gasped. Cows. A meadow. Collin's farm…the dead cow.

"I know what this is," Bizzie gasped. "It's goldenseal. It's a plant." She thought back to the day Mrs. Mason received a delivery of goldenseal by mistake. That clover was not meant for the kitchen. It was meant for here—this sanitarium. Bizzie's words tumbled out. "Poisonous. In large doses."

Francine ran a hand through her brown hair. "Goldenseal," she said and began pacing. "That would make sense. I read about it in the library's medical section. Too much goldenseal," she bit her lip and closed her eyes in concentration, "can lead to paralysis. Even death." Then, she turned to Bizzie with a furrowed brow. "But why?"

Bizzie gritted her teeth. "I wonder…" her voice trailed off as she lined up the facts tumbling through her mind. She remembered the smell of Collin's mother's tea and the feeling of a chill fever fleeing. "Goldenseal can be used to treat fevers and colds," she said and held out one hand. Then, she held out another hand. "And my editor told me that Dr. Hartman studied under some famous physician who experimented with herbs," she said. "Do you think Dr. Hartman is trying to figure out a new herbal medicine?" She locked eyes with Francine.

"Yes. That's it," Francine said. "He is testing the doses on them." She gestured to the lines of beds. "Which explains why they're basically comatose."

"Very good," came a steely voice. Bizzie gasped and jumped back. There, standing in the shadows was a tall, thin man with gray eyes and wavy brown hair. His brown trousers were held up by suspenders, and the sleeves of his white shirt were rolled up.

"But you're missing an essential part of the story," he said and took a few steps toward Bizzie, who stood frozen where she was. Francine backed into the corner. "These kids," he casually waved a hand in the direction of the rows of beds, "are no one. Orphans. They have no families. No one even knows their names," he paused. Then, with a smirk, he continued. "And yet, I'm giving their lives meaning. Because of them, thousands of other lives will be saved." His eyes shone in the flicker of Bizzie's candle flame. "I'm giving them a voice. I'm making their lives count." He walked over to the counter where goldenseal was sitting in the jar. "This," he picked up the jar in his hand, "will be available in the form of a tablet. And with just a few tablets, diseases that once would have wiped out an entire town will be cured." Bizzie looked at the rows of beds with languid children in them.

"You're wrong," her voice shook. He looked at her with questioning eyes. "These children do have names. That girl is Ella. And he," she pointed to the boy who'd first caught her attention, "is Ella's brother, Sam." She took a step closer to Dr. Hartman. "They might not come from wealth or fancy homes or even have parents," she said, thinking of Leon living at the poor farm, "but they do have names, and people do love them, and they deserve to be treated better than this." She spat out the words and stood belligerent.

Dr. Hartman tilted his head. "What did you say your name was?"

For the first time, Bizzie felt scared. She felt the anger float away and, in its place, was fear.

"Bizzie," she replied, her lips trembling.

Dr. Hartman nodded. "Ah, yes. Bizzie. I've heard about you." Bizzie heard a squeak inside the tunnel. Dr. Hartman heard it too. "Come on in," he said. "Show Bizzie who you are."

Bizzie heard footsteps and turned to see Louise standing in the shadows.

"I believe you two know each other?" Dr. Hartman asked. Bizzie covered her mouth with her hands.

Francine gasped. "Louise, no," she whispered. "You told him?"

Tears fell from Louise's eyes. A sob escaped her. "I'm so sorry," she mumbled as she crumpled to her knees, clutching herself. "I'm so sorry."

Chapter 33

SOPHIE

I waved over the waitress at Kelly's and asked her if she'd box up our appetizers. I told her I'd be back to pick them up later. Then, I rushed out of the restaurant. A quick Google search provided the name for the only assisted living facility in town—St. Therese—and the address. I zipped through town and parked my Kia in the near-empty lot. Then, I bolted through the front door.

"Hello," I greeted the woman at the front desk breathlessly, who seemed preoccupied with the latest issue of *People Magazine*. "I'm wondering if my friend might be here visiting her mother. My friend's name is Ida." I waited anxiously as the woman checked a visitor logbook.

"Looks like she's here," she noted without looking at me. "Ida's mother is in room 204, just down the hall to the left." She handed me a form to read and sign. I swapped that for a visitor badge. Before she could question further, I darted down the hall.

When I found room 204, I gently knocked. I could hear Ida talking. "Come in," she called.

"Ida," I said gingerly. "It's me." Then, I quickly added, "Please don't be mad."

Ida pursed her lips and shook her head. "How dare you follow me here? This is my mother's home."

I couldn't see Ida's mother; she was lying in bed facing the opposite direction. I heard her ask Ida what was going on. "Nothing," Ida muttered. "Absolutely nothing."

Ida marched over to me. "You have exactly three seconds to scoot out of here. Otherwise, I'll call security. And the police."

"The police?" Ida's mother hollered. "Oh hell. Don't call the police. They'll bring me in."

"Mother, this isn't about you!" Ida shouted back. I stifled a laugh.

"Please, Ida. Let me explain. Give me five minutes. After that, if you never want to see me again, I'll walk out these doors and leave Crab Orchard," I pleaded. I had to make this right. "I promise. Just five minutes."

Ida looked back at her mother, then at me. She shook her head and sighed. "Five minutes," she said sternly. She told her mother she'd be back and led me to an empty lounge. We sat down in plastic blue chairs.

"Time starts now," Ida said, crossing her arms.

I started from the beginning. I explained how I had a gut feeling Morris Hartman was trying to hide something. I told her how I'd dug deeper into the proposed demolition—both in my follow-up call and at the press conference. Then, I explained what Aaron and I had seen in the shadows after the fundraiser. I told her about the city council meeting minutes I'd found—that the demolition date had already been set. And lastly, I shared with her what Aaron had found—the hidden sanitarium.

"I think it all adds up. Morris knew his grandfather performed those experiments. As a cover-up, he's been working to acquire the property from the city and then have the buildings demolished. That way, no one will ever learn the truth." I sat back. "That's why he didn't comment about the demolition. Because he was hoping no one would ever even question him about it."

Ida leaned toward me and gently picked up the newspaper clipping I had brought with me. Then, she shook her head. "I don't believe this," she whispered. "They already agreed to demolish the building?" To herself, she added, "And we worked so hard. Oh, I was so stupid. Why else would Mr. Hartman be supporting a little cause like ours?" She scowled.

"Because he never really was supporting it," I replied. Our eyes met.

Ida gripped the newspaper clipping. "I've seen this before," she said. "In my grandmother's journal."

"What?" After a moment, I gently squeezed her hand. "What is it?" I asked again softly.

Ida turned to me, tears glistening in her eyes. "As Grandma got older, her memory started to fade. That's around the same time she

184 | THE MUCKRAKER

started talking about her days working for Dr. Hartman." Ida pointed to the newspaper clipping. "She used to say things like, 'Bizzie was right, you know.' And, 'It's not right, what they did.'"

My mind was spinning. "So, your grandmother knew something about this," I said and patted the clipping with my finger. "Wait, who—who is Bizzie?"

"I never met Bizzie. Apparently, she and my grandmother were good friends." Ida picked up the clipping, slipped on her glasses, and viewed it carefully. A minute later she took off her glasses and looked at me. "This is Bizzie," she said, sliding the article toward me. "E. Johansen. Elizabeth Johansen. Bizzie, short for Elizabeth."

Chapter 34

BIZZIE

"Uh, Bizzie?" came Dr. Hartman's steely voice. "A word?" His eyebrows were raised, but he appeared otherwise perfectly calm.

"No, please!" Louise pleaded, sobbing on the floor. "I'm so sorry, Bizzie! I didn't know...I shouldn't have..."

"Tsk, tsk," Dr. Hartman waved a finger in Louise's direction. "It's too late for that. You run along. You've done your job." He shooed a hand in Francine and Louise's direction. Bizzie thought she might be sick. A whoosh of heat overwhelmed her, and she began to sweat.

"Please, Dr. Hartman," Louise pleaded, while Francine helped her up from the floor. "She didn't mean any harm. Please let Bizzie go."

In a resolute voice, he said, "I said go. Now."

Francine's eyes were as wide as saucers. Louise bit her lip and shook her head in Bizzie's direction. Then, together, they disappeared through the dark tunnel.

Dr. Hartman smirked. Bizzie shuddered. He turned away from her and walked between the rows of children. He slowed at the end and turned back, making eye contact with Bizzie.

"Your journal, please?" he said, as if asking for a glass of milk.

"Excuse me?" Bizzie said, her voice catching.

He smiled. "The newest maid," he nodded. "That's good. What did you tell your friends at the county poor farm?"

Blood drained from Bizzie's face.

"That's right. I know who you are. Your little friend told me everything. An undercover journalist. A muckraker." He spat out that last word. He stopped at Ella's bed and suddenly pounded on the

186 | **THE MUCKRAKER**

iron frame with his fist. "Not in my house, you're not!" He shouted so loudly that Bizzie jumped. None of the children lying in their beds did, though. They didn't move. They couldn't move. "You hand over the journal immediately."

Bizzie could only gasp breath in small amounts. She was terrified. She swallowed hard. "And if I don't?"

He nodded to the jar of goldenseal on the counter. "Then, we'll find out for sure how much of that is too much." He nodded at Ella. "I've gotten close with this one. But she always manages to come back from the brink."

Bizzie couldn't stop herself. Her journalistic curiosity got the best of her. "I just don't understand. How can a man of medicine who is supposed to be saving lives also be destroying them?"

"I'm not destroying them; I'm giving their lives meaning. Their sacrifice will save others." He folded his hands behind his back and turned away from her for a few steps.

"Others like my brother. My twin, Pauly." He kept walking through the row of beds. "I'm not sure why we all called him Little Pauly. He was born twenty minutes before me and was three inches taller. Anyway," he waved a hand like that detail didn't matter, "every summer, we'd go fishing and swimming in the creek near our house. We'd sleep outside, map the constellations, and dream about becoming cowboys. One day," he chuckled, "older boys were picking on me. Pauly stepped in and told them to knock it off. They punched him square in the nose. Broke it in three places." He laughed and shook his head. Then, his voice changed.

"When Pauly was twelve, he got sick. Muscardine Fever. He was in quarantine for weeks. Mother kept saying he was going to get better. He never did. I never got to say goodbye to him. Died while I was at school one day." He frowned. "My father never was the same. Neither was Mother." He stopped pacing and turned to face Bizzie. "That's when I vowed that I'd find a way to cure diseases like that. So other little twelve-year-old boys don't have to lose their best friends and go through life alone."

Bizzie's voice was gentle. "I'm truly sorry for your loss. I nearly lost my Papa in a mining accident. I can't imagine not having him—in his chair, waiting for me to come home." She felt a lump in her throat, picturing her father. "But don't you see? This is wrong." She gestured around the room at Ella and her brother. "Let them grow up together. Let them have each other."

Dr. Hartman smiled and, for a second, Bizzie thought maybe he had a change of heart. "You must be a writer," he said, a smirk on his lips. "Always looking for a happy ending."

He sauntered over to her, his heels clicking and echoing against the stone walls. He stopped when he was inches from Bizzie's face. He bent down and locked eyes with hers.

"The journal?"

Bizzie glanced at Ella and swallowed hard. She heard the slap before she felt it. Her cheek felt like it was covered in bees, stinging her all at once. Her ear was ringing. She fell to her knees, one hand on her red cheek.

"I said give me the journal!" With a clenched jaw, Dr. Hartman spit in her face. Then he grabbed a handful of her brown hair and hissed.

Bizzie sniffed and pulled the journal out of her boot. She rubbed her thumb against the binding one time. That's when she noticed something she'd never seen before. On the cover, barely legible, was ink writing. Alice Hennings. Her mother. Her heart skipped a beat. This was her mother's journal! She'd always assumed the journal had been from Papa. But it was her mother's. A tear trickled down Bizzie's cheek. She held out the journal and Dr. Hartman snatched it away.

"Now what?" Bizzie rubbed her burning cheek.

Dr. Hartman smiled. "You'll have to wait and read the headlines," he said cryptically and winked. Bizzie's stomach dropped.

"For now, though, you run on back to your little friends and keep playing your little game. You're helping in the kitchen, right? No, no… you're a maid now, that's right." He smiled at her once more before turning back to the children. "Oh, and Bizzie? Don't get any ideas about publishing anything—even without your journal. I'd hate to read about a terrible accident in the kitchen that claimed the lives of two young maids," he said coldly. "And I suggest you leave the Oasis immediately. Or I'll make sure every paper in the country knows about a libelous journalist named Elizabeth Johansen. I doubt anyone will ever want to print anything written by her."

Bizzie stifled a gasp. She turned and ran through the tunnel, burst through the office door, and bolted through the Oasis. Tears flowed down her cheeks, but she didn't bother to wipe them away. She pushed the heavy door open and ran right into Louise and Francine.

"Bizzie!" Francine said. She grabbed Bizzie by the shoulders. "Are you hurt?"

Bizzie stared at Louise in disbelief. "Louise, all along you knew that

Dr. Hartman…"

"No!" Louise shook her head. "I swear. I didn't know what he was doing. I just—" she stopped.

"You just reveal what's going on with the staff," Francine finished, scowling. "And I trusted you!"

"I never told Dr. Hartman anything about you!" Louise sobbed, tears staining her face.

"No? Just new girls, huh?" Bizzie stomped toward the bunkhouse.

"Bizzie, wait! Where are you going?" Louise trailed after her.

"To call the police," Bizzie replied.

"You can't," Louise muttered. "They won't do anything."

"What?" Bizzie turned.

"They're on his side," Louise mumbled. "He pays them to keep quiet. He does his research in whatever way he wants and pays off the police. And nobody asks questions."

"So, you did know what Hartman was doing." Bizzie folded her arms across her chest.

"I'm so sorry, Bizzie," Louise whispered. "I don't know what to say."

Bizzie chewed on her lip and sniffed. "It's over," she wiped her nose. "It's all over. My career. The lives of those kids," she said with a gesture at the Grand Hall.

"Bizzie, no!" Louise grabbed Bizzie's arm. "Don't say that. Please!" She squeezed Bizzie's hand. "There has to be something we can do. Please, let me make this right."

Francine nodded and said in no more than a whisper, "Bizzie, those kids will die down there, and no one will ever know." She shook her head. "You can't let that happen."

"What am I supposed to do?" Bizzie flung her hands in the air. She looked at Francine and Louise.

When Francine spoke again, her voice was vehement. "A true medical professional does no harm. That's the first rule. I don't care if you can't or won't, but I must help those children."

For a moment, Bizzie was speechless. It was Louise who spoke first. "What do you suppose we do?"

"First of all, *you* will have nothing to do with this," Bizzie pointed to Louise. "You've done enough damage. Go run along to your little boss, now. I'm sure he's waiting for an update."

To Francine, Bizzie said, "The story may be dead, but those kids don't have to die with it. I have an idea."

Chapter 35

SOPHIE

THE PIECES STARTED TO CLICK together in my mind. Neither Ida nor I said anything for a moment. "We thought Grandma Francine was confused. We thought it was her dementia," Ida said, shaking her head. "Then, when I was going through her things, I came across her journal with this clipping. That's when I started to wonder..." her voice trailed off. "But no one seemed to know what I was talking about. Everyone looked at me like I was crazy. So, I put the journal away."

"What exactly did your grandmother talk about? And why do you think it took her so long to bring anything up?" I asked.

Ida took a deep breath. "She would say things like, 'Bizzie was right. But they threatened her. They made her stay silent.' Again, we didn't know what she was talking about."

"Who is 'they?'" I asked.

Ida shook her head. "I'm assuming Dr. Hartman." She shrugged, "I guess I don't know."

An idea popped into my head. "Ida, do you think your mother knows anything about this?"

Ida's eyes grew wide. It looked like she was about to speak and then she stopped herself. She hung her head. "I don't know," she muttered. "Her dementia..." her voice trailed off.

I grabbed her hand. "But it's worth a try. She must have *some* good times, right? Sometimes when her memory comes back?"

Ida bit her lip and nodded. She led me back to her mother's room. On the way, we passed a few men in wheelchairs sitting in front of a blaring television.

"Mom, I brought a friend," Ida said loudly, walking over to her mother's bedside. "This is Sophie."

Ida motioned for me to join her. I pulled a brown, plastic chair close to the bed. The room smelled stale and musty. To me, Ida said, "Sophie, this is my mother, Helen."

I smiled and nodded at Ida's mother. She was a delicate and frail woman. Thin white hair was matted on top of her head. The shades were drawn, and the room was shadowy. Ida pulled the curtains open just a bit, letting in a thin stream of light. She grabbed a Styrofoam cup and filled it with water from the bathroom sink. She returned a moment later and watered each of the plants scattered around her mother's room.

Ida's mother watched us with foggy eyes but didn't say a word.

"Mom, I brought Sophie here because she's working on a project. We thought you might be able to help us," Ida said loudly. Her mother simply stared at us.

I cleared my throat and said in a loud, clear voice, "Hello, Helen!" Ida gave me a thumbs-up.

Helen's eyes opened wide. She looked at me with a confused and cranky stare.

"Mom, Sophie found something," Ida said.

I gently reached for Helen's hand and pressed the brittle newspaper clipping into her palm. "This journalist, Elizabeth, er, Bizzie Johansen, writes about Dr. Hartman. She says that he experimented on real patients. She said—"

Ida cleared her throat. I glanced at her, and she motioned for me to slow down. I nodded.

"Do you know anything about this?" I asked.

Helen looked at me for a long moment. Then she motioned for Ida to hand her a cup of water. After a long swallow, she struggled to sit up. Ida adjusted the pillows behind her. With shaky hands, Helen reached for her plastic-rimmed glasses on her bedside table. Then, she brought the newspaper clipping to her nose and breathed in.

"Mom, what do you remember?" Ida asked, sitting up straighter on the side of Helen's bed. Helen closed her eyes.

"Mother had nightmares," Helen started, her voice quiet and crusty. "At the end, they got worse. We thought…everyone thought it was the dementia." She shook her head. "But I knew she was telling the truth." She took a raspy breath. "She was scared."

Ida leaned down. "What was she scared of, Mom?"

"Scared that, once she died, the truth would die too," Helen whispered.

Fearful we were pushing her too much, but desperate for the truth, I prompted her once more. "And what was the truth?"

Helen stuck a shaky, wrinkled finger at the newspaper clipping and nodded. "This is the truth."

My mind was reeling. The sanitarium—it had really been in operation. It was true. There was so much more I wanted to ask. So much more I needed to know, but Helen looked so tired.

"Ida," Helen whispered. Ida leaned down with wide eyes. Helen pointed to a wooden box the size of a loaf of bread sitting on her desk. Ida flitted to the desk and opened the box. She gently pulled out a tattered and fragile-looking leather journal and held it up for Helen to see. She nodded and wagged a finger, gesturing for Ida to bring it to her. Ida placed the journal in Helen's hands. With effort, she lifted that to her nose too, inhaled, and then nodded slightly. A moment later, Helen reached for me. She placed the journal in my hands and wrapped hers around mine. Without a word, she looked into my eyes, and I understood. I opened the journal and saw one name scribbled inside: Bizzie Johansen.

Chapter 36

BIZZIE

THE PLAN HAD TAKEN A FEW DAYS to come together. Francine had kept Bizzie hidden in a groundskeeper's cottage no longer in use. She'd bring her leftovers for lunch and chicken pudding for dinner. Meanwhile, Bizzie scribbled notes in her backup journal. Even though this copy didn't have the same amount of detail as the one now in Dr. Hartman's possession, it provided an outline. Bizzie had also called on a favor from a friend. Even though their plan was far from rock-solid, the girls knew this was their best—and maybe only—chance at getting the children out of the sanitarium alive.

When Francine brought Bizzie coffee and a piece of buttered toast, she gave an uncharacteristically chuckle.

"What's so funny?" Bizzie asked, slurping the bitter coffee.

"Mr. O'Brien and Mrs. Mason are going at it again," she snorted. "Mr. O'Brien's nervous." Mimicking his accent, she said, "We've never had a visitor of this, er, status." Then, she added, "I think Mrs. Mason's jealous."

Mocking the stout cook, Francine said in a high-pitched voice, "I don't see what the fuss is all about. We've had plenty of well-known politicians, doctors, and professors come through our doors. Suddenly, some pretty lady walks in and everyone goes nuts!"

Bizzie smiled and shook her head, hoping their plan would work. When she'd snuck into Mr. O'Brien's office and telephoned the Young Quinlan Shop in Minneapolis, she'd asked for Emma and held her breath. A minute later, a familiar voice came on the line. When Bizzie explained the shaky plan, she'd been hesitant but determined. Without Emma's help, their plan surely would have failed.

Francine would meet their visitor at the front door and escort her inside, where Mr. O'Brien would begin an hour-long tour. Sometime on that tour, Dr. Hartman would grace her with his presence. In the meantime, the driver would unload the carriage, full of fabrics and dresses and accessories for a trunk show which would cater to the wives of the wealthy businessmen from Minneapolis and Chicago. Then, the driver would pull behind the Oasis. That's when Bizzie would deliver each child to the carriage and transport them to safety.

With a quick hug, Francine hurried off to the Oasis. Meanwhile, Bizzie snuck behind the building. She was hiding in the shadows when the sleek, brown carriage pulled up. A breathtaking Elizabeth Quinlan stepped out.

Ms. Quinlan wore a white blouse with cap sleeves tucked neatly into a black, pleated skirt that fell below her knees. On her feet were simple black heels. Bizzie thought she looked just as graceful and confident as she had on that day on the streetcar. She floated through the air. Even stoic and serious Dr. Hartman, who stood waiting to greet her, seemed taken with her.

Bizzie watched it unfold in the shadows. "The pleasure is all mine," Ms. Quinlan said elegantly. Then, she gestured to her trunks and chests outside the door. "I've brought with me the finest fabrics and materials. I think your guests will love them." She casually touched Dr. Hartman's arm. He seemed intoxicated by her.

Bizzie moved around the back of the Oasis to the crawl space hidden beneath shrubs and bushes. She climbed down the ladder and found the children in each of their beds, just as she had found them days before. She immediately went to Ella's bedside and checked her pulse. Though pale and clammy, Bizzie felt the shadow of a heartbeat.

If she placed each child right next to one another, Bizzie thought there would be enough room in the carriage for all of them. Her plan was to climb up the ladder carrying Ella first and place her in the carriage. But even though Ella was a child and as thin as a rail, Bizzie realized she wouldn't be able to carry her by herself and climb up the ladder. In desperation, she looked at Sam, who'd been watching her, and shook her head. There was no way Bizzie could get all these kids out by herself. After realizing this, Sam tried to sit up, but didn't have the strength. Defeated and exhausted, Bizzie sat on Ella's bed and started to cry. Soon, sobs began escaping her.

"Can I help?" a voice startled her. Bizzie turned to see Louise standing in the shadows.

"Louise!" Bizzie gasped. Truly terrified, Bizzie hissed, "Is Dr. Hartman coming? What did you tell him?"

Louise raced over to Bizzie and crouched down near Ella's bed. "Bizzie, I'm so sorry. What I did…" Louise closed her eyes and shook her head. After a moment, she squared her shoulders and looked Bizzie in the eye. "But I'm here to help. You can't get these kids out of this dungeon alone. Let me help you."

Bizzie looked at Louise incredulously. "I can't trust you. Ever."

Louise bit her lip. "I brought you this." She handed Bizzie her faded, worn journal. Her mother's name was scribbled on top. "Bizzie, I'll do whatever it takes to make this right."

Bizzie heard a whisper from the other side of the room. It was Sam. "Help us," he whispered. Bizzie looked at Louise and nodded. "But, if you've set us up and Dr. Hartman's out there waiting for us, their lives," she gestured around the sanitarium, "will be lost because of you."

Louise nodded. Without a word, they lifted Ella together and climbed the ladder. Ella groaned slightly and her eyes opened just a bit.

Bizzie offered her a smile. "It's going to be okay," she said and nodded at the driver who was waiting at the top of the ladder for them. With each child, the process got a bit easier. When the girls lifted eleven children to safety, Bizzie started to climb back down the ladder. Louise followed.

"I'll help Sam climb out," Bizzie told Louise. "You stay with Ella." The ten-year-old was looking paler by the minute. Louise nodded.

As Bizzie climbed back down into the nearly empty sanitarium, Sam looked around, bewildered. "Where's Ella?" he asked with a start.

"She's safe. You're going to be okay," Bizzie said in a soft voice.

Then, as if on cue, Bizzie heard stomping echoing through the hidden hallway. A man's voice shrieked. Bizzie turned to see Dr. Hartman enter the sanitarium. His face fell when he saw the empty beds. He began flipping over mattresses and tossing beds aside. He ran to the counter where notebooks held meticulous notes about each patient. Then, he locked eyes with Bizzie and his face turned to stone.

"You," he snarled. He lunged at her. In a beat, his hands were around her throat. She flailed and ripped at him, clawing against Dr. Hartman's hands and arms. His nostrils flared and his eyes were fire. Despite her attempts to fight him off, Bizzie started to see stars dancing in front of her.

"Excuse me, sir," a no-nonsense voice breezed in, "but just what in the hell do you think you're doing?"

In a breath, Dr. Hartman's hands were off Bizzie, who fell to the ground, coughing and choking. From the ground, she saw Mrs. Mason. Francine was steps behind the cook. When she saw Bizzie on the ground on all fours, she ran over to her.

"Bizzie," she gasped. "You're alive! Louise told us…I ran to fetch Mrs. Mason, the only one I could think of…" Her words came out broken and sputtered.

Mrs. Mason looked Dr. Hartman up and down with a disapproving stare. She grunted. "So, this is what you spend your time doing, eh? Poisoning kids and strangling the help?" She walked up to Dr. Hartman, her stout body coming up to his shoulder. She pointed a meaty finger at him and looked him square in the eyes. "Let me tell you what, you disgrace of a man. You might have friends in high places. You might have more money than you can count. You might have brains in that thick head of yours. But the lot of us?" She gestured to Francine, who was now helping Bizzie to her feet. "We have something you'll never have."

Dr. Hartman scowled and tilted his head. "And what's that?"

"Morality. Honesty. Friendship." At that moment, a staggered gait could be heard coming through the tunnel. Then Mr. O'Brien appeared with sweat on his brow.

"So, it's true, then?" Mr. O'Brien asked, sounding devastated. "You've been experimenting…" his voice drifted off and he erupted in sobs. Mrs. Mason comforted him with shushes and quiet, soothing words.

"You don't have any evidence that I was doing anything wrong. I was doing research," he spat. "In fact," he said, looking at Bizzie, "you can expect to find a full spread in tomorrow's *St. Paul Pioneer Press*. I've just released a vaccination against Muscardine Fever using goldenseal. It'll be in every paper across the country and then the globe. I'll be a hero. No one will believe any other story," he jerked his head once at Bizzie, "especially one written by a woman."

Bizzie cowered, knowing he was right.

Chapter 37

SOPHIE

I REALIZED I WAS CRYING. I glanced at Ida. Tears were streaming down her cheeks too. She grabbed one of her mother's hands, and I held the other. The three of us, all in search of truth, sat in solidarity.

"Time for bed," a nurse knocked on the door. When she saw us holding hands and crying, she stepped back. "I'm sorry," she said. "I didn't mean to interrupt."

Ida waved a hand at the nurse, welcoming her into the room. "Mom, we should probably get going," Ida sniffed, patting Helen's knee.

I stood up, holding the journal. "Thank you, Helen," I said, bending down to give her a gentle hug. She patted my shoulder and whispered in my ear, "Report the truth."

Ida and I huddled outside Helen's room and flipped open the brittle journal. In small, neat handwriting were pages and pages of faded, black ink. The first entry was dated April 2nd, 1920.

"Incredible," Ida whispered.

"Wow," I murmured at the same time.

Ida shook her head and exhaled. "I can't believe Grandma Francine knew the truth the whole time. No one believed her. No one except my mom." Tears streamed down her face again and she reached into her pocket for a crumpled tissue.

She sniffed and nodded at me. "I think you have some work to do." She offered me a brief smile.

"Thank you," I said quietly. "Thank you for helping me. For giving me another chance."

Ida nodded and smiled. "There's always time to do the right thing."

I got back to my apartment after ten that night. I gently set Bizzie's journal—along with the article, the city council agenda, and all the other papers I had collected—on my coffee table. I started with the journal, filled with now-yellowed pages. Sentences, written in black ink, were crowded together. Gingerly, I turned each page, feeling like I was reading something as sacred as scripture. I reached for my notebook.

"First things first," I said to myself, tapping my pen against my lip. "How do I prove that the Hartmans aren't who they say they are?" I began scribbling in my notebook.

1. *Morris Hartman's grandfather—Dr. Hartman, the "good" doctor—owned the Oasis.*
2. *Oasis shuttered for twenty years. Preservationists trying to save it.*
3. *Morris and Crab Orchard Mayor Palmer made a deal months ago. The city owns the Oasis. MH Manufacturing bought the land and will tear it down. Plan is to build a steel mill.*
4. *Morris showed up for a fundraiser and photo shoot in good spirits. Appeared to back the preservationist efforts.*
5. *Found hidden sanitarium.*
6. *Have proof in the journal of what Dr. Hartman really did.*

I underlined and starred the "Have proof" part. I sat back on my plush couch and took a deep breath. Questions came to mind. Does Morris know what his grandfather did? Is he really aware of all the details? Is that why Morris wants to demolish the building—to forever hide the evidence and protect his family name?

Although I didn't know the answers, I knew that if Morris and his posse didn't know the ugly truth yet, they would in the morning. I whipped out my laptop and began typing as fast as my fingers would let me. I needed to send this story to Kase as soon as possible. I worked through the night, constantly flipping open my notebook to reference details. I got up only to go to the bathroom and refill my favorite mug with lukewarm coffee that had gone stale. By two a.m., I had an outline. By four a.m., I had a story. I paced around my apartment, and then gave up. I pulled on a navy blazer and jeans and drove to the office. Both jittery and exhausted, I waited anxiously for my coworkers to file in. When Jen finally breezed through the doors,

I nearly pounced on her.

"How are you? Whatcha working on? Do you know that I pulled an all-nighter last night?" I jabbed a mile a minute.

"Whoa, whoa." She waved a hand at me. "Coffee first." She pointed to the Keurig in the corner. I nodded. I turned to see Kase walk in.

"Kase!" I trotted to him. "I have something to show you. Now. Right now."

His reaction was similar to Jen's, but I didn't move out of his path towards the Keurig. He chuckled and looked at me quizzically. "Alright." He jerked his head toward an empty conference room. "Meet you there in five."

I nodded, grabbed my laptop, and bolted into the conference room. I tucked a strand of hair behind my ear, opened my laptop, and started—unconsciously—shaking my leg. A minute later, I realized I was shaking the entire table. I took a deep breath and tried to stay calm. Kase walked in.

"You've got ten minutes," he said, taking a sip of his coffee and sitting down.

I cleared my throat. "I think I have something on Hartman. Something big."

He nodded. "You mentioned that. *What* is this big piece of news?"

I dove in.

"Hartman's grandfather—Dr. Hartman—owned the Oasis, that big medical center an hour west of here along the Minnesota River. In the 1920s, he came up with that breakthrough vaccination for Muscardine Fever." I waited to make sure Kase understood. He nodded.

"The Oasis shut down about twenty years ago when the smaller Hartman Clinics across the state became more popular. It's been shuttered ever since. There've been efforts to try to save it, but nothing has stuck. Then, a couple weeks ago, I came across news that the Oasis was being torn down. When I asked Hartman about it, he had a strange reaction. Like it wasn't a big deal."

Kase held up his hands and shrugged, as if to say, "So what?"

I forged on. "I dug a little deeper. Hartman and the mayor of Crab Orchard made a deal a few months ago—before this news about tearing down the Oasis came out. Hartman's company, MH Manufacturing, bought the land and is planning to build a steel mill." I raised my eyebrows at Kase. "Don't you think that's strange that the news didn't come out sooner?"

Kase scratched his chin and squinted his eyes. He nodded slightly.

"It seemed like he was covering up for something. It was all too strange. Why wouldn't he just announce he was building a plant on the site of his grandfather's old medical center? Why did he do this all so secretly?"

Kase started to say something. I could see the doubt on his face. I broke in. "And why was the answer always 'no' to the preservationists—but yes to this steel mill?"

He paused and shrugged. "Money?"

I nodded. "Maybe. But then, I found this." I pulled the leather-bound journal out of my bag. I took a deep breath and handed it to him. He carefully opened the first page. Tucked inside was the copy of the newspaper clipping. He flipped through the pages, taking in the neat but crowded entries. He looked up at me.

"This *is* big," he said, his eyes shining. "But it's also a huge allegation. I mean…you're saying Dr. Hartman, *the* Dr. Hartman, was experimenting. On real people."

"Not just people. *Kids*. And I'm not saying it," I said, pointing to the journal. "*She* is. She *did*." I tapped the newspaper clipping.

"Then, why isn't it a known fact if there was a newspaper article about it?" Kase questioned.

I pulled out my phone and scrolled through my photos until I got to the picture of the headlines I had found in the library database. I slid my phone over to Kase.

"Because everyone else was covering this story."

Kase picked up the phone. "Dr. Hartman releases miracle vaccine against deadly disease," Kase read from the picture. He looked up at me. "So just one paper covered the hidden sanitarium?" He shook his head. "Doesn't add up."

I nodded, expecting this. "I gained access to the Oasis," I said, thinking of Aaron. Kase's eyes widened. I went on. "I found the sanitarium. I've seen it with my own eyes." I paused. "What's more…I think Morris Hartman knows about it too. He's trying to cover it up. That's why he's trying to build a steel plant on the land. It will literally demolish any remaining history of this," I handed him the letter I found in the City Hall meeting notes, "and save his family name."

Kase read through the letter, took a deep breath, and then leaned back in his chair, crossing his hands behind his head. "This is a lot to think about," he said finally.

"Tell me about it." I chewed on my lip. "I'm pretty sure the mayor had me followed the other night. It was scary as hell."

200 | THE MUCKRAKER

"These guys are threatening you now?" Kase leaned in toward me. "Why didn't you come to me sooner?"

"I wanted to make sure I had my story straight," I said, tapping the journal. "And I only just got the last piece of the puzzle."

Kase pursed his lips together. "Write me up a draft."

"Already done," I replied. Then, I followed up with, "I came in late last night. Couldn't sleep." Kase shook his head in disbelief. I shrugged.

"Let me read through the draft and we'll figure out the next steps," Kase said, standing up. "And Sophie, nice work."

I silently cheered. Finally! I proved that I could ask the tough questions and write the truth. I looked for Jen as I walked back to my desk, but she had left. I pulled out my phone to text Aaron and saw that I'd received a text from a number I didn't recognize.

Last warning. Stop or you'll be stopped.

Chapter 38

BIZZIE

SILENCE HAD FALLEN over the hidden sanitarium. Dr. Hartman nodded once at no one in particular and then began to clip through the tunnel. But, before he got too far, Mr. O'Brien cleared his throat.

"Really, Joseph?" he said quietly. No one moved. "Don't you remember where you started? Your simple clinic? Making calls on Wilson?"

Dr. Hartman turned and puffed out his chest. "Ben, some of us continue to evolve. While others," he gestured to the staff, "stay the same." He turned and continued walking through the tunnel. He called out, "Call the police if you want. But the chief's son died of Muscardine Fever. So, I don't think he'll haul me away when he learns that I have a vaccine." His laughter could be heard echoing down the tunnel.

Mrs. Mason shook her head and rested her hand on her collarbone. "Bastard," she muttered.

Mr. O'Brien looked at Bizzie, Louise, and Francine. "How did you…"

Then, Sam moaned, and the ramshackle team jumped into action. Mr. O'Brien hoisted the boy on his shoulder and carried him out of the tunnel. The rest followed closely behind.

"But what about Dr. Hartman?" Bizzie asked. "I'm not sure what to do…"

Mrs. Mason and Mr. O'Brien exchanged glances. "To get to you, he'll have to come through us," Mrs. Mason exclaimed, giving Bizzie's hand a squeeze. Mr. O'Brien winked.

Bizzie piled into the carriage. Francine climbed in too. Louise stood back.

"Well, get up there," Mr. O'Brien urged. "You're the hero of this story."

Bizzie looked at Louise with raised eyebrows.

"Of course," Mrs. Mason answered Bizzie's confused stare. "Louise came to find us. Said you were in trouble."

Bizzie smiled at Louise and patted the spot next to her. She then cleared her throat and turned her attention to Mr. O'Brien and Mrs. Mason. "Thank you. Thank you both. For everything."

She nodded to the driver, thankful that Ms. Quinlan had chosen someone willing to accommodate an unusual mission. As they trotted away from the Oasis, Sam began to speak, telling Louise, Francine, and Bizzie how he—and the eleven other children—had ended up in the hidden sanitarium.

They were all orphans from New York City on a train bound for Rapid City, South Dakota where a new orphanage promised wide open spaces. During a routine stop in Minneapolis, the conductor gave Sam and the other children in his train car ten cents. They wandered to a nearby park, looking for an ice cream treat.

Sam shrugged. "We were the lucky train car that day," he coughed. "When we got back to the station after eating ice cream and playing in the park, the train was gone. In its place was an ambulance.

"The driver said his name was Dr. Joe. He told us that he'd be bringing us to another station to catch the next train to South Dakota.

"He seemed nice enough. No one even questioned him." Sam shook his head. "But when the ambulance stopped outside a big building nowhere near a train station, I had a bad feeling in my stomach. The driver, who told us to call him Dr. Joe, took us into the building.

"He said there had been a problem with the train. He said we'd be staying at the Oasis for the night," Sam explained. "We were given delicious food. Stuff we'd never had. Roasted chicken and onions. Warm bread with honey and butter. Strawberry pie. We spent the night in a small cottage." He smiled sadly and shook his head. "We thought we were the luckiest kids in the world. We thought a fluke got us there." He rubbed his eyes and his smile disappeared. "But the next day everything changed. We were blindfolded and forced through a dark tunnel into a small room. It felt humid and smelled musty. When I asked about the train, I was slapped." Sam touched his cheek, like the wound still hurt. "And that's when it began. We were given doses of…" he shook his head and made a face, "…slimy goo. It smelled like grass or clover."

Bizzie interrupted. "Didn't you try to escape?"

Sam rolled up his nightgown sleeves and revealed a pink,

tender-looking scar. "I tried once, and this is what happened." Sam traced his finger over the top and winced. "Dr. Joe said if I tried to escape again, he'd hurt Ella next time." He shuddered and looked at his sister, who was lying still.

"Could you talk with each other?" Bizzie asked.

Sam shook his head. "I felt like I was in a fog. Like I was dreaming."

"What about using the bathroom? Or bathing?" Bizzie asked, thinking back to the outhouse at the poor farm.

"There was a girl. She would come and help us," he said. "She would bring a sponge and a bucket. She was always kind to us."

Bizzie looked at Louise who stared solemnly downward.

"I just can't believe you all survived," Bizzie said finally.

"When Ella was really sick, not waking up for days in a row, I had a dream about my parents. They died in a fire when Ella and I were young. But I had this clear picture of them in my mind. They were smiling at us. They were proud of us. They were happy. That gave me the strength to go on. I made a promise to myself. I would do whatever I had to do to make sure all twelve of us got out of there alive."

"How long were you in that room?" Bizzie asked.

"I etched lines on the wall near my bed…when I was awake enough. My last count was seventy-one. Seventy-one days."

Bizzie was speechless. The rest of the two-day journey was spent checking on the children and offering them bits of food Mrs. Mason had wrapped up and sent with them. Francine was a natural nurse. She took the pulse of each child on the hour and documented it in her notebook.

When they pulled up a familiar gravel road, Bizzie noticed the changes right away. A fresh coat of white paint covered the house. Someone had repaired the broken front steps. And Bizzie was sure she caught a whiff of fresh chocolate chip cookies in the air. The gardener was there in the front, just like last time, except now he stood up straight and gave a gentle handshake and smile. His skin was clear and his eyes bright. A patch of lilacs gave off a soft, breezy scent nearby.

"Bizzie!" Ruth said, enveloping her in a hug as Bizzie stepped out of the carriage.

Bizzie smiled. "What a change! This place," she gestured to the house, "looks so different."

Ruth smiled. "It's all thanks to Abigail. She turned this place around."

Mrs. Hendry approached them.

"Wow," Bizzie breathed. "Mrs. Hendry—"

She shook her head. "It's Abigail, please. And it took all of us to make a change. We are so glad you wrote to us." She looked different; stronger, happier. Bizzie noticed a wooden sign near the entrance of the house that read *Ruth and Abigail's Country Lodging House.*

"Bizzie, is this where you stayed before you came to us?" Louise, who'd been silent up until then, asked, looking around with curious eyes.

"That voice," Sam said, looking in Louise's direction. "I know that voice." He limped over to Louise. "It was you, wasn't it? You were in the sanitarium with us."

Bizzie jumped in. "It was also Louise who helped save you." Sam looked at Bizzie, who nodded. "She went for help. She did the right thing."

Louise bit her lip and whispered, "I'm so sorry I didn't try to help sooner. I didn't know…" Tears filled her eyes. Bizzie held her breath.

Then, Sam reached out a shaky hand and patted Louise's elbow. "Thank you," he said. Tears streamed down her cheeks, and she squeezed his hand.

One by one, the children crept out of the carriage, most of them now able to walk on their own two feet.

Ella was helped by Francine. She looked up at her brother. "So, this is our new home?" Sam nodded. "I wonder if we'll all share one room again."

Ruth chuckled. "Oh, dear girl. You'll get your own room. That is, if you choose. Here, we will make sure you have time to learn, play, and rest." She winked at Ella. "I wonder if we could find a doll with your name on it, eh?" Ella smiled. Ruth took the girl under her arm and walked her toward the house.

Bizzie pulled Abigail aside. "Thank you for welcoming them," she said. "They've had quite a journey."

"We're happy to help." Abigail smiled.

"How did you make so many changes? Where did you find the—" Bizzie paused, "—the funds?"

Abigail chuckled. "Remember my dream to build a life with John in Montana?" she shrugged. "I had a years' worth of savings built up when I got that letter from him, saying he'd met someone else. I've slowly been adding to it. I never showed Lester." Her face filled with disgust at the mention of his name. "I knew that, someday, that money would come in handy." She swept her hand across the prairie. "And it has."

Chapter 39

SOPHIE

A SHIVER RAN THROUGH ME. Should I show this text to Kase? I didn't want to appear weak, or like I was having doubts. Besides, we were almost ready to break the story. Once that happened, what could Hartman or Palmer's people do anyway? They'd have their hands full with damage control.

Still, I couldn't shake the feeling that I was being watched. As I waited to hear from Kase about the first draft, I distracted myself with an AP wire rewrite about new legislation regarding paternity leave that was sweeping Minneapolis. Finally, a few minutes before noon, Kase walked over to my desk.

"I read through your work. It's solid, Sophie. You've really done your homework. We'll go live with this tomorrow. It'll be huge. Be ready to field calls all day. In other words," he patted my shoulder, "sleep well—don't come in here in the middle of the night."

"Wait, go live? Like…me? Go live?" I asked, my mind flooded with thoughts of my panic attack on air years ago.

"Yeah, you. It's your story. We'll go live on our YouTube channel and Instagram."

"Um," I started. He winked and squeezed my shoulder once more. "Oh, and those pictures are awesome. Much better than the fuzzy photos of K!ng doing yoga. Who should we give photo credit to?"

I managed a smile. "Aaron Cooper. He's a professional photographer."

Kase nodded and walked back to his desk. I closed my eyes and tried to shake off the memories of my last live shoot.

Just then, Jen came over to my desk.

"Jen!" I said, sitting up straight. "I've been looking for you! Guess what?" Her face looked as though she'd seen a ghost. "Jen, are you okay?" I asked.

"Yeah, just another long, boring meeting," she said, waving a hand in my direction. "I want to hear your news, but I've gotta run. Chat later?"

"Okay…" I said as Jen clipped out the door.

That afternoon, Kase stopped back at my desk. "Have time for a celebratory drink?" He perched himself on my desk.

I smiled. "I'd love to, but I'm heading out. I have to tell Aaron and Ida the news. They deserve the credit here. Another time?" He nodded.

My cell phone rang as I walked to the parking lot. It was Ida.

"Just who I was hoping to chat with!" I sang into the phone.

"Oh, Sophie!" she wailed.

"What is it?" I gulped.

"It's Mom. She's—she's not doing well. I guess she had a visitor just now. Someone who had something to do with the Oasis. Someone who really upset her." Her voice was muffled. "I'm so confused!"

"Wait, what? A visitor? Who?" My mind ticked back to the threatening text I received. Her phone was cutting in and out. Then, I heard her doorbell ring.

"Oh, just a minute. Someone's at the door," she sniffed. I realized it then. If they couldn't get to me, they'd go after those around me. Ida. Helen. Aaron.

"Ida," I demanded. "Do not open your door."

Chapter 40

BIZZIE

As Ruth and Abigail helped settle the children into their new home, Bizzie, Francine and Louise gathered on the lawn.

"What will we do now?" Francine asked the group.

"Does it even matter?" Louise said glumly.

Bizzie said, "Of course, it matters. Even if I can't tell the story in the Journal—"

"Is that all you can think about right now?" Louise snapped. "Your stupid story?"

"What?" Bizzie recoiled.

"We're in this mess because of you, you know," Louise said bitterly. "I have nowhere to go because of you."

"Louise," Bizzie reached out and gently touched her arm. "You did the right thing. You helped get those kids to safety."

"Yes, and lost my job in the process."

"That wasn't a job. That was a prison sentence," Bizzie replied. "That's no life for you. You are meant for better things."

Louise shrugged. "Dr. Hartman wasn't always bad, you know. He took me in when my father died of Muscardine Fever. Mom left us when I was young," she said. "It wasn't until Dr. Hartman started rebuilding the Oasis after the tornado hit. Then, the money started flowing in. Big companies started paying him for his research. I didn't know what he was doing was wrong. I was happy he was searching for a vaccine," she sniffed. "When I realized that he was experimenting on…well, you know, it was too late. I didn't think there was anything I could do." She looked at Bizzie and Francine. "Besides, he had given me a place to live, food to eat, a bed to sleep in."

"I wonder," Francine started. "No, never mind."

"What?" Louise asked.

"I wonder, Louise, if you could work at Ruth and Abigail's. I mean, you know what it's like to lose a parent. You could really help those kids."

Louise scoffed. "Like they'd ever trust me."

Bizzie jumped in. "Yes! Louise, you would be terrific. And you saw how Sam trusted you. They've already forgiven you. You saved their lives."

Louise looked at Bizzie and Francine, her eyes bright for the first time that day. "You think so?"

Bizzie gathered Ruth and Abigail and introduced them to Louise.

"Despite losing both of her parents, she's never given up hope," Bizzie said proudly.

Louise managed to smile. "I'm looking for a new start," she murmured. "I know how to manage the laundry. And I've helped in the kitchen."

Abigail and Ruth exchanged glances. "We encourage our guests to help with the chores around the house, including laundry. But we are looking for someone to run the kitchen." Abigail looked intently at Bizzie. "But, what about you?"

Bizzie kicked the ground. "I think my career as a journalist is ruined. Who will believe my story when the entire country is singing another tune?" She shook her head. "And frankly, who will care? This new vaccine will save hundreds of thousands of lives. I mean, my God, even I'm grateful for that."

Francine pursed her lips. "What about that writer friend of yours? She lives up north—where you're from. Sarah or Sandra or something."

"Sally Salter?" Bizzie replied.

"Yes! Sally Salter." Francine nodded. "What about her? Could she help you?"

"Sally Salter…" Bizzie mumbled.

"I don't know this Sally Salter or how a big paper works, or how to even write a story like that," Ruth said. "But I do know one thing." She pointed a finger at Bizzie. "You are a determined little thing." She took a step closer to Bizzie and clasped her chin between her fingers. "You did something few people ever have. You surprised me. And you have something most lack," Ruth smiled, "tenacity. Don't let anyone—not even some famous doctor—blot that out."

Bizzie wrapped Ruth in a tight hug, tears streaming down her face. "Thank you," she whispered into the woman's shoulder.

Chapter 41

SOPHIE

"IDA, I'M CALLING THE POLICE," I spoke calmly even though my heart was pounding. I grabbed my keys and bolted to my car. "I think you're in danger."

Ida's voice grew quiet and small. "Danger?"

"Ida, get to the basement. Or the bathroom. Wherever. Hide and wait for the police." I punched in 9-1-1 and blurted out my story to the dispatcher, demanding an officer go to Ida's house in Crab Orchard immediately. Then, I jumped in my car and headed to The Coffee Fox. The drive usually takes me an hour, but I made it to the coffee shop in thirty-seven minutes. I barely put the car in park before I flung the door open and ran inside, my keys still in the ignition.

"Aaron!" I burst through the door, breathless. I rubbed my bottom lip with my finger, my scar growing more tender by the second. A woman on her laptop looked up at me while a couple snuggling in the corner eyed me. I flew to the counter where Lauren was steaming some milk.

"Lauren! Is Aaron here?" I rubbed my palms on my pants.

"No…" She squinted at me. "Are you okay?"

"No. No, I'm not." Tears pricked my eyes. "Do you know where he is?"

She shrugged. "Just headed over to City Hall for a meeting with the mayor."

"Shit!" I plunged back through the door and ran down Main Street, ignoring the quizzical looks from passersby. I dialed Aaron's number, but the call went straight to his voicemail. I yanked open the glass door to City Hall and charged toward the mayor's office.

"Can I help you?" a woman said, stopping me. I glanced at her badge. Wren. She was Aaron's friend, the woman who let me into her office.

"Yes! Yes. I'm looking for my boy—er, my friend, Aaron. I think he's meeting with the mayor?" I squeaked.

"Oh shoot. You just missed them," she replied. "They just headed out."

My nostrils flared and I must have looked terrified because she put a gentle hand on my arm.

"I'm getting the feeling that something's going on here. Do you want to come into my office?" Wren gestured to an open door.

I covered my face in my hands and shook my head. "No, no…there's no time. I need to find Aaron." I groaned, "Oh, this is all my fault." I looked up at Wren. "Do you know where they went?"

Wren shrugged. "I thought I heard the mayor say something about the Oasis…"

I nodded and flew back out the door.

"Wait," Wren followed me. "You're pretty upset. Why don't I drive you? Besides, I'm not sure you should be going off by yourself anyway."

Wren ushered me to her black Honda parked nearby. As she breezed through town, I clasped my hands together and tried to take deep breaths.

"Can you tell me what's going on?" Wren asked as we drove toward the Oasis.

I closed my eyes and rubbed my forehead. "I never meant for the story to go this far. I was just…I was just trying to tell a story that mattered."

I took a deep breath and started at the beginning. How I stumbled across news of the Oasis demolition and steel plant plan that only the mayor and Hartman knew about. What Aaron and I found buried in the belly of the Oasis. The time I was followed on the highway at night, the threatening text message I received, and now, today—the people who visited Ida, her mother, and Aaron.

"You think Aaron, Ida, and Ida's mother are all in danger?" Wren asked, glancing at me.

"Yes," I nodded. "I'm positive that the mayor and Morris are covering up the fact that Dr. Hartman did horrible things in that sanitarium. We were supposed to break the story first thing tomorrow on News Now Online. This is no coincidence."

Wren floored the Honda up the drive to the shadowy castle. She threw the car in park and we both jumped out.

"Aaron!" I cried. "Aaron!"

"Aaron!" Wren echoed. She punched the flashlight app on her phone and shined a path ahead for us. I gestured around the back of the building. In silence, we crunched along the path, finding the back door that Aaron and I used just yesterday. We slipped inside. It was hard to believe it had only been a day since we discovered the hidden sanitarium.

"What is this?" Wren whispered and pointed to the rickety ladder disappearing into the darkness.

I was about to answer when we heard voices.

"Why'd you have to go digging around here anyway?" It was the mayor. "Oh, wait. You were helping that city reporter."

"Sophie didn't have anything to do with this," we heard Aaron reply. Wren and I exchanged glances. "You've seen the sanitarium. You know it exists. Can we go?"

"I can. But you—you've seen too much. I'm sorry, Aaron. This is where the little adventure ends." The mayor continued, "The Oasis will tragically catch fire. It was a total accident, of course. And, sadly, photographer Aaron Cooper was caught in the flames. His remains were found the next morning." The mayor grunted, "Maybe that's what your little girlfriend will write for tomorrow's news." Then, the cock of a gun.

"Wait!" I blurted out and launched myself into the darkness. "Don't shoot! Don't hurt him, please!"

It took a moment for my eyes to adjust to the dark, dank room. But, after a moment, I could see the mayor on one side of the room and Aaron on the other—handcuffed to a chair. Behind him stood a man I had never seen.

The mayor chuckled, "Perfect. Now the lovebirds can end their story together. Hartman'll be happy to hear that I got rid of both of you. Now, I'll definitely get my cut in the steel plant, eh, Walter?"

The man behind us laughed. He brought his face right next to mine and whispered, "Nice to see you again, Sophie. I think we met on a dark highway not too long ago." A shiver ran through me.

"Walter, stop!" Aaron fumed. He wrestled to free his arms, but they were locked together. Our eyes met.

"Aaron, I'm so sorry," I stammered.

"Oh, now don't cry," the mayor said. "You'll have an eternity to look forward to together." He pointed the gun at me. Tears streamed down my cheeks.

"Lester, stop." A female voice demanded. Wren. The mayor paused and looked up.

212 | THE MUCKRAKER

"Who's there?" he said.

"It's over, Lester. Let them go."

The mayor shook his head. "It isn't over. You have no proof. Everything—and everyone—will burn in the fire."

"Not the evidence I have. Everything you just said," a pause, "has been recorded."

Then, another voice. "Mayor Lester Palmer, you're under arrest for assault and kidnapping with the intent to harm. Come out with your hands up."

"Damnit." The mayor stared at me and Aaron. "This ain't over." Footsteps echoed and, in a span of ten seconds, the room was filled with the sheriff and Crab Orchard police officers.

"Aaron, you doing okay?" the sheriff asked and nodded at me. "These guys won't be bothering you anymore." One of the officers unlocked Aaron's handcuffs. As he rubbed his sore wrists, I launched toward him and locked my arms around him.

"I'm so sorry," I mumbled into his neck. "I never meant..."

He smoothed my hair and grabbed me tighter. Then, his warm lips were on mine and my trembling body melted into his.

"Guys! You okay?" Wren asked, coming over to us.

I threw my arms around her. "Wren, you saved our lives. How did you—"

"I texted the sheriff before we left my office. When you showed up looking like a crazy person," she laughed, "I figured something was up."

One of the police officers came over to me. "Excuse me, ma'am, but I have your boss on the line."

Chapter 42

BIZZIE

BIZZIE AND FRANCINE PARTED WAYS at the Nicollet Avenue stop. Francine would continue north to her family farm. She planned to enroll in the Minnesota Training School for Nurses later that year.

"You saved those kids, you know," Bizzie told Francine before she got off the streetcar.

Francine shrugged. "First rule of healthcare—do no harm. Then, try to help." She clasped Bizzie in a tight hug. "Remember what Ruth said. You have tenacity. Don't quit on your dream." Bizzie grabbed Francine's hand and gave it one last squeeze before hopping off the streetcar. She waved until the streetcar was out of sight.

"News! Get your news here!" a newsboy cried out. "Dr. Hartman releases miracle vaccine!" Bizzie handed the boy a nickel and bought a copy of The Journal. She scanned the front-page full spread.

> *A preliminary analysis of the Phase 1 trial of the vaccine shows it is nearly 100% effective in preventing Muscardine Fever and causes no serious safety concerns. Dr. Joseph Hartman, who has been furiously working on a vaccine for the last decade says this is the beginning of the end of the Fever that has claimed nearly a million lives since 1900. "This is a historic moment in the fight against the Fever," says Dr. Hartman. "We hope to begin delivering vaccines to hospitals as early as next month."*

Bizzie stuffed the paper under her arm as she nodded to the receptionist at The Minneapolis Journal building and took the stairs two at a time. She walked in just as the reporters were getting their daily assignments.

"Ms. Johansen," Mr. Kavanaugh said after he'd given Floyd instructions to photograph Dr. Hartman at the Minneapolis Children's Medical Center. The children in the quarantine ward would be among the first to receive the vaccine. "Welcome back." He gestured for her to follow him into his office.

"Well, I found out what Dr. Hartman was hiding," Bizzie said. "The only problem is no one will believe me. Or even care. He traded the lives of twelve orphans for a vaccine that will ultimately save millions." She shrugged. "That's a heroic story. One that makes implicating him nearly impossible."

Mr. Kavanaugh sighed. "You think everyone is focused on *who* will benefit from the vaccine. No one's wondering *how* this came to be."

"Exactly."

"Maybe they're not focused on that now," Mr. Kavanaugh said, rubbing his hands together. "But there will come a day when the truth will be revealed. And when that day comes, we'll be the first to share the answers."

"So, what do we do with the story? What about all I learned? He'll just get away with it?" Bizzie asked.

"For now, maybe. But hopefully not forever." Bizzie dropped her head into her hands. "Your story's not dead, Ms. Johansen. Stories like these never really die. Not until the truth is told. Keep your journal. Keep your notes. The story—the truth—lives on with you. As long as you're living, so is the story."

"So…what next?" Bizzie asked, looking up.

"You've done more in your short few weeks here than most of my reporters accomplish in their whole career. Tell you what. Why don't you head home to Hibbing for a week? Take a break," Mr. Kavanaugh laughed, "take a bath. Come back and we'll figure out your next assignment."

"My next assignment…" Bizzie's voice trailed off. "Really? But how? What about my name?"

Mr. Kavanaugh shrugged. "We make up a new name. A pen name," he said, his eyes sparkling.

Bizzie smiled. "Deal."

On the train ride to Hibbing, she pulled out her journal and wrote every detail she could remember about her time at the Oasis. From her time in the kitchen with Mrs. Mason, to details about the hidden tunnel, her conversation with Sam. She wrote everything.

When she stepped off the train in her hometown, it was Collin who was waiting for her. Her heart leaped in her chest at the sight of him.

"I missed you," she said.

"Ah, you were too busy being a big city reporter to think about your farmer beau," he joked, taking her satchel and bag from her. They headed toward Bizzie's log cabin.

"Oh! Before we head out of town, I need to drop this in the mail." She pulled out an envelope that held the story—her story—she'd written on the train.

"Sally Salter, huh?" Collin asked, glancing at the letter in her hand.

"I'm hoping she can help me," Bizzie said, dropping the envelope in the postal box.

On their walk, Bizzie told Collin about lodging at Miss Chambers', meeting Emma, staying at the poor farm, and finally, investigating the Oasis.

"I risked my life for that story," she said, kicking up dust. "To think it might never be told makes my blood boil." She took a deep breath. "But we saved those kids. And that's what's really important."

"What about Dr. Hartman?" Collin asked.

Bizzie scoffed. "He's a savior, didn't you hear? He released a vaccine against Muscardine Fever." She shook her head. "What's worse is that he is just going to get more funding to do more research and more testing." She shrugged and looked at Collin. "But, I tried, right?"

"Tried?! You did better than that. You changed the lives of all those kids," Collin said. He gestured to Bizzie's cabin and handed over her satchel and bag. "I'll come by and check on you later." She nodded and hugged him goodbye.

When she walked into the log cabin, the smells of woodsmoke and bacon greeted her.

"Bizzie?" Papa's voice cracked. "Is that you?"

Bizzie skipped over to Papa waiting in his chair. She knelt down beside him, tears streaming down her face. "Oh Papa, I missed you!"

Papa took in every word about her adventures in the city. It was a few minutes after five o'clock when Bizzie's mother walked in. Surprise lined her face, but she returned to her stoic expression almost immediately.

"Elizabeth," she said, looking Bizzie up and down. "I didn't expect you to be home."

Bizzie chuckled. "Me neither."

"And what about your dream of being a journalist?" Alice asked.

Bizzie smiled. "It's no longer a dream. It's a reality." She held up copies of *The Journal* documenting her county poor farm story. "I'll be moving to Minneapolis where I'll work as a reporter."

A week later, Bizzie woke up feeling excited and refreshed. Her heart quickened at the thought of a new assignment. She dressed in her gingham dress, made a mental note to ask Emma to help her make a few new dresses, and stuffed a piece of crusty bread into her mouth. She gave Papa a long squeeze before gathering her things to leave for the train station. Her mother had already left for work.

"Bizzie," Papa said, as she gathered her satchel. "Your mother wanted me to give you something." From his chair, he handed her a small package tied with twine. She unwrapped the brown paper to find a new leather journal. Bizzie opened the front cover. There, scribbled in neat writing, was her name: E. Johansen. A lump formed in her throat, and she held the journal to her chest. Papa squeezed her hand. Then, a knock at the door.

"Hello?" Collin called out, peeking his head inside. "You ready?"

Bizzie nodded, hugged Papa once more, and gathered her bags.

As they walked to the station, Bizzie felt impending tears welling in her eyes.

"You know as well as I do that farming is not the life for you," Collin said as if he could read her mind.

"But you…Papa…Sloane," Bizzie sniffed.

"We'll be fine. I heard they hired a new teacher for the school. And, if you ever get tired of your big city life, you know where to find us."

Bizzie looked up at Collin and a tear trickled down her cheek. He wiped it away with his thumb.

"Before you go, you need to see this." He pulled something out of his back pocket and handed it to Bizzie. *The Duluth Tribune.* The headline on the front page read: *Beloved Dr. Hartman conceals hidden sanitarium; conducts experiments on real patients.* It was written by E. Johansen. Bizzie looked up at Collin. "Sally," she shook her head. "Sally pushed this through."

"That old doctor might have gotten away with it, but at least the people around here—*your* people—know the truth."

Chapter 43

SOPHIE

I GRABBED THE PHONE. "Kase?"

"Sophie, I'm so glad you're okay," Kase said.

"How did you…" My mind was swirling. "How did you…"

"Someone tipped me off," he replied. "Sophie, can you go live from the Oasis in ten minutes?"

Even though I'd just escaped being shot, my stomach dropped to my feet at the thought of going live again. Panic flooded through me. In a half-second, I was back in that snowy intersection, having a panic attack. I gulped. "A live shot?"

I told Kase I had to think about it. First, I had to find Aaron.

"Wren," I yanked her arm and pulled her away from the crowd of Crab Orchard residents starting to form. She'd been busy fielding questions. "Have you seen Aaron?"

She pointed to the sheriff's truck. "Last I heard, he was giving a statement to Sheriff Goodspeed over there."

I thanked her and jogged over to the truck. "Um, excuse me," I said. Aaron and the sheriff looked at me. "Aaron, can I talk to you for a sec?"

Aaron looked at the sheriff. "That okay with you?"

The sheriff nodded. "Sophie, I'm Sheriff Tom Goodspeed. I have to ask—how did you first discover this story?"

"The truth is another reporter did all the grunt work for me. She just couldn't catch the bad guy. So, I did," I paused, "or at least, I hope so."

"Looks like you did. Actually, there were a few bad guys. And one girl—er, woman, too," he said.

I looked at Aaron. "So, this means Ida and her mom…they're safe?"

218 | **THE MUCKRAKER**

"Safe," Sheriff Goodspeed echoed. "They're all safe." I let out a sigh of relief. "Officers got to Ida's and found," he looked down at his phone, "Hines Oberg there."

"Of course," I replied.

"Know him?" the sheriff asked.

"He's Morris Hartman's assistant," I said.

"More like his thug," Aaron scoffed.

"But then, who threatened Ida's mom?" I asked, racking my brain.

Sheriff Goodspeed looked back to his notes. "Looks like she got a visit from someone named Genesis." He shrugged and looked at me.

My mouth fell open. I closed my eyes and shook my head in disbelief. "No way."

Aaron and Sheriff Goodspeed were both looking at me with questioning eyes. "I work with Jen—er, Genesis—at News Now Online. I thought we were…friends." I suddenly felt small.

"Well, right now, she's being held in the Hennepin County Jail. Along with Hartman, Palmer, and Oberg. They could all face prison time," the sheriff replied.

"So, the public will finally learn the truth about the Hartman family?" I asked.

"Well, I think that's up to you," he said.

I took a deep breath and nodded. It was time for the public to know the truth. And time for Bizzie to finally have her story told.

―――――――――

Minutes later, I was standing in front of the Oasis, a camera staring me in the face, ready to go live on News Now Online's YouTube channel. Aaron and Wren were standing beside the cameraman, facing me. I glanced at Aaron who nodded at me and smiled. Wren gave me a thumbs-up.

"We go live in five, four, three, two, one—"

My heart raced. I closed my eyes and took a deep breath. When I opened them, I saw Aaron. I saw Wren. I saw the sparkling town of Crab Orchard down the hill.

"I'm here tonight to shed light on a story that's been more than a century in the making," I started. "The Castle on the Hill—or the 'Oasis,' as it's known by the people of Crab Orchard—has been keeping a secret. Tonight, it's time to reveal that secret." I launched into details about Hartman, Palmer, the sanitarium, and a journalist named Elizabeth Johansen.

Instead of panic, strength rose up inside me. A strength I didn't even know I had. As I spoke, pictures of Ida and her mother Helen flashed into my mind. The Coffee Fox. My first day at News Now Online. Meeting Aaron in the dark halls of the Oasis. Our fundraiser. And in less than three minutes, the story was told. And I'd done it all without breaking a sweat. Without sweaty palms. Without a racing heart.

"Reporting live from Crab Orchard," I said, my voice clear, "I'm Sophie McHale."

The camera clicked off and I handed over my microphone.

Aaron wrapped his arms around me. "Your voice didn't shake even once. You're a pro."

"More like a rockstar," Wren smiled, giving me a high-five.

The next day was a blur. News agencies across the Twin Cities had picked up the story. By noon, we were getting calls from national news outlets. And by that afternoon, Kase fielded calls from Good Morning, America and the Today Show. Apparently, they saw the story and wanted to do a live interview with me. Freya called me, freaking out.

"Girl!" she squealed into the phone. "I *so* told you. You are awesome."

Before I could focus on any media appearances, TV interviews, or even having wine with Freya, I needed a few more answers for myself. With Sheriff Goodspeed and Aaron as my escorts, I headed over to the Hennepin County Jail. I wanted to talk to Jen first.

When she came into the visiting area, I stifled a gasp. Instead of a high-end Hermes bag or fancy jewelry, she wore an orange jumpsuit. Her long hair was greasy. Dark bags under her eyes told me she hadn't slept much. Without a word, she sat down across from me and began to pick at her thumbnail. She avoided my gaze.

"You must hate me," she muttered. It looked like she'd been crying.

I wanted to reach over and grab her hand, but hesitated. "I don't hate you, Jen. I'm just confused. You had it all. You were on top of your game as a reporter. Why…why did you throw it all away?"

She shrugged. "A reporter with a measly salary. And I've got expensive tastes." She paused and let out a deep breath. "Morris came to me a few weeks after I took the job as an investigative reporter. We'd met at a press conference and hit it off. He asked if I'd keep him in the loop. You know, let him know if reporters found any dirt on him." She shook her head. "Why not? That sounded easy enough. And in return?" she smiled. "Bags, jewelry, the newest iPhone, even paid vacations."

She kept picking at her thumb. "It was easy. I mean, I would text him if his name came up in a story, or if his businesses were in the headlines. That's it. But it all changed when you took the job." She stopped picking at her thumb and looked at me for the first time. "You started asking tough questions he didn't want to answer." She closed her eyes and shook her head. "And that's when I got in over my head."

"Did you know that Morris was hiding…something?" I ventured.

"No," she replied quickly and adamantly. "I mean, he's always been private. But I had no idea that he was covering up something like this."

This time I grabbed her hand and squeezed tightly. "I'm sorry this happened," I said. I meant it. "If I can help you, call me. Really. I'm still your friend."

A tear trickled down her cheek. "Thank you, Sophie."

The security guard approached Jen. Our visit was over. Mayor Palmer had refused to see me. Apparently, he said something about it being a "waste of time." But Morris said he'd talk.

As Jen returned to her cell, I waited anxiously for Morris. The door opened and he appeared, also wearing an orange jumpsuit. I stood up and cleared my throat.

"Hello, Mr. Hartman," I said. "Thanks for meeting me."

He stood there for a minute, staring at me. I was relieved that Sheriff Goodspeed and Aaron sat at the table next to us. "You know, I remember our first meeting when you took an interest in my desk. I thought we'd hit it off. I thought you'd be another Genesis." He scoffed and took a few paces around the room.

I stood, unmoving, watching him.

"And then you brought up the demolition of the Oasis at that press conference," he laughed bitterly and shook his head. "And then I knew," he glared at me, "we would never get along."

"How long have you known the secret about your grandfather?" I asked, unfazed by his snarl.

He came within an inch of my face, anger pulsing through him. As Aaron stood up, he backed away. "My grandfather saved hundreds of thousands of lives with that vaccine. And because of you," he spat and pointed a finger at me, "he'll be remembered for being a villain."

"I said, how long have you known about your grandfather?" I asked again.

"It was those damned preservationists. This all stems from them," he said, finally sitting down, his head in his hands. I sat across from him. "A few years ago, they started leading tours through the building. I was curious. So, I signed up for one. It was on Halloween, and they promoted it as a 'haunted tour.'"

He rubbed his eyes. "The tour guide took us through the entire building. When we got to my grandfather's office, he joked and said there were rumors that Doc Hartman had a secret tunnel that originated in his office. Everyone laughed it off. But I wanted to know for sure. So, I went back when no one was there. I found the hidden tunnel. I found the sanitarium. I knew if this news ever came out, not only would my career be ruined, but my grandfather's legacy would be too. My family's legacy. So, I called on a favor from an old friend. What could be better than building a steel mill on my grandfather's property? It's the perfect happy ending." He looked at me with disgust. "Well, it was."

The security guard came back in and told Morris his visiting time was up. He stood and turned to go.

"Mr. Hartman," I said. "I am sorry for hurting your family's legacy."

He looked me over once more. Then, with his shoulders slumped, he turned to go. "My grandfather had friends in high places," he said over his shoulder. "He never faced the consequences of his actions. Now, I'm doing his jail time." With clenched teeth, he added, "But I have friends in high places too. They might not be able to get me out of prison, but they *can* even the score."

"Alright, that's enough!" Aaron jumped up and lifted a protective arm across me.

Sheriff Goodspeed hollered, "Get him out of here."

A shiver ran up and down my spine. Aaron rubbed my back. "You okay?"

I nodded. "I'm exhausted." Then, a thought. "You know what sounds good? A donut and a chai from The Coffee Fox." I poked Aaron in the ribs. "I know the guy who owns it."

Epilogue

SOPHIE

FIVE MONTHS LATER

AARON, IDA, AND I stood at the entrance of the Oasis on a chilly October morning with lattes from The Coffee Fox in our hands.

News trucks were parked in the gravel lot. Newly elected Mayor Wren Coleman was wearing a hard hat and carrying a shovel, surrounded by various city council members. They'd just finished posing for the media following a press conference.

"Today is a historic day for our town," Wren spoke into a microphone. "Today, we break ground on the new Crab Orchard Community Center, luxury apartments, and green space. This will be a work of art once the Preservation Alliance is finished with it." She winked at Ida. "And now, I'd like to introduce Sophie McHale, the reporter who wouldn't—and didn't—give up."

I walked up to the podium amid a smattering of applause. I cleared my throat. "It's because of one brave woman that we're all here today. She had a few different names: E. Johansen and later, A. Hennings." I had discovered Bizzie's other pen name during subsequent visits to the historical database at the library. "But I know her best as Bizzie."

I smiled. "Bizzie discovered this sanitarium a century ago. With the help of friends, she saved the lives of twelve children who were locked in that hidden basement. They went on to thrive at a ground-breaking farm; a one-of-a-kind, women-run, lodging house. They would go on to learn about math and history and reading. They would eat Abigail's famous chocolate chip cookies. They would play hide and seek among the lilacs. And Bizzie? She kept reporting. Because Dr. Hartman ruined her first pen name, she changed her byline to Alice Hennings, after her mother. She would go on to work for dozens of other papers, travel the world, and uncover countless stories and mysteries. She lived to be eighty-eight years old."

I paused and looked at my notes. "Never married, she retired to Hibbing where she lived on a farm with her dear friend, Collin. Now, her journal and her work will be on display here, where her career began so many years ago." I turned and looked at the Oasis, then at Aaron, Ida, Wren, and Freya. "And thank you to those who helped me launch my career too. I am so grateful to you." I smiled and left the podium to claps and cheers. Then, with Ida and Aaron, we set Bizzie's journal inside the waiting glass display box.

"Great job," Aaron said, squeezing my hand. "Now what?"

"Now, I enjoy my latte," I said, taking a sip of the chai he'd brought me from The Coffee Fox. "I start my next assignment tomorrow. I guess there's been a scandal on the North Shore."

Aaron frowned and feigned a gasp. "But that's outside of your beloved Minneapolis!"

I grinned. "I forgot to mention, I have a new title. I'm News Now Online's first investigative journalist for greater Minnesota. Small towns, here I come."

ACKNOWLEDGMENTS

Publishing *The Muckraker* has been a dream! I owe thanks to many, especially the following:

To my editors, Sarah Olson and Chelsea Farr—thank you for your patience, expertise, and guidance! You have supported me through this journey. To Deb, my writing coach. Thank you for being with me when this book was nothing more than an idea.

To my sister-in-law, Terri—thank you for urging me to write. Your faith in me kept me writing!

To my beta readers, Katie and Ali—I appreciate you!

To my parents for cheering me on from a young age. Dad, I remember dictating my first story to you while you typed at our kitchen table. Mom, you continue to be such an encouraging cheerleader for me!

And, to James, Ada, Olive, and Eric—thank you for giving me time and space to write. I love you so much!

ABOUT THE AUTHOR

MAGGIE SONNEK

MAGGIE SONNEK is a small-town momma, iced coffee aficionado, and amateur chicken farmer. She lives in the bluffs of southeastern Minnesota with her husband, three kids, two dogs, two cats, seven chickens, and one bunny. *The Muckraker* is her first novel.